PiPPi Longstocking

Knowsl@y Council

Knowsley Library Service

Please return this book on or before the date shown below

2 7 APR 2018

1 6 MAR 2013

2 9 AUG 2014

1 4 JUN 9 2 SEP 2019

Books by Astrid Lindgren

Pippi Longstocking
Pippi Goes Aboard
Pippi in the South Seas

Emil's Clever Pig
Emil and the Great Escape
Emil and the Sneaky Rat

Lotta Says 'No!'
Lotta Makes a Mess

Karlson Flies Again
Karlson on the Roof
The World's Best Karlson

The Best of
Pippi Longstocking

Astrid Lindgren

Illustrated by Tony Ross

OXFORD
UNIVERSITY PRESS

OXFORD
UNIVERSITY PRESS

Great Clarendon Street, Oxford OX2 6DP

Oxford University Press is a department of the University of Oxford.
It furthers the University's objective of excellence in research, scholarship,
and education by publishing worldwide in

Oxford New York

Auckland Cape Town Dar es Salaam Hong Kong Karachi
Kuala Lumpur Madrid Melbourne Mexico City Nairobi
New Delhi Shanghai Taipei Toronto

With offices in

Argentina Austria Brazil Chile Czech Republic France Greece
Guatemala Hungary Italy Japan South Korea Poland Portugal
Singapore Switzerland Thailand Turkey Ukraine Vietnam

Oxford is a registered trade mark of Oxford University Press
in the UK and in certain other countries

British Library Cataloguing in Publication Data
Data available

ISBN 978-0-19-279308-9

1 2 3 4 5 6 7 8 9 10

Printed in Great Britain

Paper used in the production of this book is a natural,
recyclable product made from wood grown in sustainable forests.
The manufacturing process conforms to the environmental
regulations of the country of origin.

Contents

Pippi Celebrates Christmas   1

Pippi Longstocking   7

Pippi in the South Seas   137

Pippi Goes Aboard   251

Pippi Celebrates Christmas

Astrid Lindgren

Translated by Patricia Crampton

OXFORD
UNIVERSITY PRESS

Pippi Celebrates Christmas

Have you heard of Pippi Longstocking, the strongest girl in the world? The girl who lives all alone in Villekulla Cottage, with only a horse and a monkey for company? The girl with a whole suitcase full of gold coins?

Now you're going to hear about something that Pippi did once. It was late on Christmas Eve and Christmas candles were shining in all the windows of the little town. The Christmas trees were lit up. All the children were very happy.

No, not quite all the children were happy. Three sad little children sat crying in a kitchen on the first floor of a house on Corner Street. They were Mrs Larson's children, Pelle and Bosse and tiny little Inga. They were crying because their mother had gone to hospital. In the middle of Christmas Eve, just think of that! Their daddy was a sailor, far out at sea. And they didn't even have a Christmas tree! Nor any presents! And nothing good to eat! Their mother had had no time to go shopping before she fell ill. No wonder the children were crying! Everything was just about as miserable as it could possibly be.

'This is the most miserable Christmas Eve I've ever had,' said Pelle.

Just then, just after he had spoken, they heard a fearful clumping on the stairs.

'What on earth is that?' cried Bosse. 'It sounds so strange.'

But it wasn't strange at all. There's nothing strange about a bit of clumping, when a horse is climbing up the stairs!

It was Pippi's horse that was doing the climbing. On the horse sat Pippi. And on Pippi sat a Christmas tree. It was sitting on her hair. It was covered with lighted candles and bunting and sweets. It looked exactly as if it had grown straight out of her head. Perhaps it had after all, who knows? Mr Nelson, Pippi's little monkey, was there too. He hurried ahead and opened the door.

Pelle and Bosse and Inga jumped off the kitchen sofa and stared and stared.

'What are you staring at?' said Pippi. 'Haven't you ever seen a Christmas tree before?'

'Yes, but never . . . ' stammered Pelle.

'Well, then,' said Pippi, jumping down from her horse. 'The fir is one of our commonest trees. And now we're going to thresh the corn till the floorboards rock. But first . . . '

She tossed a sack on the floor, and out of the

sack she took a whole lot of parcels and a whole lot of bags. In the bags there were oranges and apples and figs and nuts and raisins and sweets and marzipan pigs. And in the parcels there were Christmas presents for Pelle and Bosse and little Inga. Pippi stacked up all the parcels on the kitchen sofa.

'You're not getting any Christmas presents yet,' said Pippi. 'First we have to dance with the tree.'

'You mean we have to dance round the tree,' said Pelle.

'That's just what I don't mean,' said Pippi. 'Can you tell me why Christmas trees are never allowed any fun? Never allowed to join in and dance? They just have to stand stock still and stare, with people skipping and dancing round them, enjoying themselves. Poor, poor little Christmas trees!'

Pippi rolled up her eyes so that she would see the tree she was carrying on her head.

'Anyway, this Christmas tree is going to join in and have fun, I've made up my mind to that,' she said.

If anyone had looked in through Mrs Larson's window a little later on, they would have seen a remarkable sight. They would have seen Pelle and

Bosse and little Inga skipping around and dancing. They would have seen Pippi dancing, too: Pippi with a fir tree in her hair, Pippi stamping the floor with her big shoes, Pippi singing in a loud cheerful voice: 'Here I go dancing with my little fir, here I go dancing around!'

'No Christmas tree has ever had this much fun before,' said Pippi happily, when she and Pelle and Bosse and little Inga were sitting round the Christmas table later on.

'No, I don't think so either,' said Bosse, popping a fig into his mouth.

'And we've never had so much fun on Christmas Eve before,' said little Inga, swallowing down a whole marzipan pig.

And just imagine what it was like when they got to the Christmas presents! Imagine when Pelle opened his parcel and found an aeroplane and a train, and when Bosse found a steam engine and a car that could drive around on the floor when you wound it up, and when Inga found her doll and a little golden heart!

The Christmas tree lights shone down so sweetly on the children's happy faces, and on all the Christmas presents. And the tree must have been happy too. After all, it was the first Christmas tree that had ever been allowed to join in and dance!

Pippi Longstocking

Astrid Lindgren

Translated by Edna Hurup
Illustrated by Tony Ross

OXFORD
UNIVERSITY PRESS

Contents

1. Pippi Comes to Villekulla Cottage   9
2. Pippi is a Turnupstuffer and Gets in a Fight 20
3. Pippi Plays Tag with Policemen   33
4. Pippi Starts School   41
5. Pippi Sits on the Gate and Climbs a Tree   53
6. Pippi Arranges a Picnic   65
7. Pippi Goes to the Circus   77
8. Pippi is Visited by Thieves   90
9. Pippi Goes to a Tea Party   99
10. Pippi Becomes a Heroine   112
11. Pippi Celebrates her Birthday   122

1
Pippi Comes to Villekulla Cottage

AT the end of a little Swedish town lay an old, overgrown orchard. In the orchard was a cottage, and in this cottage lived Pippi Longstocking. She was nine years old, and she lived all alone. She had neither mother nor father, which was really rather nice, for in this way there was no one to tell her to go to bed just when she was having most fun, and no one to make her take cod-liver-oil when she felt like eating peppermints.

There was a time when Pippi had had a father, and she had been very fond of him. Of course, she had had a mother too, but that was long ago.

Pippi's mother had died when Pippi was just a tiny baby lying in her cradle and howling so dreadfully that no one could come near. Pippi believed that her mother now lived somewhere up in Heaven and looked down on her little girl through a hole in it. Pippi often used to wave up to her and say, 'Don't worry, I can look after myself!'

Pippi hadn't forgotten her father. He had been a ship's captain, and sailed on the great ocean. Pippi had sailed with him on his boat, at least until the time he had blown into the sea during a storm and disappeared. But Pippi was quite sure that one day he would come back, for she never believed that he had drowned. She was certain that he had come ashore on a desert island, one with lots and lots of cannibals, and that her father had become king of them all and went about all day with a gold crown on his head.

'*My* father is a Cannibal King; there aren't *many* children with so fine a father!' said Pippi, really pleased with herself. 'And when my father has built himself a boat he'll come to fetch me, and then *I* shall become a Cannibal Princess. What a life it will be!'

Her father had bought the old cottage in the orchard many years ago. He had wanted to live there with Pippi when he grew old and sailed the seas no longer. But then he had unfortunately been blown into the sea, and as Pippi expected him to return she went straight home to Villekulla Cottage, as their house was called. It stood there furnished and ready and waiting for her. One fine summer's evening she had said goodbye to all the sailors on her father's boat. They liked Pippi very much, and Pippi liked them.

'Goodbye, boys!' said Pippi, kissing each in turn on the forehead. 'Don't worry about me. I can take care of myself!'

She took two things from the boat: a little monkey whose name was Mr Nelson (he had been a present from her father) and a big suitcase full of gold pieces. The sailors stood by the rail and watched Pippi until she was out of sight. She kept on walking without turning round once, with Mr Nelson on her shoulder and the suitcase firmly in her hand.

'A remarkable child,' said one of the sailors. wiping a tear from his eye when Pippi disappeared from view.

He was right. Pippi was a very remarkable child, and the most remarkable thing about her was her strength. She was *so* strong that in all the world there was no policeman as strong as she. She could have lifted a whole horse if she had wanted to. And there were times when she *did* want to. Pippi had bought a horse of her very own with one of her gold pieces the day she came home to Villekulla Cottage. She had always longed to have her very own horse, and now there was one living on her front porch. When Pippi wanted to take afternoon tea there, she simply lifted him out into the orchard without further ado.

Next to Villekulla Cottage lay another orchard and another house. In that house lived a mother and a father with their two nice little children, a boy and a girl. The boy's name was Tommy and the girl's Annika. They were both very good and well-brought-up and obedient children. Tommy *never* bit his nails, and *always* did what his mother asked. Annika *never* fussed when she didn't get her own way, and she was always very properly dressed in freshly ironed cotton.

Tommy and Annika played nicely together in their orchard, but they had often wished for a playmate. At the time when Pippi always sailed the seas with her father, they would sometimes hang on the fence and say to each other, 'What a pity no one moves into that house! Someone ought to live there; someone with children.'

The beautiful summer's day that Pippi first crossed the threshold of Villekulla Cottage, Tommy and Annika weren't at home. They were spending the week with their grandmother, and so had no idea that someone had moved into the house next to theirs. The first day after their arrival home they stood by the gate and looked out on the street, and they still didn't know that there was a playmate so near. Just as they stood and wondered what they should do, and if possibly anything *special* would happen that day or if it would be just one of those dull days when one couldn't think of anything in particular to do, why, just then the gate to Villekulla Cottage opened and a little girl appeared. She was the most curious child Tommy and Annika had ever seen. It was Pippi Longstocking going for a morning walk. This is what she looked like:

Her hair was the same colour as a carrot, and was braided in two stiff pigtails that stood straight out from her head. Her nose was the shape of a very small potato, and was dotted with freckles. Under the nose was a really very large mouth, with healthy white teeth. Her dress was curious indeed. Pippi had made it herself. It was supposed to have been blue, but as there hadn't been quite enough blue cloth, Pippi had decided to add little red patches here and there. On her long thin legs she wore long stockings, one brown and the other black. And she had a pair of black shoes which were just twice as long as her feet. Her father had bought them in South America so she would have something to grow into, and Pippi never wanted any others.

The thing that made Tommy and Annika open their eyes widest was the monkey which sat on the strange girl's shoulder. It was little and long-tailed, and dressed in blue trousers, yellow jacket, and a white straw hat.

Pippi went on down the street, walking with one foot on the pavement and the other in the gutter. Tommy and Annika watched her until she was out of sight. In a moment she returned, walking backwards. This was so she shouldn't have to take the trouble to turn round when she went home. When she came level with Tommy and Annika's gate, she stopped. The children looked at each other in silence. At last Tommy said, 'Why are you walking backwards?'

'Why am I walking backwards?' said Pippi. 'This is a free country, isn't it? Can't I walk as I please? Why, let me tell you that in Egypt *everyone* walks that way, and no one thinks it the least bit odd.'

'How do you know that?' asked Tommy. 'You haven't been in Egypt, have you?'

'Have I been to Egypt! You can bet your boots I have. I've been all over the world and seen odder things than people who walk backwards. I wonder what you would have said if I'd walked on my hands like the people do in Indo-China?'

'That can't be true,' protested Tommy.

Pippi considered this for a moment. 'Yes, you're right,' she said sadly, 'I wasn't telling the truth.'

'It's wicked to lie,' said Annika, who at last had found her tongue.

'Yes, it's *very* wicked,' said Pippi, even more sadly. 'But I forget once in a while, you see. How can you expect a little child whose mother is an angel and whose father is a Cannibal King and who has spent her life sailing the seas to tell the truth always? And for that matter,' she said, a smile spreading over her whole freckled face, 'I can tell you that in the Belgian Congo there isn't a single person who tells the truth. They tell fibs all day and every day, begin at seven in the morning and keep it up until sunset. So if I should happen to tell a fib sometimes you must try to forgive me and remember that it's only because I've been a little too long in the Belgian Congo. We can still be friends, can't we?'

'Of course,' said Tommy, realizing suddenly that this *wouldn't* be one of those dull days.

'Why not have breakfast at my house, for that matter?' Pippi wondered.

'Well, yes,' said Tommy, 'why not? Come on, let's!'

'Yes,' said Annika. 'Right away!'

'But first let me introduce you to Mr Nelson,' said Pippi. The monkey raised his hat to them politely.

And so they went through Villekulla Cottage's tumble-down orchard gate and up the path between rows of mossy trees (trees lovely for climbing, they noticed) to the house and on to the porch. There stood the horse, munching oats from a soup tureen.

'Why on earth have you a horse on the front porch?' asked Tommy. All the horses he knew lived in stables.

'Well,' said Pippi after thinking it over, 'he'd be in the way in the kitchen, and he doesn't thrive in the parlour.'

Tommy and Annika patted the horse, and then went on into the house. There was a kitchen and a parlour and a bedroom. But it looked as if Pippi had forgotten to turn out the rooms that week. Tommy and Annika looked carefully about in case that Cannibal King should be in a corner.

16

They'd never seen a Cannibal King in all their lives. But no father was to be seen, nor any mother, and Annika asked anxiously, 'Do you live here all alone?'

'Of course not,' said Pippi, 'Mr Nelson lives here too.'

'Yes, but haven't you a mother and father here?'

'No, none at all,' said Pippi cheerfully.

'But who tells you when to go to bed at night, and that sort of thing?' asked Annika.

'I do,' said Pippi. 'The first time I say it, I say it in a friendly sort of way, and if I don't listen I say it again more sharply, and if I *still* don't listen, then there's a thrashing to be had, believe me!'

Tommy and Annika didn't quite understand all this, but they thought that perhaps it was a good arrangement. Meanwhile, they had come into the kitchen, and Pippi whooped:

> 'Here pancakes will be baked now,
> Here pancakes will be served now,
> Here pancakes will be fried now!'

At which she took out three eggs and flung them into the air. One of the eggs fell on her head and broke, and the yolk ran down into her eye. But the others she caught properly in a bowl, where they broke.

'I've always heard that egg-yolk is good for the hair,' said Pippi, wiping her eye. 'You'll see that it will grow now so fast it creaks! In Brazil, for that matter, *everyone* goes about with egg in his hair. There's not a bald head to be seen. Once there was an old man who was so odd that he *ate* his eggs instead of spreading them on his hair. He turned quite bald, too, and when he as much as showed himself on the streets the traffic stopped and they had to call out the police.'

While she was talking, Pippi carefully picked out all the broken eggshell from the bowl with her fingers. Then she took a bath-brush which hung on the wall and began beating the batter so that it splattered on the walls. At last she threw what was left on a griddle that stood on the stove. When the pancake was browned on one side she threw it halfway to the ceiling so that it turned in the air and was caught in the pan again. And when it was done, she threw it across the kitchen so that it landed on a plate standing on the table.

'Eat it!' she cried. 'Eat it before it gets cold!'

Tommy and Annika ate, and thought it a very good pancake. Afterwards, Pippi invited them into the parlour. There was only one piece of furniture in it. It was an enormous cupboard with many, many little drawers. Pippi opened them one by one and showed Tommy and Annika all

18

the treasures she kept there. There were strange birds' eggs, and unusual shells and stones, lovely little boxes, beautiful silver mirrors, a pearl necklace, and much more, all bought by Pippi and her father during their travels round the world. Pippi gave her new playmates each a little present as a keepsake. Tommy's was a knife with a gleaming mother-of-pearl handle, and Annika's a little box decorated on the lid with pieces of shell. In the box lay a ring set with a green stone.

'If you should happen to go home now,' said Pippi, 'you'll be able to come again tomorrow. Because if you don't go home, you can't very well come back, and that *would* be a shame.'

Tommy and Annika thought so too, so they went home. They went past the horse, who had eaten up all his oats, and out through the gate of Villekulla Cottage. Mr Nelson waved his hat to them as they left.

2
Pippi is a Turnupstuffer and Gets into a Fight

Annika awoke especially early the next morning. She bounded out of bed and quickly padded over to Tommy.

'Wake up, Tommy!' she said, tugging at his arm. 'Let's go and see that funny girl with the big shoes!'

In an instant, Tommy was wide awake.

'All the time I was sleeping I knew there was going to be something nice about today, though I couldn't remember just what it was,' he said, struggling out of his pyjama-top. Then they both went into the bathroom and washed themselves and brushed their teeth much faster than usual. They were merry and quick about putting on their clothes, and a whole hour earlier than their mother had expected they came sliding down the banister from the top floor and landed exactly by the breakfast table, where they sat down and shouted that they wanted their hot chocolate now, at *once*!

'And may I ask,' said their mother, 'just what it is that makes you in such a hurry?'

'We're going over to see the new girl in the house next door,' said Tommy.

'We might stay all day!' added Annika.

That morning Pippi was baking ginger-snaps. She had made a huge pile of dough, and was rolling it out on the kitchen floor.

''Cause can you imagine,' said Pippi to her little monkey, 'what earthly good a pastry board would be when you're going to make at least five hundred ginger-snaps?'

There she lay on the floor and cut out heart-shaped ginger-snaps as if her life depended on it.

'Do stop walking in the dough, Mr Nelson,' she said irritably just as the doorbell rang.

Pippi ran to open it. She was as white as a miller from top to toe, and when she shook hands heartily with Tommy and Annika a whole cloud of flour came down on them.

'How nice of you to drop in,' she said, shaking a new cloud of flour out of her apron. Tommy and Annika got so much of it in their throats, they had to cough.

'What are you doing?' asked Tommy.

'Well, if I say I'm sweeping the chimney you wouldn't believe me, as clever as you are,' said Pippi. 'As a matter of fact, I'm baking. But that will soon be out of the way. You can sit on the woodbox in the meantime.'

Pippi could work *very* fast. Tommy and Annika sat on the woodbox and watched how she cut her way forward through the dough, and how she threw the biscuits on to the tins, and how she slung the tins into the oven. They thought it was all rather like something in the films.

'All clear,' said Pippi at last, slamming the oven door after the last tins with a bang.

'What are we going to do now?' asked Tommy.

'I don't know what *you're* thinking of doing,' said Pippi, 'but as for me, I'm not one who can take things easy. I happen to be a turnupstuffer, so of course I never have a free moment.'

'What did you say you were?' asked Annika.

'A turnupstuffer.'

'What's that?' asked Tommy.

'Somebody who finds the stuff that turns up if only you look, of course. What else would it be?' said Pippi, sweeping together all the flour on the floor into a little pile. 'The whole world is filled with things that are just waiting for someone to come along and find them, and that's just what a turnupstuffer does.'

'What sort of things?' asked Annika.

'Oh, *all* sorts,' said Pippi. 'Gold nuggets and ostrich feathers and dead mice and rubber bands and tiny little grouse, and *that* kind of thing.'

Tommy and Annika thought it sounded a great deal of fun, and at once wanted to become turnupstuffers too, though Tommy said he hoped he would find a gold nugget and not a little grouse.

'We'll have to wait and see,' said Pippi. 'You always find *something*. But we'll have to hurry up so other turnupstuffers don't come first and take away all the gold nuggets and things that are waiting hereabouts.'

The three turnupstuffers set out. They thought it was best to begin hunting around the houses in the neighbourhood, because Pippi said that even if there *were* little grouse deep in the woods, the *very* best things were almost always found near where people lived.

'Though not always,' she said. 'I've seen it just the other way about. I remember a time when I was looking for things in the jungles of Borneo. Right in the middle of the wild jungle, where no man had ever put his foot, what do you suppose I found? A lovely wooden leg! I gave it away later on to an old man who was one-legged, and he told me that money couldn't buy a wooden leg like that!'

Tommy and Annika watched Pippi to see how a turnupstuffer should act. She ran from one side of the road to the other, shading her eyes with her hand, and searching and searching. Once in a while she crept on her knees, and stuck her hands in through a fence, saying in a disappointed voice, 'Strange! I was *sure* I saw a gold nugget!'

'Can you really take anything you find?' asked Annika.

'Yes, anything that's lying on the ground,' said Pippi.

A little further on, an old man lay sleeping on the lawn in front of his house.

'*That*'s lying on the ground,' said Pippi, 'and we've found him. We'll take him!'

Tommy and Annika were horrified.

'No, no, Pippi! We can't take a gentleman! That would never do!' said Tommy. 'Anyway, what would we do with him?'

24

'What we'd do with him? We could use him for *lots* of things. We could keep him in a little rabbit hutch instead of a rabbit, and feed him dandelion leaves. But if you don't want to, we can leave him here, for all I care. Still, I hate to think that some other turnupstuffer may come along and carry him off.'

They went on. Suddenly, Pippi gave a wild shriek.

'Well, I never saw the likes!' she cried, picking up an old rusty cake tin out of the grass. 'What a find! What a find! One can never have too many tins.'

Tommy looked rather suspiciously at the tin and asked, 'What can you use that for?'

'It can be used for *lots* of things,' said Pippi. 'One way is to put cakes in it. Then it will be one of those nice Tins With Cakes. Another way is *not* to put cakes in it. Then it will be a Tin Without Cakes, which isn't quite as nice, but it would do well enough too.'

She inspected the tin, which really was quite rusty, and had a hole in the bottom.

'It looks as though this one is a Tin Without Cakes,' she said thoughtfully. 'But you can put it over your head and pretend it's the middle of the night!'

And she did just that. With the tin over her

25

head, she wandered through the neighbourhood like a little tin tower, and she didn't stop before she fell on her stomach over a wire fence. There was a terrific crash when the cake tin hit the ground.

'There, you see!' said Pippi, removing the tin. 'If I hadn't had this on me, I would have fallen face first and knocked myself silly.'

'Yes, but,' said Annika, 'if you hadn't had the tin on you, why, you'd never have tripped over the fence . . . '

But before she had finished speaking, another shriek came from Pippi, who triumphantly held up an empty cotton reel.

'It seems to be my lucky day today!' she said. 'What a perfectly sweet little reel to blow soap bubbles with, or to hang on a string round my neck for a necklace! I want to go home and do it now.'

Just then, the gate to a nearby house opened, and a little boy rushed out. He looked frightened, which wasn't surprising, for hard on his heels came five other boys. They soon got hold of him and pushed him against the fence, where the whole lot attacked him. All five began hitting him at the same time. He cried and tried to shield his face with his arms.

'On him, blokes!' yelled the biggest and the strongest of the boys. 'So he'll never dare show himself in *this* street!'

'Oh!' said Annika. 'That's Willie they're beating. How can they be so horrid!'

'It's that beastly Bengt. He's always fighting,' said Tommy. 'And five against one! What cowards!'

Pippi went up to the boys and tapped Bengt on the back with her finger.

'You there,' she said. 'Do you mean to make pulp of little Willie on the spot, since five of you are at him at once?'

Bengt turned round and saw a girl he'd never met before, an unruly, strange girl who dared to poke him! At first he simply stared in astonishment, and then a broad sneer spread over his face.

'Hey, blokes!' he said. 'Let Willie go, and take a look at this. What a girl!'

He slapped his knees and laughed. In a moment the whole lot had flocked around Pippi. Everyone except Willie, who dried his tears and carefully went and stood beside Tommy.

'Have you ever seen such hair! It's a real flaming bonfire! And what shoes!' Bengt continued. 'Couldn't I please borrow one of

27

them? I'd like to go for a row, and I haven't a boat.'

Then he took hold of one of Pippi's pigtails, but quickly dropped it and said, 'Ouch! I burned myself!'

The five boys made a ring round Pippi and hopped about and yelled, 'Carrot top! Carrot top!'

Pippi stood in the middle of the ring and smiled in a friendly manner. Bengt had hoped she would become angry or begin to cry. At the very least she ought to look scared. When nothing else worked, he pushed her.

'I don't think you have particularly good manners with ladies,' said Pippi. Then she lifted him high into the air with her strong arms. She carried him to a nearby birch tree, and hung him across a branch. Then she took the next boy and hung him on another branch, and then she took the next one and sat him on the high gatepost outside the house, and then she took the *next* one and threw him right over the fence, leaving him sitting in a bed of flowers in the next-door garden. She put the last of the bullies into a little toy cart that stood on the road. Then Pippi and Tommy and Annika and Willie stood looking at the boys a while, and the bullies were quite speechless with astonishment.

Pippi said, 'You are cowards! Five of you go after one boy. That's cowardly. And then you begin to push a little defenceless girl around. Oh, how disgraceful! Nasty!'

'Come on now, let's go home,' she said to Tommy and Annika. And to Willie she said, 'If they try 'n hit you any more, just tell me about it.'

And to Bengt, who sat up in the tree and didn't dare to move, she said, 'If there's anything else you wanted to say about my hair or my shoes, it's best you see to it now, before I go home.'

But Bengt hadn't anything else to say about Pippi's shoes, nor about her hair. And so Pippi took her cake tin in one hand and the cotton reel in the other, and went off, followed by Tommy and Annika.

When they came back to Pippi's orchard, Pippi said, 'Dear hearts, what a shame. Here I've found two such fine things and you haven't found anything at all. You must look a little more. Tommy, why don't you look in that old tree? Old trees are often the very best of places for a turnupstuffer.'

Tommy said that he didn't really think that Annika and he would ever be able to find anything, but in order to please Pippi, he stuck his hand down a hollow in the tree.

'Well but—' he said, quite amazed, and pulled out his hand. Between his thumb and forefinger he held a fine notebook with a leather cover. There was a silver pen in a special holder at the side.

'Gosh! That was odd,' said Tommy.

'There, you see!' said Pippi. 'There's nothing better than being a turnupstuffer. It's only a wonder that there aren't more who take up the work. Carpenter and shoemaker and chimney sweep and that sort of thing, *that* they'll become, but turnupstuffer, mark you, that's not good enough!'

And then she said to Annika, 'Why don't you go and feel in that old tree stump? You can just about *always* find things in old tree stumps.'

Annika stuck her hand under the stump, and almost right away got hold of a red coral necklace. Tommy and she just stood and gaped, they were so surprised. They decided that from now on they were going to be turnupstuffers *every* day.

Pippi had been up half the night tossing a ball, so now she suddenly felt sleepy.

'I think I'll go in and have a bit of a snooze,' she said. 'Won't you come along and tuck me in?'

When Pippi sat on the edge of the bed taking off her shoes, she looked thoughtfully at them and said, 'He wanted to go rowing, that Bengt said. Bosh!' she snorted scornfully. 'I'll teach *him* to row, I will! Some other time.'

'I say, Pippi,' said Tommy cautiously, 'why is it you've got such big shoes?'

'Why, so I can wiggle my toes!' she answered. Then she lay down to sleep. She always slept with her feet on the pillow and her head far down under the covers.

'That's the way they sleep in Guatemala,' she explained. 'And it's the only right way to do it. This way, I can wiggle my toes while I'm sleeping, too.

'Can you go to sleep without a lullaby?' she continued. 'I always have to sing to me for a while, else I can't get a wink of sleep.'

Tommy and Annika heard a droning from under the covers. It was Pippi singing herself to sleep. They tiptoed softly out so they shouldn't disturb her. At the door they turned round and took a last look at the bed. They didn't see anything except Pippi's feet on the pillow. There she lay, wiggling her toes energetically.

Tommy and Annika bounded home. Annika clutched her coral necklace tightly in her hand.

31

'It *was* odd,' she said. 'Tommy, you don't think . . . do you, that Pippi had already put the things there herself?'

'You can't tell,' said Tommy. 'You can't really be certain about *anything* when it comes to Pippi.'

3
Pippi Plays Tag with Policemen

Everyone in the town soon knew that a little girl just nine years old was living alone in Villekulla Cottage. Mothers and fathers shook their heads and agreed that this would not do at *all*. Certainly all children had to have someone to tell them what they ought to do, and all children ought to go to school to learn the multiplication tables. And so they decided that the little girl in Villekulla Cottage should be put into a Children's Home at once.

One beautiful afternoon Pippi had invited Tommy and Annika to her house for tea and ginger-snaps. She set the tea things out on the steps of the front porch. It was sunny and pretty there, and the flowers in Pippi's garden smelled sweetly. Mr Nelson climbed up and down the porch railing, and now and again the horse would stick his nose forward expecting to be offered a ginger-snap.

'How lovely it is to be alive!' said Pippi, stretching her legs out as far as they would go.

Just then two policemen in full uniform came in through the gate.

'Oh!' said Pippi. 'This must be my lucky day, too! Policemen are the very best thing I know. Except for strawberries and cream.'

And she went forward to meet the policemen, her face shining with delight.

'Are you the girl who's moved into Villekulla Cottage?' asked one of the policemen.

'Not me!' said Pippi. 'I'm her very small aunt who lives on the third floor at the other end of the town.'

She only said this because she wanted to have a bit of fun with the policemen. But they didn't think it was the least bit funny. They told her not to try to be so clever. And then they explained that kind people in the town had arranged for her to be placed in a Children's Home.

'I'm already in a Children's Home,' said Pippi.

'What's that? Is it already arranged?' asked the policeman. 'Which Children's Home is that?'

'*This* one,' said Pippi proudly. 'I'm a child, and this is my home. There aren't any grown-ups living here, so I think that makes it a Children's Home.'

'Dear child,' said the policeman, laughing, 'you don't understand. You must come to a regular Institution where someone can look after you.'

'Are horses allowed in the stintitution?' wondered Pippi.

'No, of course not,' said the policeman.

'That's that, I suppose. I thought as much,' said Pippi gloomily. 'Well, how about monkeys, then?'

'Certainly not! I should think you'd know that.'

'I see,' said Pippi. 'Then you'll just have to find yourself kids for that stintitution of yours somewhere else. 'Cause *I* don't mean to move there.'

'Yes, but don't you see, you have to go to school,' said the policeman.

'Why do I?'

'Well, to learn things, of course.'

35

'What kind of things?' Pippi asked.

'Any number of different kinds,' said the policeman. 'A whole lot of useful things, multiplication tables, for example.'

'I've managed well enough without any pluttification tables for nine years,' said Pippi. 'So I s'pose I can keep managing.'

'Come now! Imagine how unpleasant it will be for you to be so ignorant. Just think, when you grow up and someone perhaps comes and asks you what the capital of Portugal is, you couldn't answer.'

'Oh, yes I could,' said Pippi. 'I'd just say, "If you're all that anxious to know what the capital of Portugal is, well, by all means write direct to Portugal and ask 'em."'

'Yes, but don't you think you'd be sorry you didn't know it yourself?'

'Might be so,' said Pippi. 'I s'pose I *would* lie awake sometimes at night and wonder and wonder, "What the dickens was the name of the capital of Portugal?" But then, you can't have fun *all* the time,' said Pippi, turning a few cartwheels. 'Anyway, I've been in Lisbon with my father,' she continued while upside-down and then right-side-up, for she could talk that way too.

But then one of the policemen said that Pippi shouldn't believe that she could do exactly as she pleased. She would just come along to the Children's Home, and that at *once*. He went towards her and took hold of her arm. But Pippi quickly slipped loose, hit him lightly, and said, 'Tag!' And before he could blink his eyes, she had taken a leap up the post of the porch. With a few pulls she was up on the balcony over the porch. The policemen didn't feel inclined to climb after her the same way, so they rushed into the house and up to the first floor. But when they came out on the balcony, Pippi was already halfway to the roof. She climbed on the roof-tiles very much as if she herself were a monkey. In a moment she stood on the top of the roof and jumped easily up on to the chimney. Down on the balcony both the policemen stood tearing their hair, and on the lawn below stood Tommy and Annika looking up at Pippi.

'What fun it is to play tag!' shouted Pippi. 'And how nice it was of you to come. It's my lucky day today too, that's plain to see.'

When the policemen had thought a moment they went and got a ladder which they leaned against the roof, and then they climbed up, first one and then the other, to fetch Pippi down. But they looked a little bit afraid when they climbed out on to the top of the roof and began balancing their way towards Pippi.

'Don't be scared!' cried Pippi. 'It's not dangerous—just fun!'

When the policemen came within two steps of Pippi, she leaped quickly down from the chimney, and laughing and whooping, ran along the top of the roof to the other gable. A few yards from the house stood a tree.

'Watch me dive!' shouted Pippi, and then she hopped straight down into the tree's green crown, hung fast in a branch, dangled back and forth a moment, and let herself fall to the ground. And then she dashed off on to the other gable and took away the ladder.

The policemen had looked a bit foolish when Pippi jumped, but they looked even more so when they had balanced their way back along the top of the roof and wanted to climb down the ladder. At first they became dreadfully angry and yelled at Pippi, who stood below looking up at them, that she'd better put the ladder back, or else they'd show her a thing or two.

'Why are you so angry?' said Pippi reproachfully. 'We're only playing tag, so we all ought to be friends!'

The policemen thought for a moment, and at last one of them said in a small voice, 'Um, err, I say, wouldn't you be nice and bring the ladder back so that we can get down?'

'Certainly I will,' said Pippi, and brought the ladder back at once. 'And then we can have tea and have a nice time together!'

But the policemen were very deceitful, to be sure, for as soon as they were on the ground they rushed upon Pippi and shouted, 'Now you're going to get it, you nasty child!'

But then Pippi said, 'No, now I haven't time to play any longer. Though it *is* fun, I must admit.'

Then she took a strong hold of their belts, and carried them along the orchard, and out through the gate to the road. There she set them down, and it was a long time before they could bring themselves to move.

'Wait a minute,' shouted Pippi, and ran into the kitchen. She came out with two heart-shaped ginger-snaps. 'Would you like to try one?' she said. 'I don't s'pose it makes much difference if they're a *little* burnt.'

Then she went back to Tommy and Annika, who stood there staring and filled with wonder. And the policemen hurried back to the town and said to all the good mothers and fathers there that Pippi just wasn't quite suitable for a Children's Home. They didn't talk about having been up on the roof. Everyone agreed that perhaps it was best to let Pippi stay in Villekulla Cottage. And if it should happen that she wanted to go to school, then she should arrange that herself.

But Pippi and Tommy and Annika had a really pleasant afternoon. They continued the interrupted tea-party. Pippi gobbled down fourteen ginger-snaps, and then she said, 'Those weren't what I'd call the *best* kind of policemen. No! Altogether too much silly talk about Children's Homes and pluttification and Lisbon.'

Later she lifted out the horse, and then all three of them rode on him. At first Annika was afraid and didn't want to, but when she saw what fun Tommy and Pippi were having she let Pippi lift her up on the horse's back too. And the horse trotted round and round the orchard, and Tommy sang, 'Here come the Swedes with a hullabaloo!'

When Tommy and Annika had crept into their beds that night, Tommy said, 'Annika, don't you think it's jolly that Pippi has moved here?'

'Of course I do,' said Annika.

'I don't even remember what we used to play before she came, do you?'

'Well, we played croquet and *that* sort of thing,' said Annika. 'But somehow it's lots more fun with Pippi, *I* think. And with horses and all that!'

4
Pippi Starts School

Quite naturally, Tommy and Annika went to school. Each morning at eight o'clock they trudged away hand in hand with their school books under their arms.

At that hour Pippi was usually to be found riding her horse or dressing Mr Nelson in his little costume. Or she would be doing her morning exercises, which consisted of standing bolt upright on the floor and then turning forty-three somersaults in the air, one right after the other. After this she would sit on the kitchen table and enjoy a big cup of coffee and a cheese sandwich in peace and quiet.

Tommy and Annika always looked wistfully towards Villekulla Cottage when they toiled away to school. They would much, much rather have gone to play with Pippi. If only Pippi had had to go to school too, it wouldn't have been quite so bad.

'Just think what fun we could have together on our way home from school,' said Tommy.

'Yes, and on the way there too,' Annika agreed.

The more they thought about it, the more it seemed a pity that Pippi didn't go to school. Finally they decided to try and persuade her to begin.

'You can't *imagine* what a nice teacher we have,' said Tommy artfully to Pippi one afternoon when he and Annika were visiting Villekulla Cottage after having first done all their homework.

'Oh, if you *knew* what fun it is at school,' said Annika innocently. 'I should go out of my mind if I couldn't go!'

Pippi sat on a stool washing her feet in a tub. She didn't say anything, but just wiggled her toes a little so the water splashed around.

'One doesn't have to be there so *terribly* long,' continued Tommy. 'Just till two o'clock.'

'Yes, and we get Christmas holidays and Easter holidays and summer holidays,' said Annika.

Pippi bit her big toe thoughtfully, but didn't say anything. Suddenly, without hesitation, she tossed all the water out on the kitchen floor, so that Mr Nelson, who was sitting nearby playing with a mirror, got his trousers absolutely soaked.

'It's unjust!' said Pippi sternly, without taking any notice of Mr Nelson's distress over the wet trousers. 'It's absolutely unjust. I'm not going to stand for it!'

'Not stand for what?' asked Tommy.

'In four months it's Christmas, and you'll be getting Christmas holidays. But me, what do *I* get?' Pippi's voice sounded gloomy. 'No Christmas holidays; not even the very teeniest Christmas holiday,' she complained. 'There's got to be a change here. Tomorrow I'm beginning school!'

Tommy and Annika clapped their hands with joy.

'Hurrah! Then we'll wait for you outside our gate at eight o'clock.'

'No, no,' said Pippi. 'I can't begin *that* early. And for that matter, I think I'll be riding to school.'

And she did. At exactly ten o'clock the next morning she lifted her horse down from the front porch, and a moment later all the people of the little town rushed to their windows to see what horse had run away. That is to say, they *thought* it had run away. But it hadn't. It was simply that Pippi was in a bit of a hurry to get to school. In a wild gallop she burst into the school yard, hopped off the horse at full speed, tied him with a string, and flung open the door of the schoolroom with a terrific crash that made Tommy and Annika and their classmates jump in their seats.

'Hey, hurrah!' shouted Pippi and waved her big hat. 'Am I in time for pluttification?'

Tommy and Annika had explained to their teacher that a new girl called Pippi Longstocking would be coming. The teacher had also heard about Pippi from people in the town. As she was a very kind and pleasant teacher, she had decided to do everything she could to make Pippi feel at home in school.

Pippi flung herself down into an empty seat without anyone having asked her to do so. But the teacher took no notice of her careless manner. She just said in a friendly way, 'Welcome to school, little Pippi. I hope you will be happy here and that you will learn a great deal.'

'To be sure! And *I* hope I'll get Christmas holidays,' said Pippi. ' 'Cause that's the reason I've come. Justice above all things!'

'If you'll first tell me your full name,' said the teacher, 'I shall enrol you in the school.'

'My name is Pippilotta Provisionia Gaberdina Dandeliona Ephraimsdaughter Longstocking, daughter of Captain Ephraim Longstocking, formerly the terror of the seas, now Cannibal King. Pippi is really just my nickname, 'cause my father thought Pippilotta was too long to say.'

'I see,' said the teacher. 'Well then, we shall call you Pippi too. But now perhaps we should test your knowledge a bit,' she continued. 'You're quite a big girl, so you probably know a great deal already. Let us begin with arithmetic. Now, Pippi, can you tell me how much seven and five make?'

Pippi looked rather surprised and cross. Then she said, 'Well, if *you* don't know, don't think I'm going to work it out for you!'

All the children stared in horror at Pippi. The teacher explained to her that she wasn't to answer in that way at school. She wasn't to call the teacher just 'you' either; she was to call the teacher 'ma'am'.

'I'm awful sorry,' said Pippi apologetically. 'I didn't know that. I won't do it again.'

'No, I should hope not,' said the teacher. 'And now I'll tell you that seven and five make twelve.'

'You see!' said Pippi. 'You knew it all the time, so why did you ask, then? Oh, what a blockhead I am! Now I called you just "you" again. 'Scuse me,' she said, giving her ear a powerful pinch.

The teacher decided to pretend that nothing was the matter.

'Now, Pippi, how much do you think eight and four make?'

'I s'pose round about sixty-seven?' said Pippi.

'Not at all,' said the teacher. 'Eight and four make twelve.'

'Now, now, my good woman, that's going too far,' said Pippi. 'You said yourself just now that it was seven and five that made twelve. There oughter be *some* order, even in a school. If you're so keen on this silly stuff, why don't you sit by yourself in a corner and count, and let us be in peace so we can play tag? Oh, dear! Now I said just "you" again,' she said with horror. 'Can you forgive me this last time too? I'll try to remember better from now on.'

The teacher said she would do so. But she thought that trying to teach Pippi any more arithmetic wasn't a good idea. She began to ask the other children instead.

'Can Tommy answer this question, please,' she said. 'If Lisa has seven apples and Axel has nine apples, how many apples have they together?'

'Yes, answer that one, Tommy,' Pippi chimed in. 'And at the same time answer me this one: If Lisa has a tummy ache and Axel has even *more* of a tummy ache, whose fault is it, and where had they pinched the apples?'

The teacher tried to look as if she hadn't heard, and turned to Annika.

'Now, Annika, this problem is for you: Gustav went with his friends on a school outing. He had elevenpence when he went and sevenpence when he came home. How much had he spent?'

'All right,' said Pippi, 'then *I'd* like to know why he was so extravagant, and if it was ginger beer he bought, and if he'd washed well behind his ears before he left home.'

The teacher decided to give up arithmetic completely. She thought that perhaps Pippi would be more interested in learning to read. She therefore brought out a picture of a pretty little green island surrounded by blue water. Just over the island stood the letter 'i'.

'Now, Pippi, I'm going to show you something very interesting,' she said quickly. 'This is a picture of an iiiiiiisland. And this letter above the iiiiiiisland is called "i".'

'Ow, I can hardly believe that,' said Pippi. 'It looks to me like a short line with a fly-speck over it. I'd like to know what islands and fly-specks have to do with each other.'

The teacher brought out the next picture, which was of a snake. She explained to Pippi that the letter over it was called 's'.

'Speaking of snakes,' said Pippi, 'I don't s'pose I'll ever forget the time I fought with a giant snake in India. It was such a horrid snake, you can't *imagine*; he was fourteen yards long and as angry as a bee, and every day he ate up five Indians and two little children for dessert. One day he came and wanted *me* for dessert, and he wound himself round me—krratch—but "I've learned a thing or two at sea," I said and hit him on the head—boom—and then he *hissed*—uiuiuiuiuiuiuitch—and then I hit him again—boom and—ow—well—then he died. So *that's* the letter "s"? Very interesting!'

Pippi had to catch her breath for a moment. The teacher, who was beginning to think Pippi a noisy and troublesome child, decided to let the class draw for a while. Surely Pippi would sit quietly and draw, thought the teacher. So she brought out paper and pencils and handed them out to the children.

'You may draw whatever you like,' she said,

and she sat down at her desk and began correcting copybooks. After a while she looked up to see how the children were getting on. They all sat looking at Pippi, who lay on the floor drawing to her heart's content.

'But, Pippi,' said the teacher impatiently, 'why don't you draw on the paper?'

'I used that up long ago. There isn't room enough for my whole horse on that silly little scrap of paper,' said Pippi. 'Just now I'm working on the front legs, but when I get to the tail I'll most likely be out in the corridor.'

The teacher thought hard for a moment. 'Perhaps we should sing a little song instead?' she suggested.

All the children stood up beside their seats; all but Pippi, who lay still on the floor.

'Go ahead and sing,' she said. 'I'm going to rest a bit. Too much study can break the healthiest.'

But now the teacher's patience had come to an end. She told all the children to go out into the schoolyard, because she wanted especially to talk to Pippi.

When the teacher and Pippi were alone, Pippi got up and came forward to the desk.

'Do you know,' she said, 'I mean, do you know, *ma'am*, it was really lots of fun to come here and see what it's like. But I don't think I want to go to school any more, Christmas holidays or no Christmas holidays. There's just too many apples and islands and snakes and all that. I just get flustered in the head. I hope you're not disappointed, ma'am.'

But the teacher said she *was* disappointed, most of all because Pippi wouldn't try to behave properly, and that no girl who behaved as badly as Pippi would be allowed to come to school even if she wanted to very much.

'Have I behaved badly?' asked Pippi, very surprised. 'But I didn't know that myself,' she said, looking sad. No one could look as tragic as Pippi when she was unhappy. She stood silently a minute, and then she said in a shaking voice, 'You understand, ma'am, that when your mother is an angel and your father a Cannibal King, and you've travelled all your life on the seas, you don't really know *how* you oughter behave in a school with all the apples and the snakes.'

Then the teacher said that she quite understood, and that she wasn't disappointed in Pippi any longer, and that perhaps Pippi could come back to school when she was a bit older. And Pippi said, beaming with pleasure, 'I think you're awful nice, ma'am. And look what I've got for you, ma'am!'

Out of her pocket Pippi brought a fine little

gold chain, which she laid on the desk. The teacher said she couldn't accept such a valuable gift from Pippi, but then Pippi said, 'You have to! Else I'll come back again tomorrow, and *that* would be a pretty spectacle!'

Then Pippi rushed out into the schoolyard and leaped upon the horse. All the children crowded around to pat the horse and to watch her leave.

'I'm glad I know about Argentine schools,' Pippi said in a superior manner looking down at the children. 'You ought to go *there*! They begin Easter holidays three days after Christmas holidays, and when the Easter holidays are over, it's just three days till summer holidays. Summer holidays are over on the first of November. 'Course, then there's a bit of a grind until Christmas holidays begin on the eleventh of November. But it's not too bad, 'cause at least there aren't any lessons. It's strictly forbidden to have lessons in Argentina. It does happen once in a while that some Argentine child or other hides himself in a cupboard and sits there in secret and reads, but woe betide him if his mother finds him out! They don't have arithmetic in the schools there at all, and if there's a child who knows how much seven and five is, he has to stand in the corner all day if he's so stupid that he tells it to the teacher. They have reading on Fridays only, and then only in case they happen to have some books there. But they never do.'

'Yes, but what do they do in school then?' asked a little boy.

'Eat sweets,' said Pippi without hesitation. 'A long pipe goes direct from a sweets factory in the neighbourhood to the schoolroom. Sweets shoot out of it all day, so the children are kept busy just eating.'

'But what does the teacher do?' asked a little girl.

'Picks the papers off the sweets, dunce,' said Pippi. 'Did you think they did it themselves? Hardly! They don't even as much as go to school themselves. They send their brothers.'

Pippi waved her big hat.

'Yoicks, tally ho!' she cried. 'You won't see me in a minute. But always remember how many apples Axel had, else you'll come to a bad end, hahaha!'

With ringing laughter Pippi rode out through the gate, so fast the gravel whirred around the horse's hooves and the school windows rattled.

5

Pippi Sits on the Gate and Climbs a Tree

Outside Villekulla Cottage sat Pippi, Tommy, and Annika. Pippi sat on one gatepost, Annika sat on the other gatepost, and Tommy sat on the gate. It was a warm and beautiful day towards the end of August. A pear tree, which grew by the gate, stretched its branches so far down that the children could sit and pick the ripest little yellow-red August pears with no trouble at all. They nibbled and munched, and spat the pear pips out on to the road.

Villekulla Cottage lay just where the little town ended and the countryside began, and where the street turned into a country road. The towns-people liked to go for walks out Villekulla way, for it was there the most beautiful surroundings lay.

While the children sat there eating pears, a girl came by on the road from the town. When she saw the children she stopped and asked, 'Have you seen my father pass by?'

'I don't know,' said Pippi. 'What did he look like? Did he have blue eyes?'

'Yes,' said the girl.

'Black hat and black shoes?'

'Yes, exactly,' said the girl eagerly.

'No, we haven't seen anyone like that,' said Pippi definitely.

The girl looked disappointed and went on without a word.

'Ahoy there!' Pippi shouted after her. 'Was he bald?'

'No, not in the least,' said the girl angrily.

'*That's* a bit of good luck for him!' said Pippi, and spat out a pear pip.

The girl hurried on, but then Pippi yelled, 'Did he have uncommon big ears that reached all the way down to his shoulders?'

'No,' said the girl, and then turned about,

54

astonished. 'You don't mean to say you've seen a man walk by with ears as big as that?'

'I've never seen anyone walk with his ears,' said Pippi. 'Everybody *I* know walks with his feet.'

'Oof, but you're silly! I mean, have you really seen a man with ears that big?'

'No,' said Pippi. 'There *isn't* anybody with ears that big. Why, that would be absurd. How would it look? One simply can't have such big ears.

'At least, not in *this* country,' she added after a moment's thought. 'In China it's a little different. Once I saw a Chinaman in Shanghai. His ears were *so* big he could use them for a raincoat. When it rained, he just crept in under his ears and was warm and snug as could be. Not that the ears had such a rattling good time of it, you understand. If it was *specially* bad weather, he'd invite friends and acquaintances to pitch camp under his ears too. There they sat, singing their sorrowful songs while it poured down outside. They thought a lot of him because of his ears. Hai Shang was his name. You should have seen Hai Shang running to his work in the morning! He always came charging along at the last minute because he liked sleeping late so much, and you can't imagine how lovely it looked when he came running along with his ears like two big yellow sails behind him.'

The girl had stopped and now stood with open mouth listening to Pippi. And Tommy and Annika had quite forgotten about eating more pears. They were busy enough just listening.

'He had more children than he could count, and the smallest one was called Peter,' said Pippi.

'Yes, but a Chinese child *can't* be called Peter,' objected Tommy.

'That's just what his wife told him too. "A Chinese child *can't* be called Peter," she'd say. But Hai Shang was most *awf'ly* stubborn and he said that the baby would either be called Peter or else nothing at all. And then he sat down in a corner and pulled his ears over his head and just sulked. And so his wife had to give in, of course, and the child was called Peter.'

'Oh, indeed?' said Annika.

'It was the horridest child to be found in all Shanghai,' continued Pippi. 'So fussy with his food, that his mother was quite unhappy. You prob'ly know they eat birds' nests in China? Well, there sat the mother with a whole plateful of bird's nest to feed him. "So, little Peter," she'd say, "now we'll eat a great big bite of bird's nest just for Daddy." But Peter only just clamped his lips together and shook his head. In the end Hai

Shang got so angry that he said no new food should be made for Peter before he'd eaten that bird's nest just for Daddy. And when Hai Shang said a thing, it was *so*. The same bird's nest was sent in and out of the kitchen from May till October. On the fourteenth of July the mother asked couldn't she please give Peter a meat pie, but Hai Shang said no.'

'Nonsense,' said the girl on the road.

'Just what Hai Shang said,' continued Pippi. '"Nonsense!" he'd say. "There's no reason why a child can't eat bird's nest if he only stops being contrary." But Peter just clamped his lips together the whole time from May till October.'

'Yes, but how could he live, then?' said Tommy in amazement.

'He *couldn't* live,' said Pippi. 'He died. Of contrariness. The eighteenth of October. And buried the nineteenth. And on the twentieth a swallow flew in through the window and laid an egg in the bird's nest that stood on the table. So it didn't go to waste anyway. No harm done!' said Pippi gaily. Then she gazed thoughtfully at the girl who stood in the road looking simply bewildered.

'How odd you look,' said Pippi. 'Just why's that, now? You don't think, do you, that I'm sitting here telling untruths? What's that? Just say so in that case,' threatened Pippi, and rolled up her sleeves.

'No, no, not at all!' said the girl in alarm. 'I wouldn't say you're telling untruths, exactly, but . . .'

'No, no, not at all!' said Pippi. 'But that's just what I *am* doing. I'm telling fibs till my tongue's getting black, can't you see that? Do you really believe a child can live without food from May till October? 'Course, I know well enough they can manage nicely without food three, four months, but from May till October! Why, that's silly! You certainly ought to *know* that's not true. You shouldn't let people make you believe just anything they like.'

Then the girl went her way and didn't once turn around again.

'How simple people can be,' said Pippi to Tommy and Annika. 'From May till October! Why, that's just so *silly*!'

Then she yelled after the girl, 'No, we haven't seen any bald 'uns all day today. But yesterday seventeen of 'em went by. Arm in arm!'

Pippi's orchard was really delightful. It wasn't well looked-after, to be sure, but there were lovely stretches of grass, which were never cut, and old rosebushes full of white and yellow and pink roses. They were not particularly fine roses, perhaps, but sweetly scented. Quite a number of fruit-trees grew there too, and best of all, some old, old oaks and elms which were perfect for climbing.

Climbing-trees were sadly lacking in Tommy and Annika's orchard, and their mother was always rather afraid they would fall down and hurt themselves. For this reason, they hadn't done very much climbing in their day. But now Pippi said:

'What about climbing up in that oak over there?'

Tommy jumped down from the gate at once, delighted with the suggestion. Annika was a little more doubtful, but when she saw there were big bumps on the trunk that one could climb on, she too thought it would be fun to try.

A few yards from the ground the oak divided into two branches, and where it divided it was just like a little room. It wasn't long before all three children sat there. Over their heads the oak spread its crown of leaves like a big green ceiling.

'We could have tea here,' said Pippi. 'I'll pop in and make a drop.'

Tommy and Annika clapped their hands and shouted 'Hooray!'

It wasn't long before Pippi had tea ready. And she'd baked buns the day before. She stood under the oak and began tossing up teacups, and Tommy and Annika caught them. Now and then it was the *oak* that caught them, so that two teacups were broken. But Pippi ran in and fetched new ones. Then it was the buns' turn, and for a long while a cloud of buns whirled in the air. They, at least, didn't get broken. Finally Pippi climbed up with the teapot on her head. She had milk in a bottle in her pocket, and sugar in a little box.

Tommy and Annika thought that tea had never tasted as good before. They weren't allowed to drink tea every day, but only when they were invited out. And now, after all, they *were* invited out. Annika spilled a little tea in her lap; it was warm and wet at first, and then cold and wet, but it didn't matter at all, said Annika.

When they had finished, Pippi flung the cups down to the grass below.

'I want to see how well the china made nowadays wears,' she said. One cup and all three saucers held, strange as it seems. As for the teapot, only the spout broke off.

All of a sudden, Pippi decided to climb a bit higher in the tree.

'Well, I never saw the likes of this before,' she shouted. 'The tree's hollow!'

Going right into the trunk there was a big

hole, which the leaves had hidden from the children's eyes.

'Could I climb up and see too?' said Tommy. But there was no answer. 'Pippi, where are you?' he called uneasily.

Then they heard Pippi's voice, not above them, but far below. It sounded as if it were coming from under the ground.

'I'm inside the tree. It's hollow all the way to the ground. If I peep out through a little crack I can see the teapot on the grass outside.'

'But how are you going to get *up*?' shouted Annika.

'I never can,' said Pippi. 'I'll have to stand here till I get pensioned off. And you'll have to throw food to me through the hole up there. Five, six times a day.'

Annika began to cry.

'But why worry, why complain?' said Pippi. 'Come down here instead, you two. We can play that we're languishing in a dungeon.'

'Not on your life!' said Annika. And for safety's sake, she climbed down out of the tree altogether.

'Annika, I see you through the crack,' shouted Pippi. 'Don't step on the teapot! It's a good old *cosy* teapot that never did a body any harm. And it isn't *its* fault it hasn't a spout any more.'

Annika came up to the tree, and through a little crack she saw the very tip of Pippi's forefinger. This comforted her a great deal, but she was still anxious.

'Pippi, can't you really get up?' she asked.

Pippi's finger disappeared, and in the twinkling of an eye her face popped out through the hole up in the tree.

'Perhaps I can if I really try,' she said, holding the leaves out of the way with her hands.

'Is it that easy to come up?' said Tommy, who was still in the tree. 'Well, then I want to come down and languish a little.'

'Well, first,' said Pippi, 'I think we'll fetch a ladder.'

She crawled out of the hole and slid quickly to the ground. Then she ran to fetch a ladder, struggled with it up the tree, and stuck it down the hole.

Tommy was wildly excited and couldn't wait to go down. It was quite a difficult climb up to the hole as it was rather high, but Tommy was brave. He wasn't afraid to climb into that dark tree-trunk either. Annika saw him disappear, and she wondered if she would ever see him again. She tried to look in through the crack.

'Annika,' she heard Tommy's voice say, 'you can't imagine how wonderful it is here. You must come in too. It's not the least little bit dangerous when you have a ladder to climb on. If you do it just once, you'll never want to do anything else ever.'

'Are you *sure?*' said Annika.

'Absolutely sure,' said Tommy.

So Annika climbed up into the tree again with quaking legs, and Pippi helped her with the last difficult part. She shrank back a little when she saw how dark it was inside the trunk. But Pippi held her hand and encouraged her.

'Don't be afraid, Annika,' she heard Tommy say from inside. 'I can see your legs now, and I'll be sure to catch you if you should fall.'

Annika didn't fall, but came down safe and sound to Tommy. And in a minute, Pippi followed.

'Isn't this spiffing!' said Tommy.

And Annika had to admit that it was. It wasn't nearly as dark as she had thought, because light came in through the crack. Annika went there to make sure that she too could see the teapot on the grass outside.

'We can have this for our hiding-place,' said Tommy. 'Nobody could possibly know we're in here. And if they come round here looking, we can see them through the crack. And *then* we'll laugh!'

'We can have a little stick to poke them with through the crack,' said Pippi. 'Then they'll think there are ghosts.'

With this thought the children became so happy they all three hugged one another. Then they heard the gong-gonging which rang before dinner at Tommy and Annika's home.

'How awful,' said Tommy. 'We have to go home now. But we'll come here tomorrow, as soon as we get home from school.'

'Do,' said Pippi.

So they climbed up the ladder, first Pippi, then Annika, and Tommy after. And then they climbed down the tree, first Pippi, then Annika, and Tommy after.

6
Pippi Arranges a Picnic

'We're having a holiday from school today,' said Tommy to Pippi, ''cause it's closed for cleaning.'

'Ha!' cried Pippi. 'Injustice again and again! *I* don't get a holiday, though a bit of cleaning is just what's needed here. Just look at this kitchen floor! But for that matter,' she added, 'when I really think it over, I can clean *without* leave. That's just what I mean to do now, holiday or no holiday. I'd like to see someone try and stop me! If you sit on the kitchen table you won't be in the way.'

Tommy and Annika climbed obediently up on the table, and Mr Nelson jumped up there too and lay down to sleep in Annika's lap.

Pippi warmed a big saucepan of water which she then heaved without ceremony on to the kitchen floor. Then she took off her big shoes and lay them neatly on the breadboard. She tied two scrubbing brushes to her bare feet and then skated over the floor so that it said squish-squeep as she ploughed forward through the water.

'I should have become an ice-skating queen,' she said, lifting one leg high in the air so the scrubbing brush on her left foot knocked a piece off the ceiling lamp.

'Grace and charm I do have, at any rate,' she continued, taking a nimble leap over a chair that stood in her way.

'Well, I should think it's about clean now,' she said at last, taking off the brushes.

'Aren't you going to *dry* the floor?' asked Annika.

'No, it can just vapporpate,' said Pippi. 'I don't s'pose it'll catch cold as long as it keeps moving.'

Tommy and Annika clambered down from the table and stepped across the floor as carefully as they could so as not to get wet.

Outside, the sun was shining from a bright blue sky. It was one of those golden September days when one knows it would be lovely to go into the woods. Pippi had an idea.

'What do you think of taking Mr Nelson with us and going on a picnic?'

'Oh, *yes*!' cried Tommy and Annika with glee.

'Run home then, and ask your mother,' said Pippi. 'I'll fix a picnic lunch in the meantime.'

Tommy and Annika thought that it was a fine plan. They rushed home, and it wasn't long before they were back. Pippi was already standing outside the gate with Mr Nelson on her shoulder, a stick in one hand, and a big basket in the other.

At first, the children followed the country road a little way, and then turned off into a field where a pleasant little footpath wound its way between birches and hazel trees. By and by they came to a gate, and past it lay an even lovelier field. But right in front of the gate was a cow, and she didn't look as if she intended to move. Annika shouted at her, and Tommy went bravely forward and tried to shoo her away, but she didn't move an inch, and just stared at the children with her big cow-eyes. To put an end to it all, Pippi laid the basket down, went forward, and lifted the cow away. It lumbered off through the trees in confusion.

'Imagine cows being as pig-headed as that!' said Pippi, jumping with both feet together over the gate. 'And what's the result? The pigs get cow-headed, of course! It's really disgusting to think about it.'

'What a lovely, lovely field!' cried Annika with delight, climbing up on all the rocks she saw. Tommy had taken along his knife, the one he'd got from Pippi, and he cut sticks for both himself and Annika. He cut his thumb a little too, but that didn't matter.

'Perhaps we ought to pick some mushrooms,' said Pippi, breaking off a beautiful red toadstool. 'I wonder if it's eatable,' she continued. 'Anyhow, it certainly isn't *drink*able, that much I know, so there isn't any other choice but to eat it. Perhaps it's all right!'

She bit off a big piece of the toadstool and swallowed it.

'It was!' she pronounced with delight. 'We certainly ought to cook some of these another time,' she said, throwing the toadstool high over the treetops.

'What have you got in the basket, Pippi?' asked Annika. 'Is it anything good?'

'I wouldn't tell you for all the tea in China,' said Pippi. 'First we're going to find a good place where we can set it out.'

The children eagerly began looking for such a place. Annika found a big, flat stone which she thought just right, but it was full of crawling red ants, and 'I shouldn't want to sit down with them, 'cause I don't know them,' said Pippi.

'Yes, and they *bite*,' said Tommy.

'Do they?' said Pippi. 'Bite 'em back, then!'

Then Tommy caught sight of a little glade between two hazel bushes, and that was where he thought they should sit.

'It isn't sunny enough for my freckles to thrive there,' said Pippi. 'And I do think it's nice having freckles.'

A bit further on lay a little cliff which was easily climbed. On the cliff was a sunny little ledge just like a balcony. It was there they sat.

'Now, close your eyes while I set everything out,' said Pippi. Tommy and Annika shut their eyes as tight as they could, and they heard Pippi opening the basket and rustling with paper.

'One, two, nineteen, now you can look!' said Pippi finally. So they looked. And they shouted with delight when they saw all the good things Pippi had set out on the bare rock. There were lovely little sandwiches of meatloaf and ham, a whole pile of pancakes sprinkled with sugar, little brown sausages, and three pineapple puddings.

For, you see, Pippi had learned a great deal from the cook on board her father's ship.

'Gosh, what fun it is to have a holiday!' said Tommy through a mouthful of pancake. 'We ought to have it all the time.'

'No, tell you what,' said Pippi, 'I'm not all *that* fond of cleaning. It's fun, sure enough, but not for *every* day.'

At last the children were so full they could hardly move, and they sat quietly in the sunshine and simply felt good.

'I wonder if it's hard to fly,' said Pippi, looking dreamily over the side of the ledge. The cliff dropped sharply beneath them, and it was far to the ground.

'Going *down* ought to be possible to learn,' she continued. 'It must be *lots* harder going up. But then, one can begin the easy way. I think I'll try!'

'No, Pippi!' cried both Tommy and Annika. 'Oh, dear Pippi, don't do it, please!'

But Pippi already stood at the edge.

'Fly, you flat fly, fly! and the flat fly flew,' she said, and just as she said 'flew', she raised her arms and stepped right into the air. After half a second there was a thud. It was Pippi hitting the ground. Tommy and Annika lay on their stomachs and looked fearfully down at her. Pippi got up and brushed her knees.

'I forgot to flap,' she said easily. 'And I had too many pancakes in me.'

Just at that moment the children discovered that Mr Nelson had disappeared. He had clearly gone off on an outing of his very own. They agreed that they had seen him sitting happily chewing the picnic-basket to pieces, but during Pippi's flying practice they had quite forgotten him. And now he was gone.

Pippi became so angry that she threw one of her shoes into a big, deep pool of water.

'You shouldn't ever take monkeys along when you go somewhere,' she said. 'He should have been left at home to mind the horse. It would have served him right,' she continued, walking into the pool to fetch her shoe. The water reached her waist.

'One should remember to wet the hair, too,' said Pippi, and ducked her head under the water so long it began to bubble.

'There! I won't have to bother about the hair-dresser *this* time,' she continued with satisfaction when she reappeared at last. Then she walked out of the pool and put her shoe on, and they marched off to look for Mr Nelson.

'Listen to the skwuffling when I walk,' laughed Pippi. 'It says "skwuff, skweep" in my clothes, and "skwipp, skwipp" in my shoes. It's funny! I think you should try it too,' she said to Annika, who was walking her pretty way with her fair, silky hair, pink dress, and little white leather shoes.

'Some other time,' said the wise Annika.

They went on.

'I get really angry with Mr Nelson,' said Pippi. 'He does this all the time. He ran away from me once in Sourabaya too, and took a job as a butler with an old widow.

'That isn't true, you know,' she added after a pause.

Tommy suggested that they should each go separate ways to search. Annika was a little afraid and didn't want to at first, but Tommy said, 'You're not a *coward*, are you?'

And of course Annika couldn't stand for that. So all three children went separate ways.

Tommy went across a meadow. He didn't find Mr Nelson, but he *did* find something else. A bull! Or rather, the bull found Tommy, and the bull didn't *like* Tommy, because it was an angry bull who was not in the least fond of children. With a terrible bellow and lowered head he rushed forward, and Tommy let out a wild howl of distress which could be heard through the whole wood. Pippi and Annika heard it too, and came running to see what it was Tommy had meant by his howl. The bull had already caught Tommy on his horns and had tossed him high up in the air.

'What a rude bull!' said Pippi to Annika, who was crying, quite distressed. 'One simply can't act that way. Why, he's dirtying up Tommy's white sailor suit. I'll have to go and talk sense to that stupid bull.'

And she did. She ran forward and pulled his tail.

'Excuse me for interrupting,' she said, and as she was pulling rather hard, the bull turned round and saw a new child which he also wanted to stick with his horns.

'As I said, excuse me for breaking in,' said Pippi again. 'And excuse me for breaking *off*,' she added, and broke off one of the bull's horns. 'It's not fashionable with two horns this year,' she said. 'This year, all the better bulls have only one horn. If any at all,' she added and broke off the other one too.

As bulls have no feeling in their horns, this one didn't know that his were missing. He still tried to butt her, and if it had been anyone but Pippi, there wouldn't have been anything left of that child but apple sauce.

'Hahaha, stop tickling me,' cried Pippi. 'You can't imagine how ticklish I am! Haha, stop, stop, I'll laugh myself to death!'

But the bull didn't stop, and finally Pippi jumped upon his back to get a moment's peace. It wasn't a particularly peaceful place, though, for the bull didn't like having Pippi on his back. He made the very worst sorts of twists and turns to get her off, but she just held tight with her legs and sat where she was. The bull rushed back and forth in the meadow and bellowed so that smoke came out of his nose. Pippi laughed and shouted and waved to Tommy and Annika, who stood at a distance trembling like aspen leaves. The bull turned round and tried to throw Pippi off.

'Look at me dancing with my little friend!' sang Pippi, sitting fast. Finally, the bull became so tired that he lay down on the ground and wished there were no children in the world. For that matter, he had never seen why children were necessary at all.

'Had you thought of taking your afternoon nap now?' asked Pippi politely. 'I shan't disturb you, then.'

She stepped down from his back and went over to Tommy and Annika. Tommy had cried a little. He'd been hurt on one arm, but Annika had wound her handkerchief round it, so it didn't hurt any longer.

'Oh, *Pippi!*' cried Annika, full of excitement when Pippi came.

'Ssh!' whispered Pippi. 'Don't wake the bull! He's sleeping, and if we wake him he'll just be cross.

'Mr Nelson! Mr Nelson! Where are you?' she shouted the next minute in a shrill voice without bothering about the bull's afternoon nap. 'We have to go home!'

And indeed, there sat Mr Nelson huddled up in a pine tree. He was chewing his tail, and looked very unhappy. It wasn't much fun for such a little monkey to be left alone in the woods. Now he hopped down from the pine tree and up on Pippi's shoulder, and he waved his straw hat as he always did when he was especially happy.

'So you didn't become a butler this time,' said Pippi stroking his back. 'Bosh, *that* was a true fib,' she added. 'But if it was true, how could it be a fib? Perhaps when all's said and done, he really *has* been a butler in Sourabaya, after all! Well, if that's so, I know who's going to serve dinner from now on!'

And so they wandered home, Pippi still in dripping clothes and squelching shoes. Tommy and Annika thought they had had a wonderful day, except for the bull, and they sang a song they had learned at school. It was really a summer song, and now it was almost autumn, but they thought it would do just the same.

'When summer days are warm and still
We like to go o'er wood and hill
Let the journey be as hard as it will,
We'll sing as we go, Hi ho, hi ho!
All children, hear!
Join us and sing,
O, make the air with music ring!
Our happy band will never stop,
We'll keep on climbing up, up, up,
Until we've reached the very top!
When summer days are warm and still,
We sing as we go, Hi ho, hi ho!'

Pippi sang too, but she didn't use quite the
same words. She sang like this:

'When summer days are warm and still
And I go over wood and hill
I do exactly what I will
And it drips as I go, Hi ho, hi ho!
And in my shoes,
Because I choose,
It squelches just like orange juice
Because the shoes are soaking wet.
Ho, ha, what a silly bull we met!
And I—I do like chicken croquette!
When summer days are warm and still
It drips as I go. Drip ho! drip ho!'

7
Pippi Goes to the Circus

A circus had come to the little town, and all the children ran to their mothers and fathers and begged to be allowed to go. Tommy and Annika did so too, and their kind father at once gave them some of the shiny Swedish silver coins called crowns.

With their money held tightly in their hands, they rushed over to Pippi. She was on the front porch with the horse, arranging his tail into small braids, each tied with a red ribbon.

'Today is his birthday, I think,' she said, 'so he has to be dressed up.'

'Pippi,' said Tommy, panting, for they had run so fast, 'Pippi, can you come with us to the circus?'

'I can do anything I please,' said Pippi, 'but I don't know if I can come to the sarcus, 'cause I don't know what a sarcus is. Does it hurt?'

'How silly you are!' said Tommy. 'It doesn't hurt! It's just fun! Horses and clowns and beautiful ladies who walk on a rope!'

'But it costs money,' said Annika, opening her little hand to see if her three shiny crowns still lay there.

'I'm rich as a goblin,' said Pippi, 'so I suppose I can always buy a sarcus. It's going to be crowded if I have any more horses, though. The clowns and those beautiful ladies could squeeze into the laundry-house, but it's more of a problem with the horses.'

'What nonsense!' said Tommy. 'You're not going to *buy* the circus. It costs money to go there and look, don't you see?'

'Heaven help me!' cried Pippi, shutting her eyes tight. 'Does it cost money to *look*? And here I've been going around with my eyes open all day and every day! Goodness knows how much money I've used up already!'

Then little by little she carefully opened one eye, and rolled it round and round in her head. 'Cost what it will,' she said, 'I must have a peep now!'

Tommy and Annika finally succeeded in explaining to Pippi what a circus was, and then Pippi went and took some gold pieces out of her suitcase. After that she put on her hat, which was as big as a mill-wheel, and they started off for the circus.

There was a crowd of people outside the circus tent, and in front of the ticket window stood a long queue. By and by it was Pippi's turn. She stuck her head through the window, looked hard at the dear old lady who sat there, and said, 'How much does it cost to look at *you*?'

The old lady was from a foreign country, so she didn't understand what Pippi meant. She answered, 'Liddle girl, it is costink vive crones the front rows and dree crones the back rows and wan crones the zdandinkroom.'

'I see,' said Pippi. 'But you must promise that you'll walk on the rope too.'

Now Tommy stepped in and said that Pippi would have a ticket for the back rows. Pippi gave a gold piece to the old lady, and she looked suspiciously at it. She bit it, too, to see if it were real. At last she was convinced that it really was gold, and Pippi got her ticket. She got a great many silver coins in change as well.

'What do I want with all that nasty little white money?' said Pippi crossly. 'Keep it. I'll look at you twice instead. From the zdandinkroom.'

So, as Pippi absolutely didn't want any money back, the lady changed her ticket for a front row one, and gave Tommy and Annika front row tickets as well, without their having to add any money of their own. In this way, Pippi and Tommy and Annika came to sit on some very fine red chairs by the ringside. Tommy and Annika turned round several times in order to wave to their schoolmates, who sat much further away.

'*This* is a queer hut,' said Pippi, looking about her with wonder. 'But they've spilled sawdust on the floor, I see. Not that I'm fussy, but it *does* look a bit untidy.'

Tommy explained to Pippi that there was always sawdust in circus rings for the horses to run on.

On a platform sat the circus musicians, and they suddenly began to play a rousing march. Pippi clapped her hands wildly and jumped up and down in her chair with delight.

'Does it cost something to listen, too, or can you do that free?' she wondered.

Just then the curtain was pulled back from the artistes' entrance, and the ringmaster, dressed in black and with a whip in his hand, came running in, and with him there came ten white horses with red plumes on their heads.

The ringmaster cracked his whip, and the horses cantered round the ring. Then he cracked his whip again, and they all stood with their front legs up on the railing which circled the ring. One of the horses had stopped just in front of the children. Annika didn't like having a horse so close to her, so she crouched back in her chair as far as she could. But Pippi leaned forward, lifted up the horse's front leg, and said, 'How's yourself? My horse sends his regards to you. It's *his* birthday too today, though he has bows on his tail instead of his head.'

As luck would have it, Pippi let go of the horse's foot before the ringmaster cracked his whip the next time, because then all the horses jumped down from the railing and began to canter again.

When the act was finished, the ringmaster bowed beautifully, and the horses trotted out. A second later the curtain opened again for a coal-black horse, and on his back stood a beautiful lady dressed in green silk tights. Her name was Miss Carmencita, it said in the programme.

The horse trotted round in the sawdust, and Miss Carmencita stood there calmly and smiled. But then something happened. Just as the horse passed Pippi's place, something came whistling through the air. It was none other than Pippi herself. There she suddenly stood on the horse's back behind Miss Carmencita. At first, Miss Carmencita was so astonished that she nearly fell off the horse. Then she became angry. She began to hit behind herself with her hands in order to get Pippi to jump off. But she couldn't manage it.

'Calm down a little,' said Pippi. 'You're not the only one who's going to have fun. There are others who've paid *their* money too, believe it or not!'

Then Miss Carmencita wanted to jump off herself, but she couldn't do that either, for Pippi had a steady hold round her waist. The people in the circus couldn't help laughing. It looked so silly, they thought, to see the beautiful Miss Carmencita held fast by a little red-headed scamp who stood on the horse's back in her big shoes looking as if she'd never done anything *but* perform in a circus.

But the ringmaster didn't laugh. He made a sign to his red-coated attendants to run forward and stop the horse.

'Is the act over already?' said Pippi, disappointed. 'Just now when we were having such fun!'

'Derrible child,' hissed the ringmaster between his teeth, 'go avay!'

Pippi looked sorrowfully at him. 'Well, but, now,' she said, 'why are you so angry with me? I thought everyone was supposed to have a nice time here.'

She jumped down from the horse, and went and sat down in her place. But now two big attendants came to throw her out. They took hold of her and tried to lift her.

It was no use. Pippi just sat still, and it simply wasn't possible to move her from the spot, though they tugged as hard as they could. So they shrugged their shoulders and went away.

In the meantime the next act had begun. It was Miss Elvira, who was to walk the tightrope. She wore a pink tulle dress and carried a pink parasol in her hand. With small neat steps she ran out on to the rope. She swung her legs and did all manner of tricks. It was very pretty indeed. She proved too that she could go backwards on the thin rope. But when she came back to the little platform at the end of the line and turned round, Pippi was standing there.

'What was it you said?' said Pippi, delighted to see Miss Elvira's surprised expression.

Miss Elvira didn't say anything at all, but jumped down from the rope and threw her arms around the neck of the ringmaster, who was her father. Again he sent for his attendants to throw Pippi out. This time he sent for five. But all the people in the circus shouted, 'Let her be! We want to see the little red-head!'

And they stamped their feet and clapped their hands.

Pippi ran out on the line. And Miss Elvira's tricks were nothing compared to what Pippi could do. When she came to the middle of the rope, she stretched one leg straight up into the air, and her big shoe spread out like a roof over her head. She waggled her foot a little, to scratch behind her ear.

The ringmaster was not the least bit pleased that Pippi was performing in his circus. He wanted to be rid of her. So he sneaked forward and loosened the mechanism which held the line tight, and he was sure that Pippi would fall off.

But she didn't. She began to swing the rope instead. Back and forth swayed the line, faster and faster swung Pippi, and then—suddenly—she took a leap into the air and landed right on the ringmaster. He was so frightened that he began to run.

'This horse is even more fun,' said Pippi. 'But why haven't you any tassels in your hair?'

Now Pippi thought it was time to turn back to Tommy and Annika. She climbed off the ringmaster and went and sat down, and then the next act was about to begin. There was a moment's delay, because the ringmaster first had to go out and drink a glass of water and comb his hair. But after that he came in, bowed to the audience, and said, 'Ladies and chantlemen! In ze next moment you vill zee vun of ze vunders uff all time, ze zdrongest man in ze vorld, Mighty Adolf, who nobody has effer beaten yet. And here he is, ladies and chantlemen. Mighty Adolf!'

A gigantic man stepped into the ring. He was dressed in scarlet tights, and he had a leopard skin round his stomach. He bowed to the audience, and looked very self-satisfied indeed.

'Just *look* at which mossels!' said the ringmaster, squeezing Mighty Adolf's arm where the muscles bulged like bowls under the skin.

'And now, ladies and chantlemen, I giff you a grrreat offer! Weech of you dares to try a wrestling match with Mighty Adolf, who dares to try to beat ze vorld's zdrongest man? A hundred crowns I pay to the vun who can beat Mighty Adolf. A hundred crowns, consider it, ladies and chantlemen! Step right up! Who'll giff it a try?'

Nobody came forward.

'What did he say?' asked Pippi. 'And why is he speaking Arabian?'

'He said that the person who can beat that great big man over there will get a hundred crowns,' said Tommy.

'I can do it,' said Pippi. 'But I think it would be a shame to beat him, 'cause he looks such a nice man.'

'But you could *never* do it,' said Annika. 'Why, that's the strongest man in the world!'

'Man, yes,' said Pippi. 'But I'm the strongest *girl* in the world, don't forget.'

In the meanwhile, Mighty Adolf was lifting dumb-bells and bending thick iron bars to show how strong he was.

'Now, now, goot people!' shouted the ringmaster. 'Is there rilly nobody who should like to vin a hundred crowns? Must I rilly keep them for myself?' he said, waving a hundred-crown note.

'No, I rilly don't think you must,' said Pippi, climbing over the railing to the ring.

'Go! Disappear! I don't vant I should zee you,' the ringmaster hissed.

'Why are you always so unfriendly?' said Pippi reproachfully. 'I only want to fight with Mighty Adolf.'

'Zis is no time for chokes,' said the ringmaster. 'Go avay, before Mighty Adolf hears your impertinence!'

But Pippi went right past the ringmaster and over to Mighty Adolf. She took his big hand in hers and shook it heartily.

'Now, shall we have a bit of a wrestle, you and I?' she said.

Mighty Adolf looked at her and didn't understand a thing.

'In one minute I'm going to begin,' said Pippi.

And she did. She grappled properly with Mighty Adolf, and before anyone knew how it had happened, she'd laid him flat on the mat. Mighty Adolf scrambled up, quite red in the face.

'Hurrah for Pippi!' shouted Tommy and Annika. All the people at the circus heard this, and so they shouted, 'Hurrah for Pippi!' too. The ringmaster sat on the railing and wrung his hands. He was angry. But Mighty Adolf was angrier still. Never in his life had anything so terrible happened to him. But now he would show this little red-haired girl what kind of a man Mighty Adolf was! He rushed forward and took a strong grip on her, but Pippi stood as fast as a rock.

'You can do better than that,' she said to encourage him. Then she prised herself free from his grip, and in a second, Mighty Adolf was lying on the mat again. Pippi stood beside him and waited. She didn't have to wait long. With a bellow he raised himself and stormed at her again.

'Tiddlelipom and poddeliday,' said Pippi.

All the people at the circus stamped their feet and threw their caps up in the air, and shouted, 'Hurrah for Pippi!'

The third time Mighty Adolf rushed at her, Pippi lifted him high into the air and carried him on her upstretched arms around the ring. After that, she laid him on the mat and held him there.

'Now, my boy, I think we've had enough of this sort of game,' she said. 'It won't get any more fun than this, anyway.'

'Pippi is the winner! Pippi is the winner!' shouted all the people at the circus. Mighty Adolf slunk out as fast as he could. And the ringmaster had to go forward and present Pippi with the hundred-crown note, though he looked as if he would rather have eaten her up.

'Here you are, my young lady, here is your hundred crowns!'

'That?' said Pippi scornfully. 'What should I do with that piece of paper? You can have it to wrap fish in, if you want!'

Then she went back to her place.

'This is a long-lasting circus, this one,' she said to Tommy and Annika. 'Forty winks might not do any harm. But wake me if there's anything else I need to help with.'

So she lay back in her chair and went to sleep immediately. There she lay snoring while clowns and sword-swallowers and snake-people showed their tricks to Tommy and Annika and all the other people at the circus.

'Somehow, I think Pippi was best of all,' whispered Tommy to Annika.

8
Pippi is Visited by Thieves

After Pippi's performance at the circus there was not a person in the little town who didn't know how fearfully strong she was. There had even been articles about her in the newspaper. But people who lived elsewhere naturally didn't know who Pippi was.

One dark autumn night two tramps came wandering by on the road past Villekulla Cottage. They were two nasty, shabby thieves who had set out through the countryside in order to see if they could find something to steal. When they saw that there was a light on in Villekulla Cottage, they decided to go in and ask for a sandwich.

That evening Pippi had emptied out all her gold pieces on the kitchen floor and sat counting them. She wasn't very good at counting, to be sure, but she did it anyway once in a while. Just to keep things in order.

' . . . seventy-five, seventy-six, seventy-seven, seventy-eight, seventy-nine, seventy-ten, seventy-eleven, seventy-twelve, seventy-seventeen, pooh! There must be other numbers to be had. 'Course, now I remember! One hundred and four, a thousand. Bless be! *that's* a lot of money!' said Pippi.

Just then there was a knock at the door.

'Come in or stay where you are, just as you like,' yelled Pippi. 'It's not for me to decide!'

The door opened and the two tramps came in. You can be sure their eyes grew big when they saw a little red-haired girl sitting there quite alone on the floor counting money.

'Are you at home all alone?' they asked craftily.

'Not at all,' said Pippi. 'Mr Nelson is at home too.'

The thieves couldn't very well know that Mr Nelson was just a little monkey who lay sleeping in his green-painted bed with a doll's blanket round his stomach. They thought it was the man of the house whose name was Mr Nelson, and they winked slyly at each other.

'We can come back a little later,' they meant with that wink, but to Pippi they said, 'Well, we just came in to see what your clock says.'

'Big, strong fellows who don't know what a clock says!' said Pippi. 'What kind of bringing up did you have? It says tick tock. Now I suppose you'll want to know what it does? Well, it goes and goes and never comes to the door. If you know any more riddles, just come along with them,' she said encouragingly.

The tramps thought that Pippi was probably too little to understand about clocks, so they turned and went out again without a word.

'Holy mackerel! Did you see all that money?' said one.

'What a piece of luck,' said the other. 'All we have to do now is wait until the little girl and that Nelson fellow are asleep. Then we can slip in and lay our hands on the whole lot.'

They sat down under an oak tree in the orchard to wait. A cold drizzle fell and they were very hungry. It was really quite unpleasant, but the thought of all that money kept them in good spirits.

In all the other houses, the lights went out one by one, but in Villekulla Cottage they still kept on burning. For Pippi was busy teaching herself to dance the polka, and she didn't want to go to bed before she was sure she knew how. Finally, though, the windows of Villekulla Cottage became dark as well.

The tramps waited a good while so as to be certain that Mr Nelson would be asleep. At last they sneaked forward to the back door and got ready to open it with their house-breaking tools. One of them (his name was Bloom, by the way) in the meantime tried the door by pure accident. It wasn't locked.

'They must be out of their heads!' he whispered to his comrade. 'The door's wide open!'

'So much the better for us,' answered the comrade, a dark-haired fellow called Thunder Karlson by those who knew him.

Thunder Karlson lit his torch, and then they sneaked into the kitchen. There was nobody there. In the next room was Pippi's bed, and there, too, was Mr Nelson's little doll's-bed.

Thunder Karlson opened the door and carefully looked in. It was peaceful and still, and he let the flashing light of the torch play around the room. When the stream of light fell on Pippi's bed, both the tramps saw, to their astonishment, nothing but a pair of feet resting on the pillow. As usual, Pippi had her head under the covers down at the foot of the bed.

'That must be the little girl,' whispered Thunder Karlson to Bloom. 'And she's certainly asleep. But where d'you think Nelson is?'

'*Mr* Nelson, if you don't mind,' came Pippi's calm voice from under the covers. 'Mr Nelson is lying in that little green doll's-bed.'

The tramps were so alarmed that they were about to rush out at once. But then they thought over what Pippi had said. *Mr Nelson lay in the doll's-bed!* By the light of the torch they could see the doll's-bed and the little monkey who lay in it. Thunder Karlson couldn't help laughing.

'Bloom,' he said, 'Mr Nelson is a monkey, hahaha!'

'Well, what did you think he was?' came the calm voice from under the covers. 'A lawnmower?'

'Aren't your mother and father home?' asked Bloom.

'No,' said Pippi. 'They're gone. Quite gone!'

Thunder Karlson and Bloom chuckled with joy.

'Well, little lady,' said Thunder Karlson, 'come out, we'd like to talk to you.'

'No, I'm asleep,' said Pippi. 'Was it something

about clocks again? 'Cause in that case, can you guess what kind of a clock . . . '

But before she could finish, Bloom took a firm hold of the covers and pulled them off Pippi.

'Can you dance the polka?' asked Pippi, looking him solemnly in the eyes. '*I* can!'

'You ask so many questions,' said Thunder Karlson. 'Can we ask some too? For example, where have you got the money you had on the floor?'

'In the suitcase there on the cupboard,' Pippi answered truthfully.

Thunder Karlson and Bloom grinned.

'I hope you don't mind me taking it back, little friend?' said Thunder Karlson.

'Oh, not at all,' said Pippi. ' '*Course* not!'

Whereupon he went over and lifted down the suitcase.

'I hope you don't mind me taking it back, little friend?' said Pippi, climbing out of bed and padding over to Bloom.

Bloom didn't know just how it happened, but the suitcase was suddenly in Pippi's hand.

'This is no joke,' said Thunder Karlson angrily. 'Give us that suitcase!'

He grabbed Pippi hard by the arm and tried to snatch away the much-desired prize.

'*I* wasn't joking,' said Pippi, lifting Thunder Karlson and putting him up on the cupboard. A minute later Bloom sat there too. Then the tramps both became frightened. They began to understand that Pippi was not exactly an ordinary girl. But they wanted the suitcase so much that they forgot their fears.

'All together, Bloom!' cried Thunder Karlson, and they jumped down from the cupboard and hurled themselves on Pippi, who held the suitcase in her hand. But Pippi poked them with her forefinger so that they sat down hard each in a corner. Before they were able to get up, Pippi had got out a rope, and as quick as thought she bound fast the arms and legs of both the thieves. Now they changed their tune.

'Kind, good little missie,' begged Thunder Karlson, 'forgive us, we were only joking! Don't hurt us, we're just two poor penniless tramps who came in to ask for a bit of food.'

Bloom even shed a tear or two.

Pippi put the suitcase in its proper place on the cupboard. Then she turned to her captives.

'Can either of you dance the polka?'

'Well, brrumph, that is . . . ' said Thunder Karlson. 'I should think we've both done a bit along that line.'

'Oh, what fun!' said Pippi, clapping her hands. 'Couldn't we give it a try? I've just learned how, you see.'

'Yes, by all means!' said Thunder Karlson, somewhat bewildered.

Then Pippi took a big pair of scissors and cut the ropes that bound her guests.

'Oh, but we haven't any music,' said Pippi sorrowfully. Then she had an idea.

'Couldn't you play on the comb,' she said to Bloom, 'while I dance with him?' She pointed to Thunder Karlson.

Why, yes. Bloom would certainly play the comb. And he did, so that it could be heard all over the house. Mr Nelson was startled out of his sleep and sat up in his bed just in time to see Pippi whirling about with Thunder Karlson. She was dreadfully serious, and she danced with great energy as if her life depended on it.

At the end, Bloom didn't want to play on the comb any longer, as he claimed it tickled his mouth unmercifully. And Thunder Karlson, who had been trudging along the road all day long, began to have tired legs.

'Just a little while longer,' begged Pippi, and continued dancing. There was nothing for Bloom and Thunder Karlson to do but continue too.

When it was three o'clock in the morning, Pippi said, 'Oh, I could keep on till Thursday! But perhaps you're tired and hungry?'

And that was just what they were, though they hardly dared to say so. Pippi brought out bread and cheese and butter and ham and cold steak and milk from the cupboard, and then they sat round the kitchen table, Bloom and Thunder Karlson and Pippi, and ate until they were just about square. Pippi tossed a little milk into one of her ears.

'It's good for earache,' she said.

'What a shame! Have you an earache?' said Bloom.

'No,' said Pippi. 'But I might get one!'

Finally the two tramps got up, thanked Pippi very much for the food, and asked might they please say goodbye now.

'How nice it was that you came! Must you really go so soon?' Pippi complained.

'Never have I seen anyone who could dance the polka like you, my little honey-bun!' she said to Thunder Karlson.

'Practise hard at playing on the comb,' she said to Bloom, 'then you won't feel it tickle any more.'

Just as they got to the doorway, Pippi came running and gave them each a gold piece.

'You've honestly earned this,' she said.

9
Pippi Goes to a Tea Party

T ommy and Annika's mother had invited
some ladies to a tea party, and as she had
baked so very many cakes she decided to
let Tommy and Annika invite Pippi at the same
time. In this way, she thought, she wouldn't have
any bother with her own children.

Tommy and Annika were overjoyed when they
were told this, and they ran straight away over to
Pippi to invite her. Pippi was walking about in
her orchard watering the few poor remaining
flowers with an old, rusty watering-can. As it was

pouring with rain that day, Tommy told Pippi he thought it was really rather unnecessary.

'That's all very well for *you* to say,' said Pippi indignantly. 'But I lay awake all night looking forward to getting up and watering the flowers. You can bet your boots I'm not going to let a little rain stop me!'

Now Annika came out with the wonderful news about the tea party.

'Tea party . . . *me*?' cried Pippi, becoming so nervous that she began to water Tommy instead of the rosebush in question. 'Oh, what will happen? Help! I'm so nervous! What if I can't behave myself?'

'Why, '*course* you can,' said Annika.

'Don't be too sure about that,' said Pippi. 'I do try, believe me, but I've noticed lots of times that people don't think I'm behaving even though I've really truly tried to just as nicely as ever I could. At sea we never did fuss much with such things. But I promise I'll put my shoulder to the wheel good and proper today so you won't have to be ashamed of me.'

'Fine,' said Tommy, and then he and Annika dashed home again through the rain.

'This afternoon at three, don't forget!' shouted Annika, looking out from under the umbrella.

At three o'clock that afternoon a very elegant

young lady walked up the steps of the Settergreen home. It was Pippi Longstocking. For the sake of being different, her red hair was unbraided, and it fell about her like a lion's mane. She had painted her mouth a violent red with chalk, and blackened her eyebrows so much that she looked quite dangerous. With the red chalk she had also coloured all her nails, and she had put big green bows on her shoes.

'I should think I'll be the fanciest at *this* party,' she muttered, rather pleased with herself, as she rang the doorbell.

In the parlour of the Settergreen home sat three distinguished ladies, Tommy and Annika, and their mother. A splendidly laid table stood there, and a log-fire burned cheerily in the open fireplace. The ladies talked quietly with each other, and Tommy and Annika sat on the sofa and looked at an album. It was all very peaceful.

But suddenly the peace was broken.

'Attaaaaan-*shun*!'

A piercing cry came out of the front hall, and the next minute Pippi stood on the threshold. Her cry had been so loud and so unexpected that the ladies jumped in their seats.

'Company, forward M A R C H !' came the next cry, and Pippi went forward with measured steps to Mrs Settergreen.

'Company, H A L T !' She stopped.

'Present arms, one, T W O !' she yelled, taking Mrs Settergreen's hand in both of hers and shaking it heartily.

'Knees bend!' she cried, curtsying prettily. Then she leaned forward towards Mrs Settergreen and said in her usual voice, 'The fact of the matter is that I'm shy, so if I don't do this by commands, I'd just stand in the front hall and be contrary and not dare come in.'

Thereupon she rushed up to the other ladies and kissed them on the cheek.

'Charming, charming, upon my honour!' she said, for she had once heard a very fine gentleman say that to a lady. And then she sat down in the best chair she could see. Mrs Settergreen had thought that the children would have their party up in Tommy and Annika's room, but Pippi sat calmly where she was, slapped her knees, and said with her eyes on the tea-table, '*That* certainly looks good! When do we begin?'

At the same moment, Ella, the maid, came in with the teapot, and Mrs Settergreen said, 'Shall we have tea now?'

'Bags, I'm first!' shouted Pippi, and was at the table in two leaps. She scrambled together as many cakes as she could manage on one plate, slung five lumps of sugar into a teacup, emptied half the cream-pitcher into it as well, and returned to the chair with her plunder before the ladies had even come forward to the table.

Pippi stretched her legs out in front of her and put the plate of cakes between the tips of her toes. Then she plunged each cake with gusto into the teacup and pushed so much into her mouth that she couldn't get a word out, much as she tried. In a trice she had finished all the cakes on the plate. She stood up, hit on the plate like on a tambourine, and went up to the table to see if there were any left. The ladies looked disapprovingly at her, but she didn't notice that.

Gaily chattering, she went round the table and took a cake here and a cake there.

'It was really nice of you to invite me,' she said. 'I've never been to a tea party before.'

A big cream cake stood on the table. It was decorated with a red sweet in the middle. Pippi stood with her hands behind her back and looked at it. Suddenly, she bent down and snatched the sweet with her teeth. But she had bobbed a little too quickly, for when she came up again her whole face was a block of cream.

'Hahaha,' laughed Pippi. 'Now we can play blind-man's-buff, 'cause here we certainly have the blind-man free of charge. I can't see a thing!'

She stretched out her tongue and licked off all the cream.

'Well, it's terribly too bad about this,' she said. 'And the cake's quite ruined anyway, so it's just as well if I eat it up at once.'

And so she did. She went at it with a cake spade, and within a very short time, the whole cake had disappeared. Pippi rubbed her stomach with satisfaction. Mrs Settergreen had gone out to the kitchen for a moment and knew nothing of the accident with the cake. But the other ladies looked very sternly at Pippi. *They* would have liked some of that cake, too. Pippi noticed that they looked a bit dissatisfied, and she decided to cheer them up.

'Now, you mustn't be upset about such a little accident,' she said consolingly. 'The main thing is that we have our health. And at a tea party you ought to have fun.'

With these words she took the sugar-bowl from the table and sprinkled a good deal of sugar on the floor.

'Have you ever noticed what fun it is to walk on a floor that's got sugar on it?' she asked the ladies. 'It's even *more* fun, of course, going barefoot,' she continued, tearing off her shoes and stockings. 'I think you ought to try it too, 'cause there just isn't anything that feels better, you can take my word for that.'

But now Mrs Settergreen came in, and when she saw the spilled sugar she took Pippi firmly by the arm and led her over to Tommy and Annika on the sofa. Then she went and sat with the ladies and offered them another cup of tea. That the cake had disappeared only pleased her. She thought her guests had liked it so well they had eaten it all up.

Pippi, Tommy, and Annika talked quietly on the sofa, the fire crackled in the fireplace, the ladies drank their tea, and all was peace and quiet once again. As it now and then happens at tea parties, the ladies began talking about their maids. None of them seemed to have a particularly good one, for they were not at all satisfied and they agreed that the only solution was not to have a maid at all. It was far better to do everything oneself, for then at least one could be sure that it would be properly done.

Pippi sat on the sofa listening, and after a while she said, 'My grandmother once had a maid called Martha. She had chilblains on her feet, but otherwise there wasn't anything wrong with her. The only awkwardness was that as soon as strangers came she rushed forward and bit them in the leg. And scolded! Oh, how she scolded! You could hear it all over the neighbourhood. But it was only her way of being playful. The strangers didn't always understand that, though. There was an old vicar's wife who came to see grandmother once when Martha was new to her job. When Martha came running at her and sank her teeth into the lady's shin, she let out a howl which frightened Martha so much she bit her teeth together even harder, and then she couldn't get loose. She was stuck to the vicar's wife all the week till Friday. So grandmother had to peel the potatoes herself that day. But it got done properly, anyway. She peeled them so thoroughly that when she was finished there weren't any potatoes left. Just peel. After that Friday the vicar's wife never visited grandmother any more. She couldn't take a joke. And Martha, who was so funny and cheerful! Though for all that, she could be quite touchy too, no doubt about that. Once when grandmother drove a fork in her ear she went and sulked all day long.'

Pippi looked around and gave a friendly laugh.

'Well, that was Martha, *that* was,' she said, twiddling her thumbs.

The ladies looked as if they hadn't heard anything. They continued to talk.

'If my Rosa were at least *clean* at her work,' said Mrs Bergen, 'I could possibly keep her on. But she's simply piggish.'

'Then you should have seen Martha,' Pippi chimed in. 'Martha was so filthy to the core, it was a fright to see, grandmother said. But it was all genuine washable dirt, to be sure. Once at a bazaar at the Ritz Hotel she got first prize for the mourning-borders round her nails. Nuisance and miseries, but that girl was grubby!'

'Can you imagine,' said Mrs Granberg, 'the other evening when my Britta was going out, she simply borrowed my blue silk dress without a word! Isn't that the limit?'

'Well, I should say,' said Pippi. 'She seems on the whole to be made in the same mould as Martha, I can tell that. Grandmother had a pink vest she liked an awful lot. The trouble was that Martha liked it too. Each morning grandmother and Martha had a row over who should have the vest. At last they agreed to have it every other day, so's it would be fair. But even then Martha was troublesome! Sometimes she would come running in when it wasn't her turn at *all* and say, "Here! There'll be no mashed turnip served today if I can't have the pink wool vest!" Well now, what was grandmother to do? Mashed turnip was her favourite dish. Martha got the vest! And when she'd got it, she went out to the kitchen as sweet as could be and set to beating the mashed turnip so's it splashed on the walls.'

There was a moment's silence. Then Mrs Alexanderson said, 'Now, I'm not absolutely certain, but I strongly suspect that my Hilda steals. I *know* that things have been disappearing.'

'Martha . . . ' began Pippi, but Mrs Settergreen said firmly:

'The children may go upstairs immediately!'

'Yes—but, I was just going to tell how Martha stole too,' said Pippi. 'Like a magpie! Thick and fast! She used to get up in the middle of the night and steal a thing or two 'cause otherwise she couldn't sleep well, she said. Once she pinched grandmother's piano and jammed it in the top drawer of her bureau. She was very light-fingered, grandmother said.'

Now Tommy and Annika took Pippi by the arms and pulled her up the stairs. The ladies drank still more tea, and Mrs Settergreen said, 'I shouldn't really complain about my Ella, but she *does* break a great deal of china.'

A red head appeared at the top of the stairs.

'Speaking of Martha,' said Pippi, 'perhaps you're wondering if *she* used to break any china. Well, I should say she did! She had picked a special day of the week for it. It was on Tuesdays, grandmother said. And already about five o'clock on Tuesday mornings you could hear that brick of a girl smashing china in the kitchen. She began with cups and glasses and other light things, and went on later to those deep plates, and then the flat ones, and ended up with the platters. There was just one crash in the kitchen the whole morning, so *that* was a blessing, grandmother used to say. If Martha had some extra time in the afternoon, she'd go into the parlour with a little hammer and knock down all the antique East Indian plates that hung on the walls. Grandmother bought new china on Wednesdays,' said Pippi, disappearing up the stairs like a jack-in-the-box.

Now Mrs Settergreen's patience had come to an end. She ran up the stairs, into the children's room and up to Pippi, who had just begun teaching Tommy how to stand on his head.

'You may never come here again,' said Mrs Settergreen, 'since you behave so badly.'

Pippi looked at her with surprise, and her eyes slowly filled with tears.

'Well, that's that. I might have known I couldn't behave myself!' she said. 'There's no use trying. I just never will learn how. I should have stayed at sea.'

Then she curtsied to Mrs Settergreen, said goodbye to Tommy and Annika, and walked slowly down the stairs.

But now the ladies were also leaving. Pippi sat down by the umbrella stand in the front hall and looked at them while they put on their hats and coats.

'It's a pity you don't like your maids,' she said. 'You ought to have someone like Martha! A better girl you'll never find, grandmother always used to say. Just think, once at Christmas-time when Martha was going to serve the whole roasted pig, can you imagine what she did? She'd read in a cookery book that the Christmas pig should be served with curled paper and an apple in the mouth. Poor Martha didn't understand that it was the *pig* that should have the apple. You should have seen her when she came in on Christmas Eve, dressed in a starched white apron and with a big red Pippin in her mouth. Grandmother said to her, "You are a *nut*, Martha!" and 'course Martha couldn't get a word out for an answer. She just wiggled her ears so the paper rustled. She was trying to say something, but it just became "Blubb, blubb, blubb". 'Course, she couldn't bite people in the leg as she was used to doing, either, and just when there were so many strangers coming! No, there wasn't much fun for poor little Martha *that* Christmas Eve,' said Pippi sadly.

The ladies now had their street-clothes on, and so they said a last goodbye to Mrs Settergreen. And Pippi ran up to her and whispered, 'I'm sorry I couldn't behave myself. Goodbye!'

Then she slung on her big hat and followed the ladies out. Their ways separated outside. Pippi went towards Villekulla Cottage, and the ladies in the opposite direction.

When they had gone a little way, they heard something panting behind them. Pippi came bolting up to them.

'You can bet grandmother missed Martha when she lost her. Imagine, one Tuesday morning when Martha hadn't broken more than a dozen teacups, she went her way and took to the sea. So grandmother had to break the china herself that day. And she wasn't used to it, poor thing, so she got blisters on her hands. She never saw Martha again. And that was a shame, what with such a first-rate girl, grandmother said.'

Then Pippi went, and the ladies hurried on. But when they had gone a few hundred yards they heard Pippi from far off shouting with all her might:

'S-h-e n-e-v-e-r s-w-e-p-t u-n-d-e-r t-h-e b-e-d-s, M-a-r-t-h-a!'

10
Pippi Becomes a Heroine

One Sunday afternoon Pippi sat wondering what to do. Tommy and Annika were with their father and mother, who had been invited out to tea, so she couldn't expect a visit from them.

The day had been full of pleasant things to do. She had got up early and served Mr Nelson fruit juice and buns in bed. He had looked such a dear, sitting there in his light blue night-shirt holding the glass with both hands. Then she had fed and combed the horse and told him a long story about her travels on the seas. After that, she had gone into the parlour and done a big painting on the wall. It was a picture of a fat lady in a red dress and a black hat. In one hand she held a yellow flower and in the other a dead mouse. It was a very beautiful painting, Pippi thought; it brightened up the whole room. After that, she sat down by her cupboard and looked at all her birds' eggs and shells, and then she had remembered all the wonderful places where she and her father had gathered them together, and all the pleasant little shops the world over where they had bought all the fine things that were now kept in the drawers of her cupboard. After that, she had tried to teach Mr Nelson the polka, but he hadn't wanted to learn. For a moment she had thought of trying it with the horse, but instead she crawled into the woodbox and closed the lid over herself. She pretended that she was a sardine in a tin, and it was such a pity that Tommy and Annika weren't there or they could have been sardines too.

But now it began to get dark. Pippi pressed her little potato-nose against the window pane and looked out at the autumn twilight. Then she remembered that she hadn't ridden for several days, so she decided to do so right away. It would be a nice ending to a pleasant Sunday.

So she went and put on her big hat, fetched Mr Nelson, who was sitting in a corner playing with some marbles, saddled the horse, and lifted him down from the front porch. And off they rode, Mr Nelson sitting on Pippi, and Pippi sitting on the horse.

It was so cold the roads were frozen, and there was a loud clatter as they rode along. Mr Nelson sat on Pippi's shoulder and tried to catch hold of branches as they passed them, but Pippi rode so fast he couldn't. Instead, he got a good many cracks on his ears from the whizzing-by branches, and he had a hard time keeping his straw hat in place. Pippi rode through the little town, and the alarmed people pressed themselves as close as they could against the walls of the houses as she stormed by.

All Swedish country towns have a market place, and this town had one too. Around it stood the little town hall, which was painted yellow, and several beautiful single-storeyed houses. There was one rickety big building too. It was a newly-built three-storey house which was called the Skyscraper because it was taller than any of the other buildings in the town.

On this Sunday evening, the little town seemed a very still and peaceful place. But suddenly the peace was broken by a loud cry:

'The Skyscraper's burning! Fire! Fire!'

From all directions people came running with wide open eyes. A fire-engine drove through the streets with a terrible clanging, and the little children of the town, who had always thought it such fun to see the fire-engine before, were now so frightened they began to cry because they were sure that *their* houses were going to catch fire too. The square in front of the Skyscraper was filled with people. The police tried to keep them out of the way so that the fire-engine would be able to get through.

From the windows of the Skyscraper leaping flames forced their way, and smoke and sparks surrounded the firemen who bravely set about putting the fire out.

The fire had started in the ground floor, but spread quickly to the upper floors. Suddenly the people who stood gathered in the square saw a sight which made them gasp with horror. At the very top of the house there was an attic, and at the attic window, which had just been opened by a little child's hand, stood two small boys yelling for help.

'We can't come down 'cause somebody's made a fire in the stairs!' cried the bigger.

He was just five years old, and his brother was a year younger. Their mother had gone out on an errand, and now they stood there completely alone. Many people down in the square began to weep, and the head of the fire brigade looked anxious. Of course there was a ladder on the fire-engine, but it wasn't nearly long enough to reach so high up. And it was impossible to go into the house to rescue the children. The people in the square despaired when they realized the children could not be helped. And the poor little things just stood up there and cried. It wouldn't be many minutes before the fire would reach the attic too.

Pippi sat on her horse right in the middle of the crowd in the square. She looked with interest at the fire-engine, and wondered if she ought to buy herself one like it. She liked it because it was red, and because it had made so much noise driving through the streets. Then she looked at the crackling fire, and she thought it was fun when some sparks fell on her.

By and by she noticed the little boys in the attic. To her surprise they didn't seem to be enjoying the fire at all. It was more than she could understand, and finally she just had to ask those standing around her, 'Why are the children crying?'

At first she only got sobs for an answer, but then a fat man said, 'Why d'you suppose? Don't you think *you'd* cry if you were up there and couldn't come down?'

'I never cry,' said Pippi. 'But now, if they really want to come down, why is it nobody is helping them?'

'Because it can't be done, that's why,' said the fat man. Pippi thought for a moment.

'Could someone bring a long rope here?' she said.

'What good would that do?' said the fat man. 'The children are too small to climb down a rope. And for that matter, how would you get the rope up to them?'

'Oh, one learns things at sea,' said Pippi easily. 'I need a rope.'

Nobody believed that it would do any good, but somehow Pippi got a rope anyway.

A high tree grew by the Skyscraper's gable. The top of the tree was just about the same height as the attic window, but the distance between them was at least ten feet. The tree trunk was smooth and without a single branch on which to climb. Not even Pippi could have climbed it.

The fire burned, the children in the attic cried, and the people in the square wept.

Pippi climbed off her horse and went up to the tree. Then she took the rope and tied it to Mr Nelson's tail.

'Now, you're going to be Pippi's good boy, aren't you?' she said. Then she put him on the tree trunk and gave him a little push. He understood very well what he was supposed to do, and he obediently climbed up the tree. It was no trick at all for a little monkey to do that.

The people in the square held their breath and watched Mr Nelson. He soon reached the top of the tree. There he sat on a branch and looked down at Pippi. She waved at him to come down again, and he did so. But he climbed down on the other side of the branch, so that when he reached the ground again, the rope lay across the branch and hung down double with both ends on the ground.

'Mr Nelson, how clever you are! You could be a professor any old time,' said Pippi, undoing the knot that held one end of the rope to the little monkey's tail.

Close by, there was a house under repair. Pippi ran there and fetched a long plank. She held it under her arm, grabbed hold of the rope with her free hand, and then kicked against the tree with her feet. Quickly and easily she climbed up the rope, and the people stopped weeping out of sheer astonishment. When she had reached the top, she laid the plank across a heavy branch and pushed it carefully over to the attic window. The plank lay like a bridge between the top of the tree and the window.

The people in the square watched in silence. The suspense was so great, nobody could say a word. Pippi climbed out on the plank. She smiled in a friendly way at the boys in the attic.

'You're looking a bit unhappy,' said she. 'Have you got tummy-aches?'

She ran over the plank and hopped into the attic.

'It seems rather warm in here,' she said. 'You won't need to burn anything more today, that I can guarantee. And at the most, a very small fire in the grate tomorrow, I should think.'

Then she took a boy under each arm and climbed out on the plank again.

'Now you're really going to have a bit of fun,' she said. 'This is almost like tightrope walking.'

And when she had come to the middle of the plank, she lifted one leg straight into the air just as she had done in the circus. A murmur went through the crowd, and when Pippi lost one of her shoes a moment later, several old ladies fainted. But Pippi arrived safe and sound at the tree with the boys, and the crowd cheered so that their cheers rang out in the dark evening and drowned the crackling of the fire.

Then Pippi pulled the rope up to her and fastened one end firmly to a branch. To the other end of the rope she tied one of the boys, and then slowly and carefully lowered him to his overjoyed mother, who stood waiting in the square. With tears in her eyes, she threw her arms about her boy. But Pippi shouted, 'Untie the rope, can't you? There's still another one here, and he can't fly either.'

Some of the people helped to untie the knot and free the boy. Pippi really *could* tie knots! She'd learned that at sea. Then she pulled the rope up again, and it was the other boy's turn to be lowered.

Now Pippi alone was left in the tree. She jumped out on the plank, and all the people looked at her and wondered what she was about to do. Pippi danced back and forth on the narrow plank. She raised and lowered her arms delicately and sang in a hoarse voice which could barely be heard by the people in the square:

> 'A fire is burning,
> The flames are high,
> Oh, a fire is burning bright!
> It's burning for you,
> And it's burning for me,
> And for all who dance in the night!'

As she sang, she danced more and more wildly, and many of the people in the square shut their eyes with fright, for they were sure she

120

would fall and hurt herself. Big flames curled out through the attic window, and they could see Pippi clearly in the glow from the fire. She raised her arms to the evening sky, and as a rain of sparks fell over her, she shouted, 'What a lovely, lovely, lovely fire!' Then she leaped right on to the rope.

'Wheee!' she cried, and slipped to the ground with the speed of greased lightning.

'Three cheers for Pippi Longstocking!' cried the head of the fire brigade.

'Hurrah! Hurrah! Hurrah!' the crowd shouted. But there was one who cheered *four* times. And that was Pippi.

11
Pippi Celebrates her Birthday

One day Tommy and Annika found a letter in their letterbox.

'TO TMMY AN ANIKA' it read on the outside. When they opened it, they found a card on which was written:

'TMMY AN ANIKA WIL KUM TO PIPPI FOR A BIRDAYPARTI TOMORRO AFTERNUN. DRESS: WAT YU PLEEZ.'

Tommy and Annika were so pleased, they began to hop and dance. They understood everything that was written on the card even though the spelling was a bit odd. Pippi had had fearful trouble in writing it. It is true that she hadn't known the letter 'i' the day she had been at school, but actually she could write just a little. During the time she had been at sea, one of the sailors on her father's boat had sometimes sat with her on the quarterdeck in the evenings and tried to teach her to write. Unfortunately, Pippi was not a very patient pupil. Quite suddenly she would say:

'No, Fridolf (for Fridolf was the name of the sailor), no, Fridolf, I don't give a fig for this. I'm going to climb to the top of the mast and take a look at what kind of weather we're having tomorrow.'

So it was no wonder that writing was a task for her. For a whole night she had sat and struggled with the invitation, and when the small hours of morning had come, and the stars were fading over the roof of Villekulla Cottage, she had trudged over to Tommy and Annika's house and stuffed the letter down in their letterbox.

As soon as Tommy and Annika came home from school, they began to dress for the party. Annika asked her mother to curl her hair, which she did. She tied a big pink ribbon in it too. Tommy combed his hair with water to make it lie really flat. *He* didn't have any use for curls and things! Annika wanted to put on her very best dress, but her mother said that it wasn't worthwhile, since Annika was seldom very clean and neat when she came home from Pippi; so Annika had to be satisfied with her next-best. Tommy didn't much care what he wore, as long as it was nice.

Of course they had bought a present for Pippi. They had taken the money out of their own piggy-banks, and on their way home from school they had run into the toyshop in the High Street and bought a *very* fine . . . well, just what it was can be a secret for a while. Now the present lay wrapped in green paper with lots of string round it. When Tommy and Annika were ready, Tommy took the package and they trotted away, followed by mother's anxious warnings to take care of their clothes. Annika was to carry the package for a while too, and they had agreed that when they presented it they should *both* hold it.

It was now well into November, and twilight came early. When Tommy and Annika went in through the gate of Villekulla Cottage, they held hands tightly, for it was just about dark in Pippi's orchard. The old trees, which were losing their last leaves, sighed and murmured gloomily in the wind. 'It's really autumn,' said Tommy. It was much more pleasant to see the lights shining in

Villekulla Cottage, and to know that a birthday party waited inside.

Usually Tommy and Annika scampered in the back way, but today they went to the front door. No horse was to be seen on the front porch. Tommy knocked politely on the door. From inside came a hollow voice:

'O, who comes through this cold, dark night
To knock on the door of my house?
Is it a ghost, or only just
A poor bedraggled mouse?'

'No, Pippi, it's us!' cried Annika. 'Open the door!'

Pippi opened it.

'Oh, Pippi, why did you say that about "ghost"? I got so scared!' said Annika, quite forgetting to congratulate Pippi.

Pippi laughed heartily and opened the door to the kitchen. How good it was to come into the light and warmth! The birthday party was to be held in the kitchen, for it was cosiest there. There were only two other rooms on the lower floor. One was the parlour, which had only one piece of furniture, and the other was Pippi's bedroom. But the kitchen was big and roomy, and Pippi had prettied it up and made it tidy. She had put rugs on the floor, and on the table lay a new cloth which she had sewn herself. The flowers which she had embroidered on it *did* look a bit odd, but Pippi said that such flowers grew in Indo-China, and so everything was as it should be. The curtains were drawn, and in the grate a fire burned and the sparks flew. Mr Nelson sat on the wood box hitting two saucepan-lids together, and in a far corner stood the horse. Naturally, he had been invited to the party as well.

Now at last Tommy and Annika remembered that they should congratulate Pippi. Tommy bowed and Annika curtsied, and then they held the green package forward and said, 'Many happy returns of the day!' Pippi thanked them and eagerly tore open the package. And there lay a musical box! Pippi became quite wild with delight. She hugged Tommy, and she hugged Annika, and she hugged the musical box, and she hugged the paper in which it had been wrapped. Then she turned the handle of the musical box, and with many a plink and a plonk, a melody which was supposed to be 'The More We are Together' came forth.

Pippi turned the handle round and round, and forgot all else. But suddenly she remembered something.

'Dear hearts!' she said. 'You must have *your* birthday presents too!'

'But it isn't our birthday today,' said Annika.

'No, but it's mine, so I should think I could give you birthday presents too. Or is it written somewhere in your lesson books that it can't be done? Does it have something to do with pluttification that makes it so's it can't be done?'

'No, of *course* it can be done,' said Tommy. 'Though it's not usual. But I'd *like* to have a present!'

'I, too!' said Annika.

Pippi ran into the parlour and fetched two packages which lay on the cupboard. When Tommy opened his package, he found a strange little ivory flute, and in Annika's package lay a beautiful brooch in the shape of a butterfly. The wings were set with red, blue, and green stones.

Now that everyone had a birthday present, it was time to sit down at the table. There were piles of cakes and buns waiting. The cakes had rather odd shapes, but Pippi said that they made cakes like that in China.

Pippi poured hot chocolate with whipped cream into the cups, and then they were ready to sit down. But Tommy said, 'When mother and father give a dinner, the gentlemen always get cards that say which lady they should take to the table. I think we should do that too.'

'Full speed ahead,' said Pippi.

'It won't be as good for us, though, since I'm the only gentleman,' said Tommy undecidedly.

'Nonsense,' said Pippi. 'Do you suppose Mr Nelson is a young lady then?'

'No, of course not! I forgot Mr Nelson,' said Tommy. And then he sat down on the wood box and wrote on a card:

'Mr Settergreen will have the pleasure of taking Miss Longstocking.'

'Mr Settergreen is me,' he said with satisfaction, showing the card to Pippi. Then he wrote on the next card:

'Mr Nelson will have the pleasure of taking Miss Settergreen.'

'Yes, but the horse has to have a card too,' said Pippi definitely. 'Even if he can't sit at the table!'

So as Pippi dictated, Tommy wrote on the next card:

'The horse will have the pleasure of staying put in the corner, then he will get cakes and sugar.'

Pippi held the card under the horse's nose and said, 'Read this, and tell me what you think!'

As the horse had no objections, Tommy offered Pippi his arm, and they went to the table. Mr Nelson made no effort to invite Annika, so she simply lifted him up and brought him along.

He refused to sit on a chair, but sat right on the table. He didn't want chocolate with whipped cream either, but when Pippi filled his cup with water, he held it with both hands and drank.

Annika and Tommy and Pippi tucked in, and Annika said that if these were the kind of cakes they had in China, then she was going to move to China when she grew up.

When Mr Nelson had emptied his cup, he turned it upside down and put it on his head. As soon as Pippi saw this she did the same but as she hadn't finished drinking all her chocolate, a little brown stream ran down her forehead and continued down her nose. Pippi stuck out her tongue and stopped it.

'Waste not, want not,' she said.

Tommy and Annika carefully licked out their cups before they put them on their heads.

When they were all quite full and satisfied, and the horse had been given what he was to have, Pippi promptly took hold of the four corners of the tablecloth and lifted it off so that cups and plates fell over each other as in a sack. She stuffed the whole bundle into the wood box.

'I always like tidying up a bit as soon as I've finished eating,' she said.

Then it was time to play. Pippi suggested they play a game called 'Don't Fall to the Floor'. It was very simple. All you had to do was crawl round the whole kitchen without once setting foot on the floor. Pippi shot around in one second. But it went quite well even for Tommy and Annika. You started with the kitchen sink and if you could stretch your legs wide enough, it was possible to come over to the open fireplace, and from there to the wood box, from the wood box over a shelf, and so down on to the table. From there you went over two chairs to the cupboard in the corner. Between the cupboard and the sink there was a distance of several yards, but there, luckily, stood the horse. If you climbed up on him at the tail end and slid off at the head end, and then jerked at just the right moment, you landed right on the draining board.

When they had played this a while, and Annika's dress was no longer her next-best, but only her next-next-next-best, and Tommy had become as black as a chimney sweep, they decided to think of something else to play.

'Let's go up to the attic and say hello to the ghosts,' suggested Pippi.

Annika gasped.

'A . . . a . . . are there *ghosts* in the attic?' she said.

'Are there! Lots of 'em,' said Pippi. 'It's crawling with different kinds of phantoms and

130

ghosts up there. You stumble on them without any trouble. Do you want to go?'

'Oh,' said Annika, and looked reproachfully at Pippi.

'Mother says there aren't any ghosts or phantoms,' said Tommy boldly.

'That's quite true,' said Pippi. 'Any place but here, 'cause they live in my attic, all there are. It doesn't do any good to ask them to move. But they don't do any harm. They just pinch you on the arm so's it gets black and blue, and they *howl*. And play ninepins with their heads.'

'Th . . . th . . . they play ninepins with their *heads*?' whispered Annika.

'Just what they do,' said Pippi. 'Come on, let's go up and talk to them. I'm good at ninepins.'

Tommy didn't want to show he was afraid, and in a way he really *did* rather want to see a ghost. That would be something to tell the boys at school! Besides, he comforted himself with the thought that the ghosts would never dare to try anything with Pippi. He decided to go along. Poor Annika didn't want to at all, but she happened to think that possibly a tiny ghost might slip down to her while she was alone in the kitchen. That settled the matter! Better to be with Pippi and Tommy among a thousand ghosts than alone with even the tiniest little baby ghost in the kitchen!

131

Pippi went first. She opened the door to the attic. It was pitch dark. Tommy held on tightly to Pippi, and Annika held on even more tightly to Tommy. Then they went up the stairs, which creaked and groaned at every step. Tommy began to wonder if it would have been better to forget the whole thing, and Annika didn't need to wonder. She was quite sure of it.

By and by, they had reached the top of the stairs and were standing in the attic. It was completely dark there except for a narrow stream of moonlight which fell across the floor. There were sighs and whistles in every corner as the wind blew in through the cracks.

'Hail, all ghosts!' shouted Pippi.

But if there was a ghost there, he made no reply.

'Well, of course, I might have known,' said Pippi. 'They've gone to a committee meeting of the Society of Honourable Ghosts and Phantoms!'

A sigh of relief escaped from Annika, and she hoped that the committee meeting would last a long time. But just then a terrible cry came from one corner of the attic.

'Klaawitt,' it cried, and the next moment Tommy saw something whistling towards him in the dark. He felt it fan him on the forehead, and then something black disappeared through a little window which stood open. He yelled wildly, 'A ghost! A ghost!'

Annika joined in.

'That poor fellow's going to be late for the meeting,' said Pippi. 'If it *was* a ghost! And not an owl! Anyway, there aren't any ghosts,' she continued after a while, 'so the more I think about it, the more it was an owl. If anybody says there are ghosts, I'll tweak his nose!'

'But you said so yourself!' said Annika.

'Oh, I did, did I?' said Pippi. 'Well then, I'll certainly have to tweak my nose.'

And she took hold of her own nose and gave it a sharp twist.

After this Tommy and Annika felt a bit calmer. They were even so brave that they dared to go up to the window and look out over the orchard. Big, dark clouds drove across the sky and did their best to hide the moon. The trees bent and murmured.

Tommy and Annika turned about. But then— oh, so terrible!—they saw a white figure moving towards them.

'A ghost!' Tommy screamed wildly.

Annika was so frightened that she couldn't even scream. The figure came even closer. Tommy and Annika clung to each other and shut their eyes. Then they heard it say:

'Look what I've found! Father's nightshirt was in an old seaman's chest over here. If I turn it up round the bottom I can use it myself.'

Pippi came forward to them with the nightshirt dragging round her feet.

'Oh, Pippi, I could have died of fright!' said Annika.

'But there's nothing dangerous about nightshirts,' protested Pippi. 'They never bite, 'cept in self-defence.'

Pippi decided that this was the right time to go through the seaman's chest properly. She carried it up to the window and opened the lid so that the pale moonlight fell over the contents. There were a lot of old clothes, which she tossed on the floor, a telescope, a couple of old books, three pistols, a sword, and a bag of gold pieces.

'Tiddelipom and poddeliday,' said Pippi happily.

'How exciting!' said Tommy.

Pippi gathered everything together in the nightshirt, and they went down to the kitchen again. Annika was very happy to be out of the attic.

'Never let children handle firearms,' said Pippi, taking a pistol in each hand. 'Otherwise, an accident can easily happen.' And she fired both pistols at the same time. '*That* was a good-sized bang,' she announced, looking up at the ceiling.

There were two holes in it where the bullets had gone through.

'Who knows,' she said hopefully, 'perhaps the bullets have gone straight through the roof and hit some of those ghosts in the leg. *That* will teach them to think twice the next time they mean to go scaring little innocent children. 'Cause even if they don't exist, that's no excuse for scaring people out of their wits. Would you each like a pistol, by the way?' she asked.

Tommy was thrilled, and Annika said she would like a pistol too, if it weren't loaded.

'Now we can become a band of robbers if we want to,' said Pippi, looking through the telescope. 'I can almost see the fleas in South America with this thing, I think,' she continued. 'It will be a good thing to have if we form a band of robbers.'

Just then there was a knock at the door. It was Tommy's and Annika's father, who had come to take them home. It was long past bed-time, he declared. Tommy and Annika had to hurry with thanking and saying goodbye and gathering together their possessions, the flute and the brooch and the pistols.

Pippi followed her guests to the front porch and saw them disappear down the orchard path. They turned about and waved. The light from inside fell over Pippi. There she stood with her stiff red pigtails, her father's nightshirt dragging round her feet. She held a pistol in one hand, and in the other a sword. She was presenting arms with it.

When Tommy and Annika and their father reached the gate, they heard her shouting after them. They stopped and listened. The wind was howling through the trees so that her voice scarcely reached them. But they did hear her anyway.

'I'm going to be a pirate when I grow up,' she shouted. 'Are you?'

Pippi in the South Seas

Astrid Lindgren

Translated by Marianne Turner
Illustrated by Tony Ross

OXFORD
UNIVERSITY PRESS

Contents

1. Pippi Still Lives at Villekulla Cottage   139
2. Pippi Cheers up Auntie Laura   152
3. Pippi Finds a Squeazle   160
4. Pippi Arranges a Quiz   170
5. Pippi Receives a Letter   181
6. Pippi Goes Aboard   188
7. Pippi Goes Ashore   196
8. Pippi Reproves a Shark   204
9. Pippi Reproves Jim and Buck   213
10. Pippi Gets Tired of Jim and Buck   226
11. Pippi Leaves Canny Canny Island   232
12. Pippi Longstocking Does not Want to
    Grow Up   239

1
Pippi Still Lives at
Villekulla Cottage

The tiny little town was looking very trim and cosy with its cobbled streets, its small, low houses surrounded by little gardens. Everyone who came there thought it must be a very quiet and restful town to live in. But there were not many places of special interest to a visitor—only one or two: and these were a folk museum and an ancient burial mound; that was all. Oh no!—there was just one other thing. The people in the little town had put up neat notice-boards which clearly marked the way for those who wanted to see the sights. On one of them it said in large letters: 'To the Folk Museum', and underneath there was an arrow to show the way; on another it said: 'To the Long Barrow'.

But there was still one more notice-board. It said:

To Villekulla Cottage

It had been put there recently because people kept asking the way to Villekulla Cottage—as a matter of fact, far more often than they asked the way to the folk museum or the long barrow.

One beautiful summer's day, a gentleman came driving into the little town in his car. He lived in a much bigger town; that was why he had got it into his head that he was better and more important than the people in the tiny little town. Of course, there was this about it, too, that he had a big, shining car, and he himself looked very imposing with his highly polished shoes and with a fat gold ring on his finger. It was hardly surprising, then, that he thought himself exceedingly grand and superior.

He honked loudly as he drove through the streets of the little town to make sure that people would notice him.

When the fine gentleman caught sight of the notice-boards he laughed scornfully.

'"To the Folk Museum"—'pon my word!' he said to himself. '"To the Long Barrow"—I say, how *exciting*!' he jeered. 'But what nonsense is this?' he said, when he caught sight of the third notice-board. '"To Villekulla Cottage". What a name!'

He thought for a moment. An ordinary cottage can hardly be a show-place like a folk museum or a long barrow. The board must have been put up for some other reason, he thought. Finally, he came to the conclusion, The house must be up for sale, and the board has been put there to show the way for prospective buyers. The fine gentleman had intended, for some time, to buy a house in a small town where life would be quieter than in the big city. Of course, he would not live there all the time, he would only visit it now and then when he wanted a rest. Besides, in a small town it would be more noticeable what a particularly fine and grand gentleman he really was. He decided to go and look at Villekulla Cottage at once.

He had only to follow the direction in which the arrow was pointing. The road took him to the very outskirts of the little town before he found what he was looking for. There, on a very ramshackle garden gate, was printed in red crayon:

VILLEKULLA COTTAGE

Behind the gate he saw an overgrown garden and old trees covered with moss, uncut lawns, and masses of flowers growing exactly as they liked. At the far end of the garden there was a house— but, oh dear, what a house! It looked ready to fall down at any minute. The fine gentleman stared at it, and suddenly he gave a gasp. *There was a horse standing in the porch*. The fine gentleman was not used to seeing horses in porches. That was why he gasped.

On the steps of the porch, in the brilliant sunshine, sat three little children. The one in the middle was a girl with a lot of freckles on her face and two red plaits which stuck straight out. A very pretty little girl with fair curls, and dressed in a blue-checked cotton frock, sat on one side of her, and a little boy with neatly combed hair on the other. A monkey crouched on the red-haired girl's shoulder.

The fine gentleman thought he must have come to the wrong place. Surely no one would expect to sell such a ramshackle house.

'Look here, children,' he shouted, 'is this miserable hovel really Villekulla Cottage?'

The girl in the middle, the one with the red hair, rose and walked towards the gate. The other two followed slowly.

'Answer me, can't you?' said the fine gentleman irritably, while the red-haired girl was still approaching.

'Let me think,' said the red-haired girl, frowning thoughtfully. 'Is it the folk museum?— No! The long barrow?—No! I've got it!' she shouted. 'It's Villekulla Cottage!'

'Answer me properly,' said the fine gentleman, getting out of his car. He had decided to look at the place more closely in any case.

'Of course, I could pull it down and build a new house,' he muttered to himself.

'Oh, yes, let's start straight away,' cried the red-haired girl, quickly breaking off a couple of planks from the side of the house.

The fine gentleman did not listen to her. Small children were of no interest to him, and besides, now he had something to consider. The garden, in spite of its neglected state, really looked very pleasant and inviting in the sunshine. If a new house were built, the grass cut, the paths raked and beautiful flowers planted, then even a very fine gentleman could live there. The fine gentleman decided to buy Villekulla Cottage.

He looked round to see what further

improvements might be made. The old mossy trees would, of course, have to go. He scowled at the gnarled oak tree with a thick trunk. Its branches stretched right over the roof of Villekulla Cottage.

'I'll have that cut down,' he said firmly.

The pretty little girl in the blue check dress cried out.

'Pippi, did you hear?' she called in a terrified voice.

The red-haired girl took no notice and practised hop-scotch on the garden path.

'That's it—I'll have that rotten old oak tree cut down,' said the fine gentleman to himself.

The little girl in blue looked at him imploringly.

'Oh, please don't,' she said. 'It's—it's such a good tree for climbing. And it's hollow. You can sit inside it.'

'Nonsense,' said the fine gentleman. 'I don't climb trees. You should know better than that.'

The little boy with the tidy hair also came forward. He was looking worried.

'But,' he pleaded, 'ginger-beer grows in it. And chocolate, too—on Thursdays.'

'Look here, children, I think you've been sitting out here too long and have got a touch of the sun,' said the fine gentleman. 'But that's no concern of mine. I'm going to buy this property. Will you tell me where I can find the owner?'

The little girl in the blue check started to cry, and the boy ran to the red-haired girl who was still practising hops.

'Pippi,' he said, 'can't you hear what he's saying? Why don't you do something?'

'Do something?' said the red-haired girl. 'I keep hopping as if my life depended on it, and then you come and tell me to do something. Try it yourself and see how *you* get on.'

She went over to the fine gentleman.

'I'm Pippi Longstocking,' she said, 'and this is Tommy and Annika.' She pointed at her friends. 'Can we help you in any way? If there's a house to be pulled down, or a tree to be pulled up, or anything else to be altered, you have only to say so!'

'Your name does not interest me,' said the fine gentleman. 'All I want to know is where I can find the owner of this house. I'm going to buy it.'

The red-haired girl, the one whose name was Pippi Longstocking, had gone back to her exercise.

'The owner is otherwise engaged at the moment,' she said. She hopped with great concentration while she spoke. 'Extremely engaged,' she said, hopping round the fine gentleman. 'But won't you sit down a moment, and I'm sure she'll come?'

'She?' said the fine gentleman, pleased. 'So it's a she who owns this miserable dwelling? All the better. Women don't know anything about business matters, so I may get the whole lot for a song.'

'Let's hope so,' said Pippi Longstocking.

Since there did not appear to be anywhere else to sit, the fine gentleman placed himself cautiously on the porch steps. The little monkey jumped nervously to and fro on the veranda railing. Tommy and Annika, the two charming and well cared for children, stood some distance away, looking at him anxiously.

'Do you live here?' asked the fine gentleman.

'No,' said Tommy, 'we live next door.'—

'But we come here every day to play,' said Annika shyly.

'I'll soon put a stop to that,' said the fine gentleman. 'I won't have any children running round my garden: there's nothing worse.'

'I quite agree,' said Pippi, who stopped hopping for a moment. 'Children ought to be shot.'

'How can you say such a thing?' said Tommy in an injured voice.

'What I mean is that all children *ought* to be shot,' said Pippi. 'But it wouldn't do, because then there would never be any kind old gentlemen. And we couldn't do without them, could we?'

The fine gentleman looked at Pippi's red hair and decided to pass the time by teasing her.

'Do you know what you have in common with a newly struck match?' he asked.

'No, I don't,' said Pippi, 'but I've always wanted to know.'

The fine gentleman tugged quite hard at one of Pippi's plaits.

'They're both flaming at the top,' he said, roaring with laughter.

'I wonder I didn't think of that before,' said Pippi. 'We have to hear a lot before our ears drop off.'

The fine gentleman stared at her.

'I do believe you're the ugliest child I've ever seen,' he said.

'Maybe,' said Pippi, 'but it seems to me you're no oil painting yourself.'

The fine gentleman looked offended, but made no reply. Pippi watched him in silence for a time, her head on one side.

'Do you know what we two have in common?' she said at last.

'No. Nothing, I should hope,' said the fine gentleman.

'Oh, yes,' said Pippi. 'We're both swollen headed . . . except me.'

A faint giggle was heard from the direction of

Tommy and Annika. The fine gentleman went red in the face.

'So you're impudent,' he shouted. 'We'll soon put a stop to that.'

He stretched out a fat arm to take hold of Pippi, but she instantly jumped to one side, and a second later she was sitting high up in the hollow oak tree. The fine gentleman's mouth dropped open with astonishment.

'And when are we going to start to put a stop to my impudence?' asked Pippi, making herself comfortable on a branch.

'I can wait,' said the fine gentleman.

'Good,' said Pippi, 'because I'm thinking of staying up here until the middle of November.'

Tommy and Annika laughed and clapped their hands. But that was not a very wise thing to do as it made the fine gentleman furiously angry, and since he could not get hold of Pippi, he seized Annika by the scruff of her neck and said:

'Then I'll give you a spanking instead. It seems you can do with it, too.'

Annika had never in all her life been smacked, and she cried out in her fright. There was a thud as Pippi jumped down from the tree. With one leap she reached the fine gentleman.

'Oh no, you don't,' she said. 'I won't waste

time fighting you, but I'm going to put a stop to your meddling once and for all.'

Without delay, she seized the fine gentleman about his fat waist and threw him up in the air, twice. Then she carried him at arm's length to his car and threw him into the back seat.

'I don't think we'll pull the house down till another day,' she said. 'You see, once a week I pull down houses, but never on Fridays, because then I've got the weekly turning-out to think of. So I generally vacuum the house clean on Fridays and pull it down on Saturdays. It's always best to have a routine.'

The fine gentleman struggled with great difficulty into the driving seat and drove off at high speed. He was both frightened and angry, and he was annoyed that he had not been able to speak to the owner of Villekulla Cottage, because he was very eager to buy the place and turn the horrid children out of it.

It was not long before he met one of the little town's policemen. Stopping the car, he called to the policeman:

'Could you help me find the lady who owns Villekulla Cottage?'

'With pleasure,' said the policeman. He jumped into the car and said:

'Will you drive to Villekulla Cottage?'

'She isn't there,' said the fine gentleman.

'Oh yes, she's sure to be,' said the policeman.

The fine gentleman felt safe with a policeman beside him, and he drove back to Villekulla Cottage, as the policeman had told him to do, because he wanted so very much to speak to the owner of the house.

'That's the lady who owns Villekulla Cottage,' said the policeman, pointing towards it.

The fine gentleman looked, put his hand to his forehead, and groaned. For, on the porch steps, stood the red-haired girl, that dreadful Pippi Longstocking, and in her arms she carried the horse. The monkey was sitting on her shoulder.

'Come along, Tommy and Annika,' shouted Pippi. 'Let's have a ride before the next perspective buyer comes.'

'It's *prospective* buyer,' said Annika.

'Is *that* . . . the owner of the house?' said the fine gentleman in a weak voice. 'But it's only a little girl!'

'Yes,' said the policeman. 'It's only a little girl—the strongest girl in the world. She lives there all alone.'

The horse, now carrying the three children on his back, came galloping up to the gate. Pippi looked down at the fine gentleman and said:

'It was good fun guessing riddles just now, wasn't it? I know another one, too. Can you tell me the difference between my horse and my monkey?'

The fine gentleman did not really feel like guessing any more riddles, but by then he was so afraid of Pippi that he dared not refuse to reply.

'The difference between your horse and your monkey?—I don't know, I'm sure.'

'No, it *is* rather a tricky one,' said Pippi. 'But I'll give you a clue. If you see them both under a tree and then one of them starts to climb it, it's *not* the horse.'

The fine gentleman trod on the accelerator and disappeared at top speed. He was never, never, seen again in the little town.

2
Pippi Cheers up Auntie
Laura

One afternoon Pippi was walking in her garden while she waited for Tommy and Annika to turn up. But no Tommy came, and no Annika either; so Pippi decided to go and see what they were doing. She found them in the green creeper-covered arbour in their garden. But they were not alone. Their mother, Mrs Settergreen, was there, too, with a dear old lady who had come to see them. They were just having coffee. The children were drinking orange juice.

152

Tommy and Annika ran to meet Pippi.

'Auntie Laura's here,' explained Tommy. 'That's why we didn't come over.'

'She looks sweet,' said Pippi, peering through the leaves. 'I must have a chat with her. I love dear old ladies.'

Annika looked a little anxious.

'Per . . . per . . . p'raps you'd better not talk too much,' she said, remembering the time when Pippi had come to a coffee party and talked so much that Annika's mother got quite annoyed with her. Annika was so fond of Pippi that she did not want anyone to be annoyed with her.

'And why shouldn't I talk to her?' said Pippi, offended. 'I certainly shall. You simply *have* to be nice to visitors. If I sit here saying nothing, she may think I don't like the look of her.'

'But are you quite sure you know how to speak to an old lady?' Annika said doubtfully.

'You cheer them up, that's what you do,' said Pippi emphatically, 'and that's what I'm going to do.'

She went into the arbour. First she curtsied to Mrs Settergreen. Then, with raised eyebrows, she looked at the old lady.

'Well, and if it isn't Auntie Laura!' she said. 'Getting younger every day! I wonder if I might have a little orange juice so that my throat doesn't get too dry, just in case we should want to do some talking.'

The last remark was addressed to Tommy and Annika's mother. Mrs Settergreen poured out a glass of orange juice, saying, as she did so:

'Children should be seen and not heard!'

'Indeed!' said Pippi. 'People have both eyes and ears, I should hope; and though I'm certainly a pleasure to *look* at, it won't do their ears any harm to have a little exercise as well. But some people seem to think that ears are only meant for waggling.'

Mrs Settergreen did not take much notice of Pippi, but turned to the old lady.

'And how are you feeling these days?' she asked sympathetically.

Auntie Laura looked worried.

'Oh, not at all well, my dear,' she said. 'My nerves are very bad, and I get so anxious about everything.'

''Xactly like Granny,' said Pippi, vigorously dipping a biscuit in the glass of orange juice. 'Her nerves were very bad and the least little thing upset her. If she was walking in the street and a roof tile happened to fall on her head, she would start to jump and scream and make such a terrible fuss it made you think there had been an accident. Once she went to a ball with Daddy and they were doing square-dancing. Daddy is fairly strong, and all of a sudden he happened to send Granny flying right across the ballroom into the middle of the double bass. She immediately began to scream and make a fuss again. Then Daddy took hold of her and held her at arm's length out of the fourth-floor window, just to calm her down a little, so that she wouldn't feel nervous any more. But it didn't help! "Let go of me at once," she screamed. Daddy did, of course. But just fancy!—even then she wasn't satisfied! Daddy said he'd never known such a woman for getting excited about nothing. Yes! It must be dreadful to have an ache in the nerve,' said Pippi with feeling as she dipped another biscuit.

Tommy and Annika fidgeted uncomfortably on their chairs. Auntie Laura looked bewildered and Mrs Settergreen hastened to say:

'I do hope you'll soon feel better, Auntie Laura.'

'She will,' said Pippi encouragingly. 'Granny did. She got terrific'ly well, because she took something soothing.'

'What kind of thing?' asked Auntie Laura with interest.

'Fox poison,' said Pippi. 'A level tablespoonful of fox poison. It did the trick, because afterwards she sat dead still for five days and never said a word. Calm as a cucumber! Completely cured, in fact! No more jumping about and shouting. No matter how many tiles dropped on her head, she just sat there and enjoyed herself. So there's nothing to stop Auntie Laura getting well, because, as I said, Granny did.'

Tommy crept up close to Auntie Laura and whispered in her ear:

'Don't take any notice, Auntie Laura. It's just a story she's been making up! She hasn't got a granny.'

Auntie Laura nodded to show that she understood perfectly. But Pippi's ears were good, and she had heard Tommy's whisper.

'Tommy's right,' she said. 'I haven't got a granny. None at all. So what had she got to be so terribly nervous about?'

Auntie Laura turned to Mrs Settergreen.

'My dear, something *quite* extraordinary happened to me yesterday . . . '

'It couldn't possibly have been so extraordinary as what happened to me the day before yesterday,' Pippi interrupted. 'I was travelling by train, and while the train was going at top speed a cow came flying through the open window with a big suitcase hanging from her tail. She sat down on the seat facing me and began to turn the pages of the railway timetable to find out when we were supposed to arrive at Hayfield junction. I was just eating my sandwiches—I had tons of sandwiches with pickled herrings and sausages in them—and I thought maybe she was hungry, so I offered her one. She took a sandwich with pickled herring in it and ate it up.'

Pippi went silent.

'That was really most extraordinary,' said Auntie Laura kindly.

'Yes, cows like that don't grow on trees,' said Pippi. 'Fancy choosing a pickled herring sandwich when there were masses of sausage sandwiches to be had.'

Mrs Settergreen refilled the coffee cups and gave the children some more orange juice.

'What I was going to tell you, when we were interrupted by our little friend here,' said Auntie Laura, 'was about a strange meeting yesterday . . .'

'Talking of strange meetings,' said Pippi, 'I'm sure you'd be amused to hear about Agathon and Theodore. Once, when Daddy's ship sailed to Singapore, we needed a new mate. So we got Agathon. Agathon was two and a half yards tall and so thin that his joints rattled like the tail of an angry rattlesnake when he walked. His hair was black as a raven and reached to his waist. He had only one tooth in his mouth, but it was all the bigger for that, and it stuck out far below his chin.

Daddy thought Agathon was on the ugly side and at first would not take him on board, but then he thought Agathon might be a useful person to have in case he wanted to frighten any horses into a gallop. Later on, we arrived at Hong Kong. There, we needed another mate. So Theodore came. He was two and a half yards tall, had hair as black as a raven which reached to his waist, and one big solitary tooth in his mouth. Agathon and Theodore were really enormously alike. Especially Theodore. As a matter of fact they were as alike as twins.'

'That certainly was strange,' said Auntie Laura.

'Strange!' said Pippi. 'What was strange about it?'

'That they were so alike,' said Auntie Laura. 'Very strange, don't you think?'

'No,' said Pippi. 'Not at all. They *were* twins. Both of them. Right from the time they were born, even.'

She looked reproachfully at Auntie Laura.

'I really don't know what you mean, Auntie. Do you think it's worth while making a to-do because two poor twins are a bit alike? They can't help it. You may be certain, dear Auntie, that no one would willingly look like Agathon. Not like Theodore either, for that matter.'

'Very well,' said Auntie Laura. 'But why did you mention these strange meetings, then?'

'If I could just be allowed to get a word in edgeways at this party,' said Pippi, 'I'd tell you of some strange meetings. You see, both Agathon and Theodore were extremely pigeon-toed. At each step they took, the big toe of the right foot bumped into the big toe of the left one. If that wasn't a strange meeting I'd like to know what is. Certainly the big toes thought so.'

Pippi helped herself to another biscuit. Auntie Laura rose to leave.

'But, Auntie Laura, you were going to tell us about a strange meeting yesterday,' said Mrs Settergreen.

'I think I'll put it off till another time,' said Auntie Laura. 'When I come to think of it, it wasn't so very strange after all.'

She said goodbye to Tommy and Annika. Then she gave Pippi's red head a pat.

'Goodbye, my little friend,' she said. 'You were right. I think I'm better already. I feel much less nervous now.'

'I *am* glad,' said Pippi and gave Auntie Laura a hearty hug. 'D'you know, Auntie Laura? Daddy was quite pleased when we got Theodore in Hong Kong. He said now we could frighten exactly twice as many horses into a gallop.'

3
Pippi Finds a Squeazle

One morning Tommy and Annika came,
as usual, bounding into Pippi's kitchen
and shouted, 'Good morning!' But there
was no answer. Pippi was sitting in the middle of the
kitchen table with Mr Nelson, the little monkey, in
her arms, and with a happy smile on her face.

'Good morning,' said Tommy and Annika
again.

'Can you believe it?' said Pippi dreamily. 'Can
you believe it was *me* that thought of it? Me, of all
people, that made it up?'

'What is it you've made up?' asked Tommy and Annika both together. It did not surprise them in the least that Pippi had made something up—she was always doing it—but they wanted to know what it was. 'But what *is* it, Pippi?'

'A new word,' said Pippi, looking at Tommy and Annika as if she had only just caught sight of them, 'a brand new word.'

'What word?' asked Tommy.

'A really super word,' said Pippi, 'one of the superest I've ever heard.'

'Tell us!' said Annika.

'Squeazle,' said Pippi triumphantly.

'Squeazle?' repeated Tommy. 'What does it mean?'

'I only wish I knew,' said Pippi. 'All I know is that it doesn't mean a vacuum cleaner.'

Tommy and Annika thought for a moment. At last Annika said:

'But if you don't know what it means, it's not much use, is it?'

'No, that's just what annoys me,' said Pippi.

'I wonder who first decided what words should mean,' said Tommy.

'A lot of old professors, I suppose,' said Pippi. 'I must say, people are pretty queer! Think of the words they make up! "Basin" and "trowel" and "string" and things like that. It's a mystery where they get them from. But squeazle, which really is a good word, they simply leave out. Wasn't it lucky I thought of it! And I'm jolly well going to find out what it means, too.'

She thought for a moment.

'Squeazle! I wonder if it's the top of a blue-painted flagpole,' she said doubtfully.

'There aren't any blue flagpoles,' said Annika.

'No, that's true . . . Well then, I really don't know. Could it be the sound you hear when you walk in mud and it gets between your toes? Let's see how it sounds: "Annika was walking about in the mud, making the most wonderful squeazly sound."'

She shook her head.

'No, it won't do. It should be "making the most wonderful squelchy sound".'

She scratched her head.

'This is getting more and more mysterious. But whatever it is, I'm certainly going to find out. Perhaps they've got it in a shop. Let's go and ask!'

Tommy and Annika thought this was a good idea. Pippi went to find her suitcase which was full of gold coins.

'Squeazle,' she said. 'Sounds expensive. I think we'd better take a gold coin.'

So she got ready. As usual Mr Nelson jumped

162

on to her shoulder and Pippi lifted the horse down from the veranda.

'We'd better be quick,' she said to Tommy and Annika. 'We'll ride. Otherwise there may not be any squeazles left when we get there. I shouldn't be a bit surprised if the mayor had bought the last one already.'

When the horse went galloping through the streets of the little town with Pippi, Tommy, and Annika on his back, his hooves made such a noise on the cobbles that all the children of the town heard it and came running, because they were all very fond of Pippi.

'Pippi, where are you going?' they shouted.

'I'm going to buy squeazles,' said Pippi, holding in the horse for a moment.

The children stopped short and looked bewildered.

'Are they good to eat?' asked one little boy.

'I should jolly well think they are,' said Pippi, licking her lips. 'They're delicious. At least, it sounds as though they are!'

She jumped off the horse outside a sweet shop and lifted down Tommy and Annika. They walked in.

'I'd like a quarter of squeazles,' said Pippi, 'the scrunchy kind.'

'Squeazles?' said the pretty girl behind the

counter thoughtfully. 'I don't believe we've got any.'

'Oh, you must have,' said Pippi. 'I'm sure they've got them in all well-stocked shops.'

'But we've just run out of them, I'm afraid,' said the girl, who had never heard of squeazles, but did not like to admit that her shop was not so well-stocked as the others.

'Did you have them yesterday, then?' cried Pippi, eagerly. 'Please, please tell me what they looked like. I've never seen any squeazles in all my life. Did they have red stripes?'

The girl blushed prettily and said:

'I'm afraid I don't know what they are! In any case we haven't got them here.'

Very disappointed, Pippi walked out.

'Well, I've just got to go on hunting,' she said. 'I'm not going home without squeazles.'

The shop next door was an ironmonger's. An assistant bowed politely to the children.

'I want a squeazle, please,' said Pippi. 'But it must be the very best quality—the kind you kill lions with.'

The assistant looked artful.

'Let's see,' he said, scratching his head. 'Let's see!'

He went over to fetch a small garden rake and handed it to Pippi.

'Will this one do?' he asked.

Pippi looked at him indignantly.

'That thing is what the professors call a rake,' she said. 'But it so happens I want a squeazle. You shouldn't try to swindle an innocent little child!'

The assistant laughed and said:

'I'm afraid we haven't got one of those you ask for. Try the draper's at the corner.'

'The draper's,' Pippi murmured when they were out in the street. 'You can't get it *there*; that's one thing I'm quite sure about.'

She looked discouraged for a moment, but she soon brightened up.

'Perhaps, after all, squeazles is a disease,' she said. 'Let's go and ask the doctor!'

Annika knew where the doctor lived, because she had been to him for vaccination.

Pippi rang the bell. A nurse opened the door.

'Can I see the doctor, please?' said Pippi. 'It's a matter of life and death.'

'Follow me,' said the nurse.

The doctor was sitting at his writing desk when the children came in. Pippi went straight up to him, shut her eyes, and put her tongue out.

'Well, what's your trouble?' asked the doctor.

Pippi opened her bright blue eyes and drew in her tongue.

'I'm afraid I've caught squeazles,' she said. 'I itch all over and my eyes won't stay open when I'm asleep. Sometimes I hiccup, and last Sunday I didn't feel at all well after I'd swallowed a plateful of shoe-polish and milk. I eat quite well, but very often the food goes down the wrong way and then it's just wasted. It must be attacks of squeazles. And please tell me—is it infectious?'

The doctor looked at Pippi's rosy little face, glowing with health, and said:

'I think there's less wrong with you than with most people. I'm sure you don't suffer from squeazles.'

Pippi grabbed hold of his arm.

'But there *is* a disease called squeazles, isn't there?'

'No,' said the doctor, 'there isn't. But even if there was such a disease, I don't think it would attack you.'

Pippi looked depressed. She curtsied to the doctor and said goodbye, and Annika did the same. Tommy bowed. They trailed off to the horse which was waiting by the doctor's garden fence.

Not far from the doctor's there was a tall three-storeyed house. On the top floor a window was open. Pippi pointed at the open window and said:

166

'I shouldn't be at all surprised if the squeazle wasn't in there. I'll pop up and have a look.'

Hand over hand, she quickly swarmed up the gutter pipe. When she had climbed to the level of the window, she threw herself recklessly across and caught hold of the window ledge, heaved herself up, and thrust her head in.

Two ladies were sitting inside the room, talking. Imagine their surprise when a red head suddenly appeared above the window ledge, and they heard a voice say:

'Have you got a squeazle in here, by any chance?'

The two ladies started in alarm.

'Good gracious, child, what's that you're saying? Has one escaped?'

'That's just what I should very much like to know,' said Pippi politely.

'Oh dear, supposing he's under the bed,' shouted one of the ladies. 'Does he bite?'

'I think so,' said Pippi. 'It sounds as if he had hefty tusks.'

The two ladies clung to each other in fright. Pippi looked round the room with interest, but at last she said sadly:

'No, there isn't so much as a sniff of a squeazle here. Sorry to trouble you, but I thought I'd better just make sure as I was passing by.'

She lowered herself down the gutter pipe again.

'There isn't a single squeazle in this town, worse luck. Let's go home.'

When they reached the porch and jumped down from the horse, Tommy nearly trod on a small beetle which was crawling on the sandy garden path.

'Oh, careful, Tommy, there's a beetle,' shouted Pippi.

They all three bent down to look at him. He was very small. His wings were green and shimmered like metal.

'Isn't he pretty?' said Annika. 'I wonder what it's called.'

'It isn't a cockchafer,' said Tommy.

'Well, it isn't a may-bug, and not a stag-beetle either,' said Annika. 'I wish I knew what kind it is.'

A blissful smile ran over Pippi's face.

'I know,' she said. 'It's a squeazle.'

'Are you sure?' said Tommy doubtfully.

'Do you think I don't know a squeazle when I see one?' said Pippi. 'Did you ever see anything so squeazlish in all your life?'

Carefully she removed the beetle to a safe place where nobody could tread on him.

'My pretty little squeazle,' she said tenderly. 'I

knew I'd find one in the end. But it's rather odd, I must say. We've spent hours and hours hunting all over the town for a squeazle, and all the time he was right in front of Villekulla Cottage!'

4

Pippi Arranges a Quiz

One day the lovely long summer holidays came to an end, and Tommy and Annika went back to school again. Pippi still thought herself clever enough without going to school, and she made it quite clear that she did not intend ever to put her foot inside one—at least not until the time came when she felt she *must* know how to spell the 'ea' sound in 'seasick'.

'But as I'm never seasick I shan't have to bother about the spelling for a long time,' she said. 'And *if* I do get seasick I shall have other things to think of than trying to spell it.'

'I don't suppose you'll ever be seasick,' said Tommy.

He was quite right. Pippi had sailed the oceans with her father before he became Cannibal King and before she settled at Villekulla Cottage. But she had never been seasick.

Sometimes Pippi rode over to the school and brought back Tommy and Annika. This pleased them very much. They thoroughly enjoyed riding, and there are certainly not many children who can go home from school on a horse.

'I say, Pippi! Do come and fetch us this afternoon,' said Tommy one day, when he and Annika were about to return to school after their lunch hour.

'Yes, please do,' said Annika, 'because it's today that Miss Rosenbloom is going to give prizes to good and diligent children.'

Miss Rosenbloom was a rich old lady who lived in the little town. She was not very free with her money, but once a term she came to the school with gifts for the children. Not for all of them—oh no! Only the very good and hard-working children received prizes. To find out which children were really good and hard-working, she first held long oral examinations.

This was why all the children in the little town lived in a constant state of terror. Every day, when they were supposed to be doing their homework and were thinking of something pleasanter to do instead, their mothers and fathers would say:

'Now, don't forget Miss Rosenbloom!'

It was certainly a terrible disgrace to come home to their parents and small brothers and sisters, on the day that Miss Rosenbloom had visited the school, without a penny or a bag of sweets, or even a vest. Yes, a vest! Because Miss Rosenbloom also gave clothes to the poorer children. But however poor you were, it made no difference if you could not give the right answer when Miss Rosenbloom asked how many inches there are in a mile. No wonder the children in the little town were terrified of Miss Rosenbloom. They were afraid of her soup, too! They knew that Miss Rosenbloom would have them weighed and measured to see if any of them appeared to have too little food at home. All the thin and weedy-looking children had to go every day to Miss Rosenbloom's house at lunch-time and eat a large plateful of pea soup. It would have been all right if there had not been a lot of horrid husks in the soup.

The great day had now come when Miss

Rosenbloom would visit the school. The lessons finished earlier than usual, and all the children gathered in the school yard. A big table had been placed in the middle of the yard, and at the table sat Miss Rosenbloom. She had two secretaries with her who wrote down everything about the children—how much they weighed, and whether they could answer the questions; whether they were poor and in need of clothes; how many marks they had gained for good behaviour; whether there were any younger brothers and sisters who also needed clothes. There seemed no end to the things Miss Rosenbloom wanted to know. On the table in front of her she had a box of money, many bags of sweets, and great piles of vests and socks and woollen pants.

'Now, children, you're all to stand in lines,' shouted Miss Rosenbloom. 'In the first line, those without any younger brothers and sisters—in the second, those with one or two brothers or sisters—in the third, those with more than two brothers and sisters.'

Miss Rosenbloom was very methodical. And, of course, it was only fair that children with many brothers and sisters at home should have larger bags of sweets than those with none.

And so began the examination. How the children trembled! Those who could not answer had to stand in a corner and later they would go home without a single sweet for their little brothers and sisters.

Tommy and Annika, of course, were very good at their lessons. But all the same, the bow in Annika's hair shook with nervous excitement as she stood in the row beside Tommy; and Tommy's face got whiter and whiter the closer he came to Miss Rosenbloom. When it was his turn to answer, there was a sudden upheaval in the line of 'children without brothers and sisters'. Someone was pushing from behind. It was none other than Pippi. She burst through the line and walked straight up to Miss Rosenbloom.

'Excuse me,' she said, 'but I wasn't here at the beginning. Which is the line for people without fourteen brothers and sisters when thirteen of them are naughty little boys?'

Miss Rosenbloom looked most disapproving.

'You may stay where you are for the time being,' she said, 'but I should imagine it won't be long before you will be joining the group of children in the corner.'

Then the secretaries had to take down Pippi's name, and they weighed her to see if she needed soup. But she was four pounds too heavy for that.

'No soup for you, my girl,' said Miss Rosenbloom sternly.

'What a lucky escape!' said Pippi. 'Now I only have to try and keep clear of the pants and vests, and then I'll be out of the wood.'

Miss Rosenbloom did not listen. She was turning the pages of the spelling book to find a difficult word for Pippi to spell.

'Pay attention, girl,' she said at last. 'I want you to tell me how you spell "seasick".'

'With the greatest of pleasure,' said Pippi. 'S-e-e-s-i-k.'

Miss Rosenbloom smiled sarcastically.

'Oh,' she said, 'the spelling book has different ideas.'

'It's jolly lucky, then, that you asked me how *I* spell it,' said Pippi. 'S-e-e-s-i-k, that's the way I've always spelt it and it never did me any harm.'

'Make a note of it,' said Miss Rosenbloom to the secretaries. Her mouth was set in a thin line.

'Yes, do,' said Pippi. 'Take down this extra good spelling, and make sure it's put into the spelling book as soon as possible.'

'Well now, my girl,' said Miss Rosenbloom. 'Tell me this. When did Charles I die?'

'Oh, dear me!' exclaimed Pippi. 'Is *he* dead now? It makes you sad to think of how many people pop off nowadays. And I'm quite sure it need never have happened if only he'd changed his shoes when they got wet.'

175

'Put it down,' said Miss Rosenbloom in an icy voice to the secretaries.

'Yes,' agreed Pippi. 'And write down, too, that it's a good thing to put leeches on the body. And before going to bed you should drink a little warm paraffin. It keeps you wide awake!'

Miss Rosenbloom shook her head.

'Why has the horse ridges on his molars?' she asked severely.

'But are you quite sure he *has*?' said Pippi doubtfully. 'You could ask him if you wanted to. He's standing over there,' and she pointed to her own horse which she had tied to a tree.

'Wasn't it lucky I brought him?' she said happily. 'Or else you'd never have found out why he has ridges on his teeth. Quite honestly, I haven't any idea and I'm not specially interested, either.'

Miss Rosenbloom's mouth was by now set in an even thinner line.

'This is outrageous,' she muttered, 'quite outrageous.'

'That's just what I think,' said Pippi, with great satisfaction. 'If I go on being as clever as this it doesn't look as if I should be able to avoid having a pair of pink woolly pants.'

'Put it down,' said Miss Rosenbloom to the secretaries.

'No, don't bother,' said Pippi. 'I'm not so very keen on pink woolly pants, but you can put me down for a large bag of sweets, if you like.'

'You shall have one final question,' said Miss Rosenbloom in a strangled voice.

'Go ahead,' said Pippi. 'I like this sort of quiz.'

'Do you know the answer to this?' said Miss Rosenbloom. 'Peter and Paul are to share a cake. If Peter gets a quarter of it what does Paul get?'

'A tummy ache,' stated Pippi. She turned to the secretaries. 'Take notes,' she said solemnly. 'Write down that Paul gets a tummy ache.'

By this time Miss Rosenbloom had had quite enough of Pippi.

'You're the most ignorant and unpleasant child I ever met,' she said. 'Go and stand in the corner at once and feel ashamed of yourself.'

Pippi stalked off obediently, but she muttered angrily to herself:

'It's not fair! I answered every single question!'

When she had walked a few steps she suddenly remembered something and quickly made her way back to Miss Rosenbloom.

''Scuse me,' she said, 'but I forgot to give you my chest measurement and altitude. Take notes,' she said to the secretaries. 'It's not that I want soup—far from it—but the book-keeping must be correct.'

'If you don't go and stand in the corner at once,' said Miss Rosenbloom, 'I know of one little girl who will soon have a good spanking.'

'Poor child,' said Pippi. 'Where is she? Send her to me and I'll defend her. Make a note of that!'

Pippi then went to stand with the children who were supposed to be ashamed of themselves. They were feeling far from happy. Many of them sobbed and wept with the thought of what their parents and their brothers and sisters would say when they came home without any money and without sweets.

Pippi looked round at the weeping children and swallowed once or twice. Then she said:

'We're going to have a quiz all on our own!'

The children cheered up a little, but they did not quite grasp what Pippi meant.

'Stand in two lines,' said Pippi. 'All those who know that Charles I is dead, stand in one line; and those who haven't yet heard that he is dead, stand in the other.'

But as all the children knew that Charles I was dead, there was only one line.

'This will never do,' said Pippi. 'There have to be at least two lines, or else it's not proper. Ask Miss Rosenbloom; she'll tell you.'

She thought for a moment.

'I know!' she said at last. 'All children fully qualified in pranks, line up here.'

'And who's going to be in the other line?' eagerly asked a little girl who would not admit that she was full of pranks.

'The other line is for those who are *not yet* qualified,' said Pippi.

At Miss Rosenbloom's table the examination was in full swing, and now and then a small, weepy child came slowly over to join Pippi's group.

'Now comes the difficult question,' said Pippi. 'Now we shall see if you've done your homework properly.'

She turned to a thin little boy in a blue shirt.

'Pay attention!' she said, imitating Miss Rosenbloom. 'Tell me the name of someone who's dead.'

'Old Mrs Pettigrew at No. 57.'

'Good!' said Pippi. 'Do you know of anyone else?'

No, he could not think of anyone. Pippi cupped her hands round her mouth and whispered loudly:

'Charles I, of course!'

After that, Pippi asked all the children in turn if they knew of anyone who was dead, and they all answered:

'Old Mrs Pettigrew at No. 57 and Charles I.'

179

'This examination is going better than I expected,' said Pippi. 'I've got just one more question. If Peter and Paul are to share a cake, and Peter blankly refuses to eat more than one measly little quarter of it, who will then have to sacrifice himself by golloping all the rest?'

'Paul,' shouted all the children.

'My goodness! There can't be many children as clever as you,' said Pippi. 'You shall have your reward.'

And out of her pocket she brought handfuls of gold coins and gave one to each child. Then they each received a large bag of sweets which Pippi took from her rucksack.

And so it happened that there was great joy among all the children who had been put in the corner. When Miss Rosenbloom had finished her examining and it was time for everybody to go home, there were none who ran faster than those who had stood in the corner. But first, they all came up to Pippi.

'Thank you, dear Pippi,' they said. 'Thank you for the money and the sweets.'

'Oh, that's nothing,' said Pippi. 'You needn't thank me for *that*. But don't ever forget that I saved you from pink woolly pants.'

5
Pippi Receives a Letter

The weeks went by and soon it was autumn. Then autumn was over and winter followed. It was a long and cold winter which seemed as if it would never end. Tommy and Annika had to work very hard at school, and each day that passed they felt more and more tired and found it harder and harder to get up in the morning. Mrs Settergreen began to get quite anxious about their pale cheeks and their poor appetites. Then, on top of it all, both of them caught measles and had to stay in bed for two weeks.

These two weeks would have been very dull if Pippi had not come each day and done acrobatics outside their window. The doctor had forbidden her to go into the sickroom because of the risk of infection. Pippi obeyed, although she claimed she could undertake to squash one or two billion measle germs with her nails in an afternoon. But nobody had forbidden her to do acrobatics outside the window. The nursery was on the second floor, so Pippi had set up a ladder against the window. It was very exciting for Tommy and Annika, lying in their beds, to try and guess what Pippi would look like when she appeared at the top of the ladder, because she never looked the same two days running. Sometimes she was dressed as a chimney-sweep, sometimes as a ghost in a white sheet, and sometimes she was a witch. On other days she would act amusing plays outside the window, taking all the parts herself. Now and then she did physical exercises on the ladder—and *what* exercises! She would stand on one of the topmost rungs and let the ladder sway backwards and forwards, so that Tommy and Annika screamed with fright and thought she would tumble down at any moment. But she never did. When she wanted to climb down to the ground she always went head first just to make it more amusing for Tommy and Annika to watch. Every day she went into the town and bought apples and oranges and sweets. She put them all in a basket and tied a long string to the handle. Then she sent Mr Nelson up with the end of the string to Tommy, who opened the window and hauled up the basket. Sometimes Mr Nelson brought a letter from Pippi when she happened to be busy and could not come herself. But that was not often, because Pippi spent nearly all day and every day on the ladder. Sometimes she pressed her nose against the window pane and turned her eyelids inside out and made the most horrible faces. She told Tommy and Annika that they would each have a gold coin if they did not laugh, but it was quite impossible not to do so. Tommy and Annika laughed so much they nearly fell out of their beds.

By and by, they got well and were allowed up. But—oh, how thin and pale they were! Pippi sat with them in the kitchen on their first day up and watched them eating porridge. That is to say, they were supposed to be eating porridge, but they were not getting on with it at all well. Their mother felt really anxious when she saw them pecking at their food.

'Eat up your lovely porridge,' she said.

Annika stirred the porridge round in her plate, but she could not bring herself to swallow even a spoonful.

'*Why* must I eat it?' she asked plaintively.

'*What* a silly thing to ask,' said Pippi. 'Of course you must eat your lovely porridge. If you don't, you won't grow big and strong. And if you don't grow big and strong you won't be able to make *your* children one day eat *their* lovely porridge. Oh, no! Annika. Think of the dreadful muddle there would be over the porridge-eating in this country if everyone talked like that.'

Tommy and Annika ate two spoonfuls of porridge each. Pippi watched them sympathetically.

'What you need is a sea voyage,' she said, rocking her chair to and fro. 'That would soon teach you to eat. I remember once, when I sailed in my father's ship, that Fridolf, one of our sailors, suddenly found he couldn't eat more than seven platefuls of porridge for breakfast. Daddy nearly went out of his mind with worry over Fridolf's poor appetite. "My dear Fridolf," he said, almost in tears, "I am very much afraid that you are suffering from a wasting disease. I think you'd better stay in your bunk today until you feel better and can eat like other people. I'll come and tuck you up and give you some strengthening meducin!"'

'It's *medicine*,' said Annika.

'And Fridolf tottered off to bed,' continued Pippi, 'because he was worried himself, and wondered what terrible plague had struck him so

184

that he could only manage seven platefuls of porridge. He was lying in his bunk wondering if he would live till nightfall when Daddy brought the meducin. It was a black, nasty meducin, but say what you will about it—it was certainly strengthening.

'As soon as Fridolf had swallowed the first spoonful a flame of fire seemed to shoot out of his mouth. He shouted so loudly that the *Hoppetossa* shook from bow to stern and they could hear it on ships fifty sea-miles away. The cook hadn't cleared away the breakfast things yet when Fridolf came up from his cabin, steaming, and uttering loud roars. He threw himself down at the table and began to eat porridge, and after the fifteenth plateful he was still calling for more. But there was no porridge left, and the only thing the cook could think of was to keep throwing cold boiled potatoes into Fridolf's open mouth. The moment the cook looked like stopping Fridolf growled angrily, so the cook knew he'd have to go on, if he didn't want to be eaten up himself. But unfortunately he had only got a mere 117 potatoes, and when he had thrown the last one into Fridolf, he dashed outside the door and locked it. And all of us stood outside and watched Fridolf through the window. He whimpered like a hungry little child, and one after another he quickly gobbled up

185

the bread board and the water jug and fifteen plates. After that he started on the table; he broke off all four legs and ate so rapidly that the sawdust flew from his mouth, but he did say that, for asparagus, it was rather woody. He seemed to like the table top better, because he smacked his lips when he ate it, and said it was the best sandwich he'd had since he was a little boy. But by this time Daddy felt that Fridolf had recovered from his wasting disease, and he went in and told Fridolf that he'd have to try and manage without any more food for the two hours until dinner-time, and then he would get mashed turnips and boiled bacon. "Aye, aye, Cap'n," said Fridolf, wiping his mouth. "But just a moment, Cap'n," he added, and his eyes gleamed with eagerness, "when is supper-time and couldn't we have it a bit earlier?"'

Pippi put her head on one side, looked at Tommy and Annika, and then at their porridge plates.

'As I was saying, you certainly need a little sea voyage. That would soon cure your poor appetites.'

The postman was just passing the Settergreens' house on his way to Villekulla Cottage. He caught sight of Pippi through the window and shouted:

'Pippi Longstocking, there is a letter for you here!'

Pippi was so surprised that she nearly fell off the chair.

'A letter? For me? A real letter, I mean, a real letter? I shan't believe it until I see it.'

But it *was* a real letter—a letter with a lot of foreign stamps on the envelope.

'You read it, Tommy; you're good at that,' said Pippi.

'My dear Pippilotta,' Tommy read aloud. 'When you receive this, you might as well go down to the harbour and look for the *Hoppetossa*, because I am coming to take you to Canny Canny Island for a holiday. I think it's only right that you should see the country where your father has become such a mighty monarch. It's quite cosy here and I think you will like it. My faithful subjects are also very much looking forward to seeing the famous Princess Pippilotta. So there are no buts about it. You're coming—it is my royal and fatherly command.

A great big kiss and much love from your old father

KING EPHRAIM I, Longstocking,
Supreme Ruler over Canny Canny Island.'

When Tommy had finished reading the letter, you could have heard a pin drop in the kitchen.

6
Pippi Goes Aboard

One fine morning the *Hoppetossa* sailed into the harbour, decorated with flags and streamers from stem to stern. The members of the little town's brass band were standing on the quay, blowing a lively tune of welcome with all their might. Everyone in the little town had turned up to see Pippi meet her father, King Ephraim I, Longstocking. A photographer was also ready to take a picture of their first meeting.

Pippi was so impatient that she was jumping

up and down, and no sooner had the gangway been lowered than Captain Longstocking and Pippi hurled themselves together with loud shrieks of joy. Captain Longstocking was so glad to see his daughter that he threw her several times up in the air. Pippi was just as excited, so she threw her father high in the air even more times. The only unhappy person was the photographer, because it was quite impossible for him to get a good picture when all the time either Pippi or her father were flying through the air.

Then Tommy and Annika came up to greet Captain Longstocking, but oh, how pale and miserable they looked! It was the first time they had come out after their illness.

Pippi had to go on board, of course, to see Fridolf and all her other friends among the seamen. Tommy and Annika were allowed to come with her. It was a new experience to walk about on a ship which had come from so far away, and Tommy and Annika were agog to see all there was to see. They looked specially eagerly for Agathon and Theodore, but Pippi said that they had left the ship long ago.

Pippi gave each of the sailors such a hug that they had difficulty in breathing for the next five minutes. Then she picked up Captain Longstocking, put him on her shoulders, and carried him through the crowd and all the way home to Villekulla Cottage. Tommy and Annika walked behind hand in hand.

'Long live King Ephraim!' shouted everybody. They regarded this as a great day in the history of the town.

A few hours later, Captain Longstocking was in bed at Villekulla Cottage, asleep, and snoring so hard that the whole house trembled. Pippi, Tommy, and Annika were sitting at the table in the kitchen, where the remains of an excellent supper were still to be seen. Tommy and Annika sat quiet and thoughtful. What could they be thinking about? Well, Annika was thinking that, all things considered, she would rather be dead. And Tommy was trying to remember if there really was anything in the world that made life worth living, but there seemed to be nothing at all. Life was like a desert, he thought.

But Pippi was as happy as a lark. She stroked Mr Nelson, who was walking carefully, to and fro, between the plates on the table, she patted Tommy and Annika on the back, she whistled and sang, and now and then she danced a few steps and did not seem to notice that Tommy and Annika were so depressed.

'It'll be grand to go to sea again,' she said. 'Think of it—the sea—where you're free as a bird!'

Tommy and Annika sighed.

'I shall be jolly pleased to see Canny Canny Island, too. It'll be lovely to lie stretched out on the beach with my toes washed by the good old South Seas, and only have to open my mouth for a ripe banana to drop straight into it.'

Tommy and Annika sighed.

'And what fun to play with the little island children down there,' continued Pippi.

Tommy and Annika sighed.

'What are you sighing for?' asked Pippi. 'Don't you like sweet little island children?'

'Oh yes,' said Tommy. 'It's only that we keep on thinking what a long time it'll be before you come back to Villekulla Cottage.'

''Course,' said Pippi gaily. 'But that doesn't worry me at all. I think p'raps it'll be even more fun on Canny Canny Island.'

Annika turned a pale and despairing face towards Pippi.

'Oh, Pippi,' she said, 'how long d'you think you'll be away?'

'It's hard to say, really. Till around Christmas time, I should think.'

Annika gave a sob.

'Who knows?' said Pippi. 'P'raps it's so nice on Canny Canny Island that I shall want to stay there for ever. Hoppety-hop,' said Pippi and

191

danced round again. 'A Cannibal Princess! That's not so dusty a job for one who's not been to school much.'

Tommy and Annika's eyes began to look strangely watery in their pale faces. Suddenly Annika flopped on the table and burst into tears.

'But come to think of it, I don't expect I shall want to stay there for ever,' said Pippi. 'You *can* have enough of court life and get sick of it all. So one fine day I expect I shall say: "Tommy and Annika! How about a trip home to Villekulla Cottage for a change?"'

'Oh, how lovely it'll be when you write and tell us you're coming,' said Tommy.

'Write!' said Pippi. 'Haven't you got ears in your heads? I'm not going to write. I'm just going to *say*: "Tommy and Annika, we're off home to Villekulla Cottage."'

Annika lifted her head from the table and Tommy said:

'What do you mean by that?'

'Mean?' said Pippi. 'Don't you understand plain English? Or could I really have forgotten to tell you that you're coming to Canny Canny Island? I felt quite sure that I'd told you.'

Tommy and Annika *leapt* from their chairs. They were breathing fast . . . But Tommy said:

'The things you say! Mummy and Daddy will never let us go.'

'Oh yes, they will,' said Pippi. 'I've already arranged it with your mother.'

There was complete silence in the kitchen of Villekulla Cottage for precisely five seconds. Then two loud shrieks were heard. They came from Tommy and Annika who hooted with joy.

Mr Nelson, who was sitting on the table trying to spread butter on his hat, looked up in surprise. His surprise was even greater when he saw Pippi, Tommy, and Annika join hands and start to dance round and round the room. They danced and shrieked so loudly that the ceiling lamp came loose and fell down to the floor. Mr Nelson threw the butter knife out of the window and he, too, started to dance.

'Is it really true?' asked Tommy when they had calmed down and crawled into the wood box to talk things over. Pippi nodded.

Yes! It was really true. Tommy and Annika were to go to Canny Canny Island. Of course, nearly all the ladies in the little town came to Mrs Settergreen and said:

'You *don't* mean to say that you're going to let your children go far away to the South Seas with *Pippi Longstocking*? You can't be serious!'

But Mrs Settergreen said:

'And why shouldn't I? The children have been ill, and they need a change of air; the doctor says so. All the time that I've known Pippi, she's never done anything which has been bad for Tommy and Annika. No one could be kinder to them than she is.'

'But, my dear! *Pippi Longstocking!*' said the ladies disapprovingly.

'Exactly,' said Mrs Settergreen, 'Pippi Longstocking may not have very good manners, but she has a kind heart.'

And so it happened that, on a chilly evening in early spring, Tommy and Annika left the tiny little town for the first time in their lives to go out into the wide wide world together with Pippi. They were standing at the taffrail, all three of them, while the fresh evening breeze filled the sails of the *Hoppetossa*. Three of them? Well, there were five, really, because the horse and Mr Nelson were on deck, too.

All the children's school friends were standing on the quay and they were nearly in tears with sorrow and envy. Tomorrow they would have to go to school as usual. And they had been told to learn the names of all the islands in the South Seas for their geography homework. Tommy and Annika would have no homework to do for a long time. 'Health is more important than school work,' the doctor had said. 'And they'll have the South Sea Islands on the spot,' said Pippi.

Tommy and Annika's mother and father were also standing on the quayside, and Tommy and Annika felt a sudden tugging at their heart-strings when they saw their parents take out their handkerchiefs to wipe away a tear. But Tommy and Annika just could not help being happy all the same; they were so happy that it nearly hurt.

Slowly the *Hoppetossa* glided away from the quay.

'Tommy and Annika,' Mrs Settergreen called out, 'when you get to the North Sea, don't forget to put on *two* vests and . . . '

The rest of what she was about to say was drowned in the farewell shouts of the people on the quay, the wild neighing of the horse, Pippi's joyous shrieks, and Captain Longstocking's trumpeting when he blew his nose.

The voyage had begun. The *Hoppetossa* sailed away under the stars. Slabs of ice danced before the bow and the wind sang in the rigging.

'Oh, Pippi,' said Annika, 'I feel so excited. I think I want to be a pirate, too, when I'm grown up.'

7
Pippi Goes Ashore

'Land ho—Canny Canny Island straight ahead,' shouted Pippi one morning, when the dazzling rays of the sun were beating down out of a cloudless sky. She was standing by the look-out, dressed in nothing but a small piece of cloth tucked round her tummy.

They had sailed for days and nights, for weeks and months—over stormy oceans, and calm friendly seas; they had sailed by starlight and moonlight, under dark, threatening skies and in scorching sun. Yes, they had sailed for so long

196

that Tommy and Annika had almost forgotten what it felt like to live at home in the little town.

Their mother would certainly have been surprised if she could have seen them as they were now. No more pale cheeks! Healthy and sunburnt and bright-eyed, they climbed about in the rigging, just like Pippi. The climate became warmer and warmer and they peeled off their garments, one by one, so that, in the end, the two children (who had crossed the North Sea so warmly clad, wearing two woollen vests) had turned into little brown berries without a stitch on except a cloth wound round their middles.

'Oh, we are lucky,' said Tommy and Annika every morning, when they woke up in the cabin which they shared with Pippi. Pippi was generally already up by then and steering the ship.

'A better sailor than my daughter never sailed the seven seas,' Captain Longstocking often said. He was quite right, too: Pippi could guide the *Hoppetossa* with a firm hand through the roughest breakers and past the most dangerous hidden rocks.

But now the voyage was over.

'Canny Canny Island straight ahead,' shouted Pippi.

And there it lay, covered with green palms and surrounded by the bluest of blue water.

Two hours later, the *Hoppetossa* ran into a little bay on the western side of the island. All the Canny Cannibals, men, women, and children, were waiting on the shore to receive their king and his red-haired daughter. The crowd surged forward when the gangway was lowered.

Shouts of 'Ussamkura, kussomkara,' were heard, which meant:

'Welcome back, fat white chief!'

King Ephraim, dressed in his blue corduroy suit, strode majestically down the gangway, as Fridolf, on the foredeck, played the new Canny Cannibal national anthem on a concertina: 'Here the conquering hero comes!'

King Ephraim raised his hand in greeting and shouted: 'Muoni manana!' which meant: 'Hallo, chums!'

Pippi walked behind him. She was carrying the horse! A murmur went through the crowd of Canny Cannibals. They had heard tales of Pippi and of her enormous strength, certainly, but it was quite a different matter to see it for themselves. Sedately Tommy and Annika walked ashore, too, and the whole of the crew followed, but at the time the Canny Cannibals had no eyes for anyone but Pippi. Captain Longstocking lifted her up and stood her on his shoulders, so that they could see her clearly, and once more a murmur passed through the crowd. But when, a moment later, Pippi herself lifted Captain Longstocking up on one of her shoulders and the horse on the other, the murmur rose to a roar, almost as loud as a hurricane.

The entire population of Canny Cannibal Island was no more than 126 people.

'It's just about the right number of subjects to have,' said King Ephraim. 'I couldn't keep track of them if I had more.'

They all lived in cosy little huts among the palm trees. The largest and finest one belonged to King Ephraim. The crew of the *Hoppetossa* had huts of their own, too, for living in when the *Hoppetossa* was anchored in the little bay, and where, as a matter of fact, she nearly always stayed nowadays. Only on rare occasions was it necessary to make an expedition to an island fifty miles to the north. You see, there was a shop there where they could buy snuff for Captain Longstocking.

A very pretty little hut had been newly built, specially for Pippi, underneath a coconut palm. There was ample room for Tommy and Annika in it, too. But before they could go into the hut to wash off the stains of travel, Captain Longstocking had something to show them. He grabbed Pippi's arm and led her down to the shore again.

'Here,' he said, pointing with a fat forefinger, 'here's the identical spot where I floated ashore that time when I was blown into the sea.'

The Canny Cannibals had raised a monument there to celebrate such a remarkable event. On the stone was the following inscription in Canny Cannibalish:

Across the great wide ocean came our fat white chief. This is the place where he floated ashore when the bread-fruit trees were in bloom. May he ever remain as fat and splendid as when he came.

Captain Longstocking read the inscription aloud to Pippi, Tommy, and Annika in a voice which trembled with emotion. Afterwards he blew his nose vigorously.

When the sun began to set and it was about to disappear into the vast bosom of the South Seas, the Canny Cannibals' drums called all the people to the royal square in the centre of the village where they held their feasts. There stood King Ephraim's splendid throne which was made of bamboo sticks and decorated with red hibiscus flowers. It was on this throne that he sat when he held his court. The Canny Cannibals had made a slightly smaller throne for Pippi, and had put it beside her father's. They had even hastily constructed two small bamboo seats for Tommy and Annika as well.

The rolling of the drums grew louder and louder as King Ephraim, with great dignity, sat on his throne. He had shed his corduroy suit and was dressed in royal attire with a crown on his head, a straw skirt round his waist, a necklace of shark's teeth round his neck, and thick rings round his ankles. Pippi, quite unconcerned, perched herself on her throne. She was still wearing the same little cloth as before, but, to make herself look nice, she had stuck a few red and white flowers in her hair. So had Annika. But *not* Tommy—not for anything would he wear flowers in *his* hair.

King Ephraim had, of course, been away for a long time from his work of reigning, and now he began to reign for all he was worth. Meanwhile, the little Canny Cannibal children approached Pippi's throne. The nearer they came to Pippi and Tommy and Annika, the more awestruck they became. And besides, Pippi was a princess. When they had come close to Pippi they all, with one accord, knelt down and touched the ground with their foreheads.

Pippi quickly jumped down from the throne.

'Good gracious!' she said. 'If you're hunting the thimble I'd like to join in!'

She knelt down and moved her nose all over the ground.

'Somebody must have been here before us,' she said after a time. 'I'm definitely certain there isn't even a pin here.'

She sat on the throne once more. But no sooner had she done so than all the children again bent their heads to the ground in front of her.

'Have you lost something?' enquired Pippi. 'It isn't there anyway, because I've looked, so you might as well get up.'

Luckily, Captain Longstocking had been on the island for so long that some of the Canny Cannibals had learnt a little of his language. Of course, they did not know the meaning of difficult words like 'postal order' and 'Major-General', but they had picked up quite a lot just the same. Even the children knew some common expressions like 'don't touch' and so on. One small boy, called Momo, could speak the white people's language quite well, because he often stood near the huts of the crew, listening to their chatter. There was also a pretty little girl, called Moana, who knew almost as much.

Momo tried to explain to Pippi why they were kneeling before her.

'You be velly fine white princess,' he said.

'I not be velly fine white princess,' said Pippi in broken Canny Cannibalish. 'I be, on the whole, only Pippi Longstocking, and now be blowed to all this throning.'

She jumped down from the throne. So did King Ephraim, because he had finished his reigning business for the time being.

The sun sank like a red globe into the South Seas, and soon the sky was alight with stars. The Canny Cannibals lit an enormous camp fire in the royal square, and King Ephraim, Pippi, Tommy, Annika, and the crew of the *Hoppetossa* settled down on the grass to watch the Canny Cannibals dancing round the fire. The muffled rolling of the drums, the weird dance, the exotic scents from thousands of unseen flowers in the jungle, the stars twinkling in the sky above their heads—all these strange things filled Tommy and Annika with wonder, accompanied, as they were, by the unceasing sound of the restless waves of the ocean.

'I think it's a jolly good island,' said Tommy later, when Pippi, Annika, and he had snuggled into bed in their cosy little hut under the coconut palm.

'So do I,' said Annika. 'Don't you, Pippi?'

But Pippi lay quiet, with her feet on the pillow as she always did.

'Listen to the roar of the ocean,' she said dreamily.

8

Pippi Reproves a Shark

Very early next morning Pippi, Tommy, and Annika crawled out of their hut. But the Canny Cannibal children had already been awake for hours. Filled with excitement, they were sitting under the coconut palm, waiting for the white children to come out and play. They chattered sixteen to the dozen in Canny Cannibalish and their teeth flashed white in their black faces when they laughed.

Pippi led the whole crowd of children down to the shore. Tommy and Annika leapt for joy when they saw the fine white sand (where you could dig yourself in), and the very inviting blue sea. A coral reef, just off the island, served as a breakwater. Inside it, the water lay still and smooth as a mirror. All the children, the white ones and the black, threw off their clothes and rushed, shouting and laughing, into the water.

After the swim they rolled in the white sand, and Pippi and Tommy and Annika agreed that black skin was much the best because white sand on a black background looked so very funny. But, when Pippi had dug herself into the sand right up to her neck so that nothing but a freckled face and two red plaits were visible, that looked quite funny, too. All the children squatted round her for a chat.

'Tell about white children in white children's country,' said Momo to the freckled face.

'White children love pluttification,' said Pippi.

'It's multiplication,' said Annika. 'And besides,' she continued in an offended tone of voice, 'you can hardly say that we *love* it.'

'White children love pluttification,' persisted Pippi. 'White children go crackers if white children not have big doses pluttification every day.'

She was quite worn out with the effort of

speaking broken Canny Cannibalish and went on in her own language.

'If you come across a white child crying you can be pretty sure that the school has either gone up in flames, or that a half-term holiday has broken out, or that the teacher has forgotten to set homework for the children in pluttification. I hardly like to tell you what it's like when they're breaking up for their summer holidays. There's so much weeping and moaning it makes you wish you were dead when you hear it. There isn't a dry eye when the school door is shut for the summer. All the children walk home sobbing bitterly and they fairly hiccup with weeping when they think that it'll be several months before they have pluttification again. No misfortune can compare with it,' said Pippi, sighing heavily.

'What nonsense you do talk!' said Tommy and Annika.

Momo did not know the meaning of 'pluttification' and asked what it was. Tommy was on the point of explaining when Pippi forestalled him.

'Well, you see,' she said, 'it's like this: 7 times 7 is 102. Fun, isn't it?'

'It's not 102 at all,' said Annika.

'No—because 7 times 7 are 49,' said Tommy.

'Don't forget that we're on Canny Canny Island now,' said Pippi. 'The climate is quite different and it's much more fertile, so 7 times 7 are a lot more here than in other places.'

'Rubbish,' said Tommy and Annika.

The arithmetic lesson was interrupted by Captain Longstocking who came and told them that he and the whole crew and all the Canny Cannibals intended to sail to another island to hunt wild boar for several days. Captain Longstocking was feeling in the mood for some fresh roast pork. The Canny Cannibal women were going with them to drive the boar out into the open with wild screams. This meant that the children would be left alone on Canny Canny Island.

'You don't mind, do you?' said Captain Longstocking.

'I give you three guesses,' said Pippi. 'The day that I hear of children minding being left to look after themselves without grown-ups, I'll learn all the pluttification tables backwards.'

'That's the spirit,' said Captain Longstocking.

And he, and all his subjects, armed with shields and spears, stepped into their big canoes and paddled away from Canny Canny Island.

Pippi put her hands round her mouth and shouted after them:

'Go in peace! But if you're not back in time for my fiftieth birthday I shall have an SOS sent out for you on the radio.'

When they found themselves alone, Pippi and Tommy and Annika and Momo and Moana and all the other children looked at each other delightedly. Now they had a lovely South Sea Island all to themselves for several days.

'What shall we do?' asked Tommy and Annika.

'First of all we're going to fetch our breakfast down from the trees,' said Pippi.

She herself quickly climbed up a palm tree for coconuts. Momo and the other Canny Cannibal children picked breadfruit and bananas. Pippi made up a fire on the beach and roasted the delicious breadfruit over it. The children sat down in a circle round her, and they all had a large breakfast of breadfruit, coconut milk, and bananas.

There were no horses on Canny Canny Island, so all the island children were very taken with Pippi's horse. Those who were brave enough were allowed to have a ride on his back. Moana said she would like to go one day to the white people's country where they had such wonderful animals.

Mr Nelson was nowhere to be seen. He had

gone off on an expedition into the jungle, and there he had found some of his relations.

'What shall we do now?' said Tommy and Annika when they had all had enough of riding.

'White children want to see fine caves, yes, no?' asked Momo.

'White children certainly want to see fine caves, yes, *yes*,' said Pippi.

Canny Canny Island was a coral island. High coral cliffs fell steeply into the sea on the south side and there the sea waves had dug out the most splendid caves. Some of them were on the waterline and were filled by the sea, but there were others higher up in the cliff, and that was where the Canny Cannibal children used to play. They had stored up large quantities of coconuts and other good things to eat in the biggest cave. It was quite an adventure getting there. You had to work very carefully along the face of the cliff while hanging on to projecting stones and rocks. If you did not take care, you might easily fall into the sea. This would not, of course, have mattered much in the ordinary way, but in this particular place there were plenty of sharks that were very greedy to eat small children. In spite of this, the Canny Cannibal children used to amuse themselves by diving for pearl oysters; but then one of them always had to stand guard and shout,

'Shark! Shark!' the moment the fin of a shark appeared. Inside the big cave the Canny Cannibal children had a hoard of gleaming pearls which they had found in the oysters. They used the pearls for marbles, and they had no idea that those pearls were worth untold wealth in the lands of the white people. Captain Longstocking sometimes took a pearl or two with him when he went to buy snuff. In exchange, he brought back numerous things which he thought his subjects needed, but on the whole he felt that his faithful Canny Cannibals were better off as they were. And he had nothing against the children continuing to play marbles with the pearls.

Annika was horrified when Tommy told her to climb along the cliff to the big cave. The first part of the way was not very difficult. There was a fairly wide ledge to walk on, but it gradually became narrower and narrower, and for the last few yards to the cave you had to scramble and step wherever you could find a foothold.

'I can't,' gasped Annika. 'I can't!'

To move along a cliff where there was hardly anything to cling to, thirty feet above a sea full of sharks all waiting for you to fall down was not Annika's idea of having a good time.

Tommy got very angry.

'One should never bring sisters to the South Seas,' he said as he began to climb on the wall of rock. 'Just watch me! This is all you have to do—'

'Plop' was heard when Tommy tumbled into the water. Annika gave a loud shriek. Even the Canny Cannibal children were terrified. 'Shark! Shark!' they screamed, pointing at the sea. There was a fin showing in the water which was moving rapidly towards Tommy.

'Plop' was heard once more. It was Pippi jumping in. She reached Tommy about the same time as the shark. Tommy was screaming with fright. He felt the shark's pointed teeth scraping against his leg, but, at the very same moment, Pippi seized the bloodthirsty beast with both hands and held it up out of the water.

'What do you think you're doing?' she said. The shark looked round, surprised and uneasy; he could not breathe so well out of the water.

'Now promise not to do it any more and I'll let you go,' said Pippi severely. Then, with all her strength, she threw the shark far out to sea, and he wasted no time in swimming away from that place, and decided that, as soon as possible, he would go to the Atlantic instead.

Meanwhile, Tommy had climbed on to a little ledge where he sat trembling all over. His leg was bleeding. Pippi went to him. She behaved very oddly. First she lifted Tommy in the air and then she hugged him so hard that he nearly lost all his breath. Then she let go of him suddenly and sat down on the rock. She put her face in her hands and wept. Pippi wept! Tommy and Annika and all the Canny Cannibal children looked at her in surprise and alarm.

'You weep because Tommy nearly eaten,' suggested Momo.

'No,' said Pippi sulkily, wiping her eyes. 'I weep because poor little hungry shark not have any breakfast today.'

9
Pippi Reproves Jim
and Buck

The shark's teeth had only just grazed the skin on Tommy's leg, and when he had recovered from his fright he still wanted to go to the big cave. So Pippi made a rope of hibiscus fibre which she tied to a knob of rock. Then, nimble as a mountain goat, she nipped across to the cave where she fastened the other end of the rope. Even Annika was now brave enough to climb to the cave. With a stout rope to hang on to it was as easy as it could be.

It was a wonderful cave, so big that there was plenty of room for all the children.

'This cave is even better than our hollow oak tree at Villekulla Cottage,' said Tommy.

'No, not better, but just as good,' said Annika, who felt a heart-throb at the thought of the oak tree at home, and she would never admit that anything could be better than that.

Momo showed the three children the pile of coconuts and the cooked breadfruit which they had stored up in the cave. They could live there for weeks without starving. Moana brought and showed them a hollow bamboo cane full of the most splendid pearls and she gave Pippi and Tommy and Annika a handful each.

'Good place for marbles this, isn't it?' said Pippi.

It was simply beautiful to sit in the mouth of the cave and look out over the glittering sea. It was fun, too, to lie on one's tummy and see who could spit furthest out to sea. Momo was an expert at it, but was easily beaten by Pippi whom no one could equal.

'If it seems to be pouring with rain over in New Zealand today,' she said, 'it's my fault.'

Pippi shielded her eyes with her hand and looked out across the sea.

'I can see a ship over there,' she said. 'It's a very, very small steamer. I wonder what it's doing here.'

And she might well wonder. The steamer was approaching Canny Canny Island at a good speed. There were some sailors on board and also two white men, whose names were Jim and Buck. They were tough-looking, rough men, like real bandits. And that is exactly what they were.

Once, when Captain Longstocking had visited the shop to buy snuff, Jim and Buck were there, too. They saw Captain Longstocking put two unusually big and beautiful pearls on the counter, and they heard him say that on Canny Canny Island the children used pearls like these for marbles. Since that day, their one and only ambition had been to sail to Canny Canny Island to try and get hold of the pearls. They knew that Captain Longstocking was as strong as a giant, and they also had a great respect for the crew of the *Hoppetossa*, so they waited, and intended to act as soon as all the men folk went away hunting. Their chance had now come. Hidden behind a nearby island they watched through their binoculars until Captain Longstocking and all the sailors and Canny Cannibals had paddled away from Canny Canny Island. They waited just long enough for the canoes to get well out of sight.

'Let go the anchor,' shouted Buck when the ship had come close to the island. Pippi and all the children were watching them in silence from the cave above. The ship now lay at anchor. Jim and Buck jumped into a dinghy and rowed ashore. The sailors had been ordered to stay on board.

'We'll slip up to the village and take them by surprise,' said Jim. 'I expect only the women and children are at home.'

'Right-o,' said Buck. 'I saw so many women in the canoes, that I guess only the children are left on the island. I hope they're playing marbles! Ho-ho-ho!'

'Why?' shouted Pippi from the cave. 'Do you like playing marbles? I think leap-frog's just as much fun.'

Jim and Buck turned round in astonishment and caught sight of the heads of Pippi and all the children as they leant out of the cave. The men's faces broke into gratified smiles.

'Here they are,' said Jim.

'Good!' said Buck. 'We'll soon settle them.'

But they decided they had better use some cunning. After all, they did not know where the children kept their pearls, and the best plan would be to pretend to be friendly. They did not let it be known that they had come to Canny Canny Island to get pearls. No, indeed! 'We're out for a little pleasure trip,' they said. They were feeling hot and sticky, and Buck suggested they should have a swim, to begin with.

'I'll go back and fetch our swimming trunks,' he said.

He rowed away in the dinghy and Jim was left alone on the shore.

'Is this a good place for bathing?' he shouted to the children in a wheedling voice.

'Couldn't be better,' said Pippi. 'Couldn't be better for sharks. They bathe here every day.'

'Nonsense,' said Jim, 'I can't see a single shark.'

But he felt rather worried all the same, and when Buck returned with the trunks he repeated what Pippi had said.

'What rot,' said Buck. Then he shouted to Pippi: 'Was it you who said it's dangerous to bathe here?'

'No,' replied Pippi. 'I never said it was.'

'That's queer,' said Jim. 'Didn't you tell me there were sharks here?'

'Yes, I did . . . but dangerous? No, hardly that. My own grandfather bathed here last year.'

'Well, that's all right, then,' said Buck.

'And Grandfather came home from hospital only last Friday,' continued Pippi, 'with the smartest wooden legs an old man ever wore.'

She spat thoughtfully into the water.

'So you can hardly say it's dangerous. But you can expect to part with the odd arm or leg if you want to bathe here. Wooden legs cost only a shilling a pair, and I don't think you need feel you have to go without a health-giving swim just for the sake of economy.'

She spat once more.

'Grandfather takes quite a childish delight in his wooden legs. He says he doesn't know how he could manage without them when he's in for a fight.'

'Do you know what I think?' said Buck. 'I think you're lying. Your grandfather must be an old man. He surely wouldn't want to fight.'

'Wouldn't he just,' shouted Pippi, shrilly. 'He's the fiercest old man that ever banged his enemy on the head with a wooden leg. If he's not allowed to fight from morning till night he doesn't know what to do with himself and bites his own nose with rage.'

'What nonsense!' said Buck. 'How could he bite his own nose?'

'He can,' Pippi assured him. 'He climbs up on a chair to do it.'

Buck wrestled with the problem for a moment, then he swore and growled:

'I'm sick of listening to your absurd stories. Come on, Jim, let's get undressed.'

'Another thing,' said Pippi, 'is that Grandfather has the world's longest nose. He has five parrots, and all five of them can sit, one beside the other, on his nose.'

At this Buck became really angry.

'Let me tell you something, you red-headed little brat! You're certainly the biggest liar I ever met. You ought to be ashamed of yourself. Do you really expect me to believe that five parrots can sit in a row on your grandfather's nose? Own up that you're lying.'

'Yes,' said Pippi sadly. 'It is a lie.'

'There you are!' said Buck. 'Just what I said.'

'It's a terrible, wicked lie,' said Pippi more sadly still.

'I knew it all the time,' said Buck.

'’Cos the fifth parrot,' shouted Pippi, bursting into a flood of tears, 'the fifth parrot *has to stand on one leg.*'

'Go to blazes,' said Buck, and he and Jim went behind a bush to undress.

'But, Pippi, you haven't got a grandfather,' said Annika reproachfully.

'No,' Pippi replied in a cheerful tone of voice. 'Are they compulsory?'

Buck was the first to appear in swimming trunks. He dived skilfully from a rock and swam out to sea. The children watched him intently from the cave. Suddenly, they saw the fin of a shark flash above the water.

'Shark! Shark!' shouted Momo.

Buck, who was enjoying himself greatly and was treading water, turned his head and caught sight of the fearful, hungry fish coming straight towards him.

No one could ever have swum faster than Buck did then. In two frantic seconds he reached dry land and rushed out of the water. He was frightened and angry, and he evidently blamed Pippi for the sharks in the water.

'You ought to be ashamed of yourself,' he shouted. 'The sea is *full* of sharks.'

'That's just what I told you,' said Pippi, smugly. 'I don't always tell lies, you see.'

Jim and Buck retired behind the bush to put their clothes on again. They felt that now was the time to begin to think about the pearls. Nobody knew how long Captain Longstocking and the others would be away.

'Listen, my dears,' said Buck, 'I've been told there's supposed to be good pearl fishing in these parts. Is it true, d'you know?'

'I should jolly well say there is,' said Pippi. 'The pearl oysters fairly rattle round your feet wherever you walk on the bottom of the sea. Just you go down and try for yourself.'

But Buck had no wish to do so.

'There are large pearls in every oyster,' said Pippi. 'Like this one.'

She held up a huge, gleaming pearl.

Jim and Buck were so excited that they could hardly restrain themselves.

'Have you got any more of those?' asked Jim. 'We'd like to buy them from you.'

This was not true, because Jim and Buck had no money for pearls. It was just a trick by which they hoped to steal them.

'Well, I should say we've got at least eight or nine pints of pearls in the cave,' said Pippi.

Jim and Buck could not hide their pleasure.

'Good,' said Buck. 'Just bring 'em here and we'll buy the lot.'

'Oh no, you won't,' said Pippi. 'What d'you think the poor children would play marbles with then?'

There was much discussion before Jim and Buck realized that they could not obtain the pearls by trickery. But what they could not have by cunning they would take by force. And now they knew where the pearls were. All they had to do was to climb up to the cave and seize them.

Climb up to the cave? Yes! While the discussion went on, Pippi, just to make sure, had untied the hibiscus rope. It was now lying safely inside the cave.

Jim and Buck were far from eager to try and climb across to the cave. But there did not seem to be anything else they could do.

'Go on,' said Buck.

'No-o, you go, Buck,' said Jim.

'You *go*, *Jim*,' said Buck. He was the stronger of the two. So Jim began to climb. Desperately he grabbed hold of any projections he could reach, while cold sweat ran down his back.

'Mind you hang on and don't fall in,' said Pippi encouragingly.

And then Jim fell into the sea. Buck, on the beach, shouted and swore. Jim shouted, too, because he saw two sharks making straight for him. When they were not more than a yard away, Pippi threw down a coconut right in front of their noses. This frightened them away long enough for Jim to reach the shore and climb up to the little ledge. His clothes were dripping with water and he looked a miserable sight. Buck cursed him.

'If you think it's so easy, go and do it yourself,' said Jim.

'All right,' said Buck, '*I'll* show you how it's done,' and he began to climb.

All the children peeped out at him. Annika felt rather frightened when he came nearer and nearer.

'Hi! Don't step there, you'll fall in,' said Pippi.

'Where?' said Buck.

'There,' said Pippi, pointing at his feet. Buck looked down . . .

'It's a dreadful waste of coconuts,' said Pippi a second later as she threw one into the sea to stop the sharks eating up Buck, who was wriggling unhappily in the water. But up he came again, angry as a bull, for he was not one to be easily frightened. He immediately started on another climb, because he was determined to reach the cave and get hold of the pearls.

This time he found it easier. When he had nearly reached the mouth of the cave he shouted triumphantly:

'Now I'll make you pay for everything.'

Then Pippi put out a finger and poked him in the stomach.

Splash!

'I wish you'd taken the coconut with you when you dropped off,' shouted Pippi after him, hitting an inquisitive shark on the nose. But other sharks came, and she had to throw more coconuts. One of them happened to fall on Buck's head.

'Oh *dear*, was that you?' said Pippi when Buck yelled with pain. 'From here you look exactly like a horrid big shark.'

Jim and Buck now decided to wait until the children left the cave.

'Sooner or later hunger will bring them out of there,' said Buck grimly. 'And then they'll be sorry.'

He shouted to the children:

'It seems a pity that you'll have to sit in that cave until you starve to death.'

'Very kind of you,' said Pippi. 'But you needn't worry about us for the next fortnight or so. Perhaps after that, we may have to start to ration the coconuts a little.'

She cracked a large coconut, drank the milk, and ate some of the delicious kernel.

Jim and Buck cursed loudly. The sun was beginning to set, and they prepared to spend the night on the beach. They dared not row out to the steamer to sleep there, because that would have given the children the chance to run off with all the pearls. They lay down on the hard rock in their wet clothes. It was very uncomfortable.

Inside the cave sat all the children, their eyes twinkling, and they feasted on coconuts and breadfruit. It tasted very good, and everybody was excited and happy. Every now and then they popped their heads out to look at Jim and Buck. Because of the gathering darkness they could hardly see the two bandits on the ledge of rock, but they could hear swearing down below.

Suddenly the rain started pelting down, the violent kind of rain which you get in the tropics. A solid sheet of water poured from the sky. Pippi put the merest tip of her nose outside the cave.

'I must say, some people are lucky,' she shouted to Jim and Buck.

'Just what do you mean?' asked Buck hopefully. He thought that perhaps the children had now changed their minds and would let them have the pearls. 'What do you mean by some people being lucky?'

'I was just thinking how jolly lucky you were to be soaked already before this *torrent* of rain started. Otherwise the rain would have made you wet through, wouldn't it?'

There was swearing below on the ledge, but you could not tell whether it came from Jim or Buck.

'Good night to you both, and sweet dreams,' said Pippi. 'That's what we're going to have, anyway.'

The children all lay down on the floor of the cave. Tommy and Annika nestled at Pippi's side with her hands in theirs. They were warm and cosy in the cave, and they could hear the rushing sound of the rain outside.

10
Pippi Gets Tired of Jim and Buck

The children slept soundly all night—but not so Jim and Buck. They kept on swearing at the rain, and when it stopped, they began quarrelling for a change. Jim blamed Buck, and Buck blamed Jim for not seizing the pearls, and whose stupid idea was it, anyway, to come to Canny Canny Island? But when the sun rose and dried their wet clothes and they saw Pippi's bright face in the entrance to the cave and heard her cheery 'Good morning,' they were more determined than ever to seize the pearls and leave the island as rich men. The trouble was that they could not think how they were going to do it.

Pippi's horse had started to wonder what had become of Pippi, Tommy, and Annika. Mr Nelson had returned from the meeting with his kinsfolk in the jungle, and he, too, was puzzled; and he was worried about what Pippi would say when she discovered that he had lost his little straw hat.

The horse, with Mr Nelson, who had jumped up on to his hindquarters, trotted off to look for Pippi. After some time he reached the southern side of the island . . . Then he saw Pippi's head pop out of a cave. He neighed happily.

'Look, Pippi! There's your horse!' shouted Tommy.

'And Mr Nelson is sitting on his back!' shouted Annika.

Jim and Buck overheard the children talking. They learned that the horse, trotting along the shore, belonged to Pippi, that red-headed nuisance in the cave above them.

Buck went up to the horse and grabbed his mane.

'Listen, you little devil,' he shouted. 'I'm going to kill your horse.'

'Oh, surely you wouldn't kill my lovely horse,' said Pippi, 'my dear kind little horse. You can't mean it.'

'Looks as if I should have to,' said Buck. 'That is, if you don't bring us the pearls. All of them, mind you! If you don't I'll kill the horse this very instant.'

Pippi looked at him seriously.

'Please,' she said. 'Oh, please don't kill my horse, and please let the children keep their pearls.'

'You heard what I said,' retorted Buck. 'Bring the pearls at once! Or else . . . '

Then he whispered to Jim:

'I'll teach her! When she brings the pearls, I'll beat her black and blue to pay her out for last night. We'll take the horse with us and sell it on some other island.'

He shouted to Pippi:

'Well, what about it? Are you coming, or not?'

'I might as well,' said Pippi. 'But don't forget, it was your idea.'

She leapt nimbly from one small ledge to another as easily as if there had been the smoothest path, and then down to the level place where Buck, Jim, and the horse were standing. She stopped in front of Buck and stood there, small and slight, with the little cloth round her tummy and the two red plaits sticking straight out. Her eyes had a dangerous glint in them.

'Where are the pearls?' Buck shouted.

'There aren't going to be any pearls today,' said Pippi. 'There's going to be leap-frog instead.'

When Buck heard this, he roared so fiercely that Annika trembled with fright as she stood listening in the cave above.

'This is the limit. Now I'm going to kill both you and the horse,' he yelled, and charged at Pippi.

'Steady on, my good man,' said Pippi. Grasping him round the waist, she threw him three yards into the air, and he landed with a bump on the rock. Then Jim went into action. He aimed a terrible blow at Pippi, but she jumped to one side with a confident smile, and a second later Jim, also, was sailing skywards. Jim and Buck sat side by side on the rock, groaning loudly. Pippi went up to them and gripped them both by the scruffs of their necks.

'You're *much* too fond of playing marbles,' she said. 'It's high time you did some work and stopped thinking of nothing but fun and games.'

She carried them to the dinghy and threw them in.

'Off you go, home to your mother, and ask her if you can have twopence to buy stone marbles with,' she said. 'They're just as good as pearls.'

Very soon, their ship steamed away from Canny Canny Island, never to be seen again in those waters.

Pippi patted her horse. Mr Nelson jumped up on her shoulder. And from behind the furthest point of the island a long line of canoes appeared. Captain Longstocking and his company were joyfully returning home from their hunting. Pippi shouted and waved to them, and they waved back with their paddles.

Pippi quickly secured the rope again, so that Tommy, Annika, and the others could leave the cave in safety. And when, a little later, the canoes anchored in the little bay beside the *Hoppetossa*, the whole crowd of children were already there on the shore to welcome them.

Captain Longstocking patted Pippi.

'And how have you fared while I've been away?' he asked.

'Oh, fine,' said Pippi.

'But, Pippi, we haven't,' said Annika. 'Lots of awful things nearly happened.'

'Oh yes, of course, I forgot,' said Pippi. 'We haven't been getting along fine at all, Daddy. The moment you turn your back things begin to happen.'

'My dear child, what's been happening?' exclaimed Captain Longstocking anxiously.

'Something awful,' said Pippi. 'Mr Nelson lost his straw hat.'

11
Pippi Leaves Canny Canny Island

Happy days followed, happy days in a warm, enchanted world, full of sunshine and glittering blue water and sweet-smelling flowers.

Tommy and Annika were by this time so brown that you could hardly tell the difference between them and the Canny Cannibal children. And there was not the tiniest bit of Pippi's face which did not have a freckle on it.

'This trip is a real beauty treatment for me,'

she said contentedly. 'I'm frecklier and more beautiful than ever now. If I go on like this I shall soon be quite irresistible.'

But Momo and Moana and all the other Canny Cannibal children thought Pippi irresistible already. They had never had such a good time in their lives before, and they were just as fond of Pippi as Tommy and Annika were. Of course, they liked Tommy and Annika, too, and Tommy and Annika liked them back. So they all had a wonderful time together, playing from morning till night. They were often in the cave. Pippi had put some blankets there, and when they wanted to do so, they could sleep in the cave, even more comfortably than on that first night. She had also made a rope ladder which led to the water below the cave, and all the children climbed up and down it, bathed and splashed to their heart's content. Yes, it was quite safe to bathe there now. Pippi had fenced in a large area with a net, so that the sharks could not get near them. It was great fun to swim in and out of the caves which had water in them. Even Tommy and Annika had learnt how to dive for oysters. The first pearl that Annika found was a large beautiful pinky one. She made up her mind to take it home and have it set in a ring as a souvenir of Canny Canny Island.

Sometimes they pretended that Pippi was

Buck, trying to make his way to the cave to steal pearls. Then Tommy would pull up the rope ladder and Pippi had to climb up the face of the cliff the best way she could. All the children shouted, 'Buck's coming, Buck's coming,' when she put her head into the cave. Then, one after another, they were allowed to poke her in the tummy so that she toppled over backwards down into the sea. There she splashed about with only her feet showing out of the water, and the children laughed so much that they nearly fell out of the cave.

When they tired of the cave, they could go to their bamboo house. Pippi and the children had shared in the building of it, but Pippi had done most of the work. It was large and square, and was made of slender bamboo canes. You could climb in it and on it just as you liked. A tall coconut palm was growing close to the house. Pippi had chopped steps in the trunk of the palm tree so that you could go right up to the top and see a fine view from there. Between two other palm trees Pippi had fixed a swing, made of hibiscus rope. It was an extra specially good one. If you swung really high, and then threw yourself at top speed out of the swing, you landed in the water. Pippi swung so enormously high that she flew far out to sea. 'One fine day I expect I'll land in Australia, and it won't be much fun for the person whose head I drop on to,' she said.

The children sometimes made trips into the jungle to a place where there was a high mountain and a waterfall which tumbled down a steep part of it. Pippi had made up her mind to ride down the waterfall in a barrel, and sure enough she did. She brought one of the barrels from the *Hoppetossa*, and got into it. Momo and Tommy put the lid on and gave the barrel a push towards the waterfall. It hurtled down the fall at a colossal speed and was finally smashed to pieces. All the children saw Pippi disappear in the swirling torrent, and they thought they would never see her again. But before long she bobbed up to the surface, came out of the water, and said:

'These water-butts go a pretty good pace, I must say.'

The days went by, and the rainy season was about to begin, when Captain Longstocking would shut himself in his hut and contemplate. He was afraid Pippi would find it dull during the rains on Canny Canny Island. Tommy and Annika thought more and more often about their mother and father, and wondered how they were getting on. They were also very eager to be home for Christmas, so they were not so disappointed as one might think when Pippi said, one morning:

'Tommy and Annika, what about spending some time at Villekulla Cottage for a change?'

It was a sad day for Momo and Moana and the other Canny Cannibal children when Pippi, Tommy, and Annika went on board the *Hoppetossa*. But Pippi promised that they would come back to Canny Canny Island very, very often. The Canny Cannibal children had made garlands of white flowers which they hung round Pippi, Tommy, and Annika's necks as a parting gift. While the ship sailed away, a sad song of farewell was heard coming across the water. Captain Longstocking was also standing on the shore. He had to stay behind to rule his subjects. It was Fridolf who had taken on the duty of seeing the children home. Captain Longstocking blew his nose a number of times in a handkerchief smelling of snuff as he waved goodbye. Tears gushed out of Pippi, Tommy, and Annika's eyes and they waved and waved to Captain Longstocking and the children until they could see them no longer.

A fair wind carried them on their way.

'We'd better bring out your woolly vests in good time before we reach the North Sea,' said Pippi.

'Oh! What a bore,' said Tommy and Annika.

It was soon evident that the *Hoppetossa*, in spite

of the fair wind, could not possibly reach home in time for Christmas. Tommy and Annika were very disappointed when they were told. Think of it! No Christmas tree and no presents!

'We might just as well have stayed on Canny Canny Island,' said Tommy, huffily.

Annika thought of her mother and father, and felt that she would be glad to get home in any case, but it was certainly disappointing to miss Christmas. Tommy and Annika were agreed about that all right.

One dark evening at the beginning of January, Pippi, Tommy, and Annika caught sight of the welcoming light of the little town. They were home at last.

'Well, here's the end of *that* South Sea trip,' said Pippi, as she walked down the gangway with the horse.

No one was on the quay to meet them, for nobody knew when they would arrive. Pippi lifted Tommy, Annika, and Mr Nelson on to the horse, and off they went to Villekulla Cottage. The horse had to lift his legs high, because the streets and the roads were deep in snow. Tommy and Annika could hardly see through the whirling snow. Soon they would be with their mother and father. And suddenly they felt they could not wait any longer.

There was a light shining from the Settergreens' house, and through the window Tommy and Annika could see their mother and father sitting by the dining-table.

'There's Mummy and Daddy,' said Tommy, sounding very pleased.

But Villekulla Cottage was in complete darkness and was covered in snow.

Annika could not bear the thought of Pippi going in there all alone.

'Please, Pippi, stay with us the first night,' she said.

'No, but many thanks all the same,' said Pippi, and stepped deep into the snow outside the gate. 'I've got to get things organized at Villekulla Cottage.'

She plunged on through the deep snow-drifts into which she sank right up to her waist. The horse followed.

'But it'll be so cold,' Tommy protested, 'there hasn't been a fire in the cottage for ever so long.'

'Nonsense,' said Pippi. 'So long as the heart's warm and ticks properly, you don't feel the cold.'

12
Pippi Longstocking Does
not Want to Grow Up

Oh, how Tommy and Annika's mother and father hugged and kissed their children! Then they gave them a good supper and tucked them up in bed. They sat for a long time by the children's beds, listening to the tales of all the exciting things which had happened on Canny Canny Island. They were all very happy to be together again. There was only one fly in the ointment—they had not been at home for Christmas. Tommy and Annika did not want their mother to know how disappointed they were to have missed the Christmas tree and the presents, but they were sad about it all the same. It always takes a little time to settle down when you have been away and it would have helped enormously to have come back on Christmas Eve.

Tommy and Annika also felt a little sorry when they thought of Pippi. By now she would be in bed at Villekulla Cottage with her feet on the pillow, and there would be no one there to tuck her up. They decided to go and see her as early as they could on the following day.

But, on the following day, their mother did not want to part with them as she had not seen them for such a long time. Besides, their grandmother was coming to dinner, specially to see the children now they had come home. Tommy and Annika wondered anxiously what Pippi could be doing all day by herself, and when it began to get dark they could not bear it any longer.

'Please, Mummy, we *must* go and see Pippi,' said Tommy.

'Off you go, then,' said Mrs Settergreen. 'But don't stay long.'

Tommy and Annika scampered off.

When they reached the garden gate of Villekulla Cottage they stopped short and could hardly believe their eyes. The picture they saw was just like a Christmas card. The whole house was covered in soft snow and there were cheerful lights shining from every window. The flame of a burning torch outside the front door threw flickering beams across the gleaming snow. The path had been cleared, so Tommy and Annika could now walk up to the porch without sinking into drifts of snow.

They were just stamping the snow off their boots in the porch when the door opened, and there stood Pippi.

'A happy Christmas to you in this cottage,' she said. Then she pushed them into the kitchen. Heavens! If there wasn't a Christmas tree! The candles were lit, and seventeen sparklers, hooked on to the Christmas tree, were burning and spluttering and giving out a lovely smell. The table was laden with every kind of Christmas food: a large ham, coated in breadcrumbs, and decorated with fringes of tissue-paper, home-made sausages, and Christmas pudding. Pippi had even made ginger biscuits, in the shapes of boys and girls, and saffron bread. A roaring fire burned in the kitchen range, and close to the wood box stood the horse, pawing the floor delicately with his foot. Mr Nelson was jumping about in the tree in between the sparklers.

'He's supposed to be the Christmas angel,' said Pippi, severely, 'but do you think I can get him to sit still at the top?'

Tommy and Annika were speechless.

'Oh, Pippi,' said Annika at last, 'how beautiful! But how did you manage to do it all in the time?'

'I have an industrious disposition,' said Pippi.

Tommy and Annika were filled with sudden joy and happiness.

'I *am* glad we're home at Villekulla Cottage again,' said Tommy.

They sat down at the table and ate their fill of ham, sausages, pudding, ginger biscuits, and saffron bread, and they thought the feast tasted even better than bananas and breadfruit.

'But, Pippi! It isn't Christmas time,' said Tommy.

'Yes, it is,' said Pippi. 'Villekulla Cottage's calendar has lost a lot of time. I shall have to take it to a calendar repairer and have it seen to, so that it catches up again.'

'*What* a good thing!' said Annika. 'So we didn't miss our Christmas, after all—though, of course, we didn't get any presents.'

'Ah, I was thinking the very same thing,' said Pippi. 'I've hidden your presents. You'll have to look for them.'

Tommy and Annika went red in the face with excitement. Before you could wink twice they got up from the table and started hunting. In the wood box Tommy found a large parcel; on it was written 'TOMMY'. It contained a splendid paint-box. Underneath the table Annika found a parcel with her name on it, and inside the parcel was a pretty red sunshade.

'I shall take it with me next time we go to Canny Canny Island,' said Annika.

Inside the chimney corner hung two parcels. One contained a toy jeep for Tommy, and the other, a doll's tea-service for Annika. A little parcel was hanging from the horse's tail and in it was a clock for the mantelpiece of Tommy and Annika's nursery.

When they had found all their presents they both gave Pippi a big hug. She was standing by the kitchen window, looking at the quantities of snow in the garden.

'Tomorrow, we're going to build a big igloo,' she said. 'And we'll have a candle burning in it in the evenings.'

'Oh yes, let's,' said Annika, feeling more and more pleased to be home again.

'And let's make a ski-slope running down from the roof and into the snow below,' said Pippi. 'I want to teach the horse to ski, but I'm blowed if I know whether he will need four skis, or only two.'

'Hurray! We're going to have a lovely time tomorrow,' said Tommy. 'Wasn't it lucky we came in the middle of the Christmas hols?'

'We shall always have a lovely time here at Villekulla Cottage and on Canny Canny Island and everywhere,' said Annika.

Pippi nodded in agreement. All three were now sitting on the kitchen table. A shadow suddenly passed across Tommy's face.

'I never want to grow up,' he said firmly.

'Nor me,' said Annika.

'No, that's nothing to pine for,' said Pippi. 'Grown-ups never have any fun. All they have is a lot of dull work and stupid clothes and corns and nincum tax.'

'It's called income tax,' said Annika.

'It's all the same rubbish,' said Pippi. 'And they're full of superstition and silly ideas. They think it's bad luck to put a knife in your mouth when you eat, and things like that.'

'And they don't know how to play,' said Annika. 'Ugh! Fancy having to grow up!'

'And who said we have to?' asked Pippi. 'If I remember rightly, I've got some pills somewhere.'

'What kind of pills?' said Tommy.

'Awfully good pills for those who don't want to grow up,' said Pippi, jumping down from the table. She searched in all the cupboards and drawers, and after a short time she brought out what looked exactly like three yellow dried peas.

'Peas!' said Tommy in surprise.

'That's what *you* think,' said Pippi. 'It isn't peas. It's squigglypills. An old Red Indian Chief gave them to me a long time ago in Rio when I happened to mention that I didn't care very much for growing up.'

'Is that all you have to do—just take those little pills?' asked Annika doubtfully.

'Yes,' Pippi assured her. 'But you must eat them in the dark and say:

'Little squiggle, you are clever,
I do not want to *grew* up ever.'

'You mean "grow", don't you?' said Tommy.

'I said "grew", and I mean "grew",' said Pippi. 'That's the whole secret, you see. Most people say "grow" and that's the worst thing you can do, because it makes you grow more than ever. Once there was a boy who ate pills like these. He said "grow" instead of "grew" and he began to grow so much it was frightening. Lots and lots of yards every day. It was tragic. Mind you, it was all very well so long as he could walk about and graze straight out of big apple trees, rather like a giraffe. But it wasn't long before he got too tall for that. When his aunts came on a visit and they wanted to say: "What a fine big fellow you've grown into", they had to shout to him through a megaphone. All you could see of him was his long thin legs, like two flagpoles, which disappeared in the clouds. We never heard a sound from him again except once, when he took it into his head to lick the sun and got a blister on his tongue. Then he yelled so loudly that the flowers down on Earth all wilted. That was the very last sign of life we ever had from him. But I suppose his legs are still walking about in Rio and causing a lot of disturbance in the traffic, if I'm not much mistaken.'

'I daren't take a pill,' said Annika, frightened, 'in case I say the wrong thing.'

'You won't,' said Pippi, consolingly. 'If I thought you'd do that, I wouldn't let you have one, because it would be so dull to have only your legs to play with. Tommy and me and your legs—that would be a queer sight!'

'Don't be silly, Annika,' said Tommy. 'Of course you won't say it wrong.'

They blew out all the candles on the Christmas tree. The kitchen was quite dark except near the stove, where you could see the fire glowing behind the bars. The children sat down silently in a circle in the middle of the floor. They held hands. Pippi gave Tommy and Annika a squigglypill each. They could feel the excitement creeping up and down their spines. Imagine it— in a moment or two they would have swallowed the strange pills and then they would never, never have to grow up. Wasn't it wonderful?

'Now!' whispered Pippi.

They swallowed their pills, saying, all three together:

> 'Little squiggle, you are clever,
> I do not want to grew up ever.'

It was all over. Pippi lit the lamp.

'Good!' she said. 'Now we shan't have to grow up and have corns and other miseries. Of course, the pills have been in my cupboard for so long that I can't be *quite* sure they haven't lost their goodness. But we must hope for the best.'

Something had just occurred to Annika.

'But, Pippi!' she cried in dismay, 'you were going to be a pirate when you grew up!'

'Oh, I can be a pirate anyway,' said Pippi. 'I can be a teeny-weeny ferocious pirate, spreading death and destruction, all the same.'

She looked thoughtful.

'Supposing,' she said, 'supposing that after many, many years have gone by, a lady comes walking past here one day and sees us running in the garden and playing. Perhaps she will ask you, Tommy, "And how old are you, my little friend?" And you say: "Fifty-three, if I'm not mistaken."'

Tommy laughed heartily.

'I shall be rather small for my age, I think,' he said.

'Yes,' admitted Pippi, 'but you can always say that you were bigger when you were smaller.'

Tommy and Annika now remembered that their mother had told them not to stay long.

'I'm afraid we've got to go home,' said Tommy.

'But we'll be back tomorrow,' said Annika.

'Good,' said Pippi. 'We're starting on the igloo at eight o'clock.'

She saw them off at the gate and her red plaits bobbed round her head as she ran back to Villekulla Cottage.

'Well!' said Tommy a little later when he was brushing his teeth. 'If I hadn't known they were squigglypills I could have sworn they were just ordinary peas.'

Annika was standing by the nursery window in her pink pyjamas, looking towards Villekulla Cottage.

'Look! I can see Pippi!' she shouted in delight.

Tommy rushed to the window. Yes! So could he! Now that the trees were bare you could see right into Pippi's kitchen.

Pippi was sitting by the table, leaning her head on her arms. She was gazing dreamily at the flickering light of a small candle in front of her.

'She's . . . she's looking so lonely, somehow,' said Annika; and her voice trembled a little. 'Oh, Tommy, I wish it was morning and we could go to her straight away.'

They stood there, silently looking out into the winter night. The stars were shining above the roof of Villekulla Cottage and Pippi was inside. She would always be there. It was wonderful to remember that. The years would pass, but Pippi and Tommy and Annika would never grow up. That is, if the squigglypills were still good! Spring and summer would come, and then autumn and winter, again and again, but their games would continue. Tomorrow they would build an igloo and make a ski-run from the roof of Villekulla Cottage. In the spring they would climb in the hollow oak tree where ginger-beer grew. They would hunt the thimble, they would sit in the wood box and tell stories. They would, perhaps, go to Canny Canny Island sometimes, and see Momo and Moana and the others. But they would always come back to Villekulla Cottage. Yes! It was a very comforting thought—Pippi would always, always be there.

'If only she'd look this way we could wave to her,' said Tommy.

But Pippi only gazed in front of her with dreamy eyes.

Then she blew out the candle.

Pippi Goes Aboard

Astrid Lindgren

Translated by Marianne Turner
Illustrated by Tony Ross

OXFORD
UNIVERSITY PRESS

Contents

1. Pippi still lives at Villekulla Cottage   253
2. Pippi goes Shopping   257
3. Pippi writes a Letter and goes to School   276
4. Pippi goes on a School Outing   287
5. Pippi goes to the Fair   301
6. Pippi is Shipwrecked   320
7. Pippi has a Grand Visitor   343
8. Pippi gives a Farewell Party   355
9. Pippi goes Aboard   367

1
Pippi still lives at
Villekulla Cottage

If a stranger, coming to the little Swedish town, should one day happen to find himself in a particular place on the outskirts, he would see Villekulla Cottage. Not that the cottage is much to look at: it is rather a tumble-down old cottage with an overgrown garden round it, but the stranger might perhaps pause to wonder who lived there, and why there was a horse in the porch. If it was really late and almost dark, and if he caught sight of a little girl striding round the garden looking as if she had no intention of going to bed, he might think:

'I wonder why that little girl's mother doesn't see that she goes to bed? Other children are fast asleep by this time.'

If the little girl came up to the gate—and she would be certain to do so, because she enjoyed talking to people—then he would have the chance of taking a good look at her, and would probably think:

'She's one of the freckliest and most red-headed children I've ever seen.'

Afterwards perhaps he would think:

'Freckles and red hair are really rather nice—at least when a person has such a happy appearance as this child.'

It would perhaps interest him to know the name of this little red-head who was strolling about by herself in the dusk, and if he was close to the gate, he might ask:

'What's your name?'

A merry voice would reply:

'Pippilotta Provisiona Gaberdina Dandeliona Ephraims-daughter Longstocking, daughter of Captain Ephraim Longstocking, formerly the terror of the seas, now Cannibal King: but everybody calls me Pippi!'

When she said that her father was a Cannibal

King, she firmly believed it, because he had once been blown into the water and disappeared when Pippi and he had been out sailing on the sea. Since Pippi's father was somewhat stout, she was absolutely sure he had not been drowned. It seemed reasonable to suppose that he had been washed ashore on an island and become king over all the cannibals there, and this is exactly what Pippi thought had happened. If the traveller went on chatting to Pippi, he would find out that, except for a horse and a monkey called Mr Nelson, she lived quite alone at Villekulla Cottage. If he had a kind heart, he probably could not help thinking:

'How does the poor child live?'

He really need not have worried about that.

'I'm rich as a troll,' Pippi used to say. And she was. She had a whole suitcaseful of golden coins which her father had given her, and she managed splendidly without either mother or father. Since there was no one to tell her when to go to bed, Pippi told herself. Sometimes she did not tell herself until about ten o'clock, because Pippi had never believed that it was necessary for children to go to bed at seven. That was the time when you had the most fun. So the stranger should not be surprised at seeing Pippi striding round the garden, although the sun had set and the air was getting chilly, and Tommy and Annika had been tucked up in bed for ages. Tommy and Annika were Pippi's playmates, who lived in the house next to Villekulla Cottage. They had both a father and a mother, and both the father and the mother believed that it was best for children to go to bed at seven.

If the stranger lingered after Pippi had said goodnight and had left the gate, and if he saw Pippi go up to the porch and lift the horse high in her strong arms and carry him out into the garden, he would surely rub his eyes and wonder if he was dreaming.

'What a remarkable child this is,' he would say to himself. 'I do believe she can lift the horse! This is the most remarkable child *I've* ever seen!'

In that he would be right. Pippi was the most remarkable child—at least in that town. There may be more remarkable children in other places, but in that little town there was no one like Pippi Longstocking, and nowhere in the world, neither in that town nor anywhere else, was there anyone so strong as she was.

2
Pippi goes Shopping

I t was a beautiful spring day, the sun was shining, the birds were twittering and snow water ran in all the ditches. Tommy and Annika came skipping over to Pippi's. Tommy had brought two lumps of sugar for the horse, and both he and Annika stopped for a moment in the porch to pat it before they went inside to see Pippi. Pippi was asleep when they came in. Her feet were on the pillow, and her head was far down under the bedclothes. She always slept that way. Annika pinched her big toe and called:

'Wake up!'

Mr Nelson, the little monkey, was already awake and sitting on the lamp hanging from the ceiling. Presently there was movement underneath the bedclothes, and suddenly a red head popped out. Pippi opened her bright eyes, grinned, and said:

'Oh, it's you! I dreamt it was my father, the Cannibal King, looking to see if I had any corns.'

She sat up, put her legs out and pulled on her stockings, one brown and the other black.

''Course not! You don't get any corns from these,' she said, putting on her big, black shoes which were exactly twice as long as her feet.

'Pippi,' said Tommy, 'what shall we do? Annika and I have a holiday today.'

'Ooh,' said Pippi, 'let's think up something nice. We can't dance round the Christmas tree, because we threw it out three months ago. Otherwise we could have played Christmas games all morning. It would be fun to dig for gold, but we can't do that either, because we don't know where the gold is. Besides, most of the gold is in Alaska, and you can't move an inch there for gold diggers. No, we must think of something else.'

'Yes,' said Annika, 'something *really* nice.'

Pippi did her hair into two tight plaits that stuck straight out. She was thinking.

'What about going into town to do some shopping?' she said at last.

'But we haven't got any money,' said Tommy.

'I have,' said Pippi, and to prove it she went at once and opened her suitcase which was full of gold coins. She took out a large handful and put the coins in a big pocket in the front of her apron.

'Now, if I could only find my hat,' she said, 'I'd be ready to start off.' The hat was nowhere to be seen. First Pippi took a look in the wood-box, but strange to say it was not there. Then she looked in the breadbin, but there was nothing in it except a suspender, a broken alarm clock, and a small rusk. Finally she looked on the hat rack, but found only a frying pan, a screw-driver, and a piece of cheese.

'There's no order in nothing, and I can't find everything,' said Pippi irritably. 'Though I've missed the cheese for a long time: good thing that was found.'

'Come here, hat,' she shouted, 'are you coming shopping or not? If you don't come at once, you'll be too late!'

No hat came.

'Well, it has no one but itself to blame when it's so obstinate, but I won't put up with any complaints when I come back,' she said sternly.

Soon afterwards they could be seen walking along the road leading to the centre of the town, Tommy and Annika and Pippi with Mr Nelson on her shoulder. The sun shone brilliantly, the sky was very blue, and the children were very happy. There was a gurgling in the ditch beside the road. It was a deep ditch with lots of water in it.

'I like ditches,' said Pippi, and without further ado she stepped down into the water. It went above her knees, and when she jumped really hard it splashed Tommy and Annika.

'I'm a boat,' she said, and ploughed through the water. As she said this she stumbled and went under.

'I mean a submarine,' she went on quite unperturbed as soon as her head was above water again.

'Oh, Pippi,' said Annika anxiously, 'you're wet through.'

'What's wrong with that?' said Pippi. 'Who said children must be dry? Cold showers are supposed to be good for you, I've heard. It's only in this country they've got the idea that children shouldn't walk in ditches. In America the ditches are so full of children that there isn't any room for the water. They stay in the ditches all the year round. In the winter, of course, the children freeze into them, and their heads pop out through the ice. Their mothers have to take fruit salad and steak and kidney pudding to them, because they can't go home for dinner. But, you bet, they're as strong and fit as can be.'

The little town looked lovely in the spring sunshine. The narrow, cobbled streets seemed to wind their way anyhow between the rows of houses. Nearly every house was surrounded by a small garden with snowdrops and crocuses in it. There were lots of shops in the little town. On this fine spring day plenty of people were going in and out of them, and the shop bells rang continuously. The housewives arrived with baskets on their arms to buy coffee and sugar and soap and butter.

Quite a lot of children were out buying toffees or packets of chewing gum, but most of them had no money to spend, and these poor things stood outside the shops and could only *look* at all the sweets behind the glass.

When the sun was shining most brightly, three small people appeared in the High Street. They were Tommy, Annika, and Pippi—a very moist Pippi, who left a wet trail behind her as she sauntered along.

'Aren't we lucky?' said Annika. 'Look at all the shops, and we have a pocketful of gold coins!'

Tommy was so happy when he thought of this that he jumped for joy.

'Shall we start then?' said Pippi. 'First of all I'd like to buy a piano.'

'But, Pippi,' said Tommy, 'you can't play the piano!'

'How should I know when I've never tried?' said Pippi. 'I've never had a piano to practise on, and I tell you, Tommy, to play the piano without having a piano needs a lot of practice.'

There was no piano shop in sight. Instead the children saw a chemist's. A large jar of freckle cream stood in the window, and beside the jar was an advertisement, saying: DO YOU SUFFER FROM FRECKLES?

'What does it say?' asked Pippi.

She could not read much, because she never wanted to go to school like other children.

'It says: "Do you suffer from freckles?"' said Annika.

'Oh, does it?' said Pippi thoughtfully. 'Well, a polite question should have a polite answer. Come along, let's go in!'

She pushed the door open and walked in, closely followed by Tommy and Annika. An elderly lady was standing behind the counter. Pippi went straight up to her.

'No,' she said firmly.

'What do you want, dear?' said the lady.

'No,' said Pippi again.

'I don't know what you mean,' said the lady.

'No, I do *not* suffer from freckles,' said Pippi.

Then the lady understood, but, glancing at Pippi, she exclaimed:

'But, my dear child, your face is full of freckles!'

'Of course,' said Pippi, 'but I don't suffer from them. I like them! Good morning!'

She started to walk out, but in the doorway she turned round and called:

'But if you get any cream that makes *more* freckles, send me about seven or eight jars.'

Next to the chemist's there was a shop which sold ladies' clothes.

'We haven't done much shopping yet,' said Pippi. 'We really must get down to it.'

They walked in, first Pippi, then Tommy, and then Annika. The first thing that caught their eye was a very elegant dummy in a blue silk dress. Pippi went up to the figure and grasped its hand cordially.

'How do you do?' she said. 'I suppose you're the lady who owns this shop. Pleased to meet you,' she said, shaking the dummy's hand even more vigorously.

But then something awful happened. The

figure's arm came loose and slid out of its silk covering, and there was Pippi with a long white arm in her hand. Tommy caught his breath in dismay, and Annika nearly burst into tears. The assistant rushed forward and began to scold Pippi dreadfully.

'Keep your hair on,' said Pippi when she got tired of listening. 'Isn't it self service here, then? I was thinking of buying this arm, you see.'

The assistant became angrier still, and said that the dummy was not for sale. In any case an arm could not be sold by itself, but Pippi would certainly have to pay the cost of the whole dummy, since she had broken it.

'That's queer,' said Pippi. 'It's a good thing they don't treat you like this in every shop. Suppose, next time I want to have pork chops for dinner, the butcher makes me buy a whole pig!'

While speaking she pulled out a couple of gold coins with a flourish from her apron pocket and threw them down on the counter. The assistant was thoroughly taken aback.

'Does the female cost more than that?' asked Pippi.

'Oh no, indeed not. It doesn't cost anything like so much,' answered the assistant very politely.

'Keep the change, then, and buy your children

some sweets with it,' said Pippi, moving towards the door. The assistant ran after her, asking respectfully to what address he might have the dummy sent.

'All I want is this arm, and I'll take it with me,' said Pippi. 'You can give the rest to the poor. Goodbye.'

'What *are* you going to do with that arm?' asked Tommy curiously, when they were out in the street again.

'Oh *that*,' said Pippi. 'What am I going to do with it? Haven't some people false teeth and false hair? Even false noses, sometimes. So why shouldn't I have one small false arm? Besides, I can tell you, it's jolly useful having three arms. I remember once when I sailed with Daddy on the high seas coming to a town where everyone had three arms. Not bad, eh? Just imagine! When they were eating, with a fork in one hand and a knife in the other, and suddenly they wanted to scratch their noses or ears, then it wasn't such a bad idea to get out the third arm. They saved a lot of time that way.'

Pippi looked thoughtful.

'Oh, dear me, I'm telling fibs,' she said. 'Queer, how suddenly such a lot of tales bubble up in me, and I can't help it. They didn't really have three arms at all in that town. Only two.'

She was silent for a moment, thinking.

'In fact, quite a lot of them only had one,' she said, 'and to tell the whole truth, there were even people who had none, and when they wanted to eat they had to lie down and lap from the plate. They couldn't scratch their own ears at all, they had to ask their mothers to do it for them.'

Pippi shook her head sadly.

'The fact is that I've never seen so few arms anywhere as in that town, but it's just like me: I'm an awful swank, trying to be important, and pretending that people have more arms than they really have.'

Pippi marched on with the false arm slung jauntily across her shoulder. She stopped at a sweet shop. A group of children was outside, gazing at all the wonderful things displayed in the window: large jars full of red and blue and green sweets, long rows of chocolate bars, piles and piles of chewing gum, and the most tempting toffee lollipops. No wonder the little children gazed and now and then heaved a heavy sigh, because they had no money, not even one little penny.

'Pippi, shall we go in?' said Tommy, eagerly tugging at Pippi's dress.

'We're *going* into this shop,' said Pippi. '*Far* into it!'

And they entered.

'Please may I have thirty-six pounds of sweets,' said Pippi, waving a gold coin in the air. The assistant only gaped. She was not used to anyone buying so many sweets at one time.

'You mean you want thirty-six sweets,' she said.

'I mean that I want thirty-six *pounds* of sweets,' said Pippi. She put the gold coin on the counter. The assistant hurriedly began pouring sweets into large bags. Tommy and Annika pointed to the sweets they thought the best. There were some red ones which were delicious; when you had sucked them for a while a lovely soft mixture oozed out. There were some green acid drops that were not bad either. The jelly babies and liquorice allsorts were jolly good, too.

'Let's have six pounds of each,' suggested Annika. And they did.

'Then if you give me sixty lollipops and seventy-two small packets of toffee, I don't think I need to take more than one hundred and three chocolate cigarettes for today,' said Pippi, 'except perhaps a small cart to carry them in.'

The assistant said she thought a cart could be bought at the toy shop close by.

By this time a lot of children had gathered outside the sweet shop. They were all staring through the window and gasped when they saw Pippi's way of doing her shopping. Pippi hurried into the toy shop, bought a cart, and loaded it with all the bags of sweets. She looked round and called out:

'Is there a child here who does *not* eat sweets? If so, will he or she please step forward.'

No one stepped forward.

'Strange!' said Pippi. 'Does there happen to be a child who *does* eat sweets, then?'

Twenty-three came forward, Tommy and Annika with them, of course.

'Tommy, open the bags!' said Pippi.

Tommy did so. A sweet-eating began, the like of which had never been seen in the little town. All the children filled their mouths with sweets, the red ones with the luscious juice inside, and the green acid ones, and the liquorice allsorts, and the jelly babies—all higgledy-piggledy. You could also have a chocolate cigarette in the corner of your mouth, because the taste of chocolate and jelly mixed was very nice. More children came running from every direction, and Pippi shared out handfuls all round.

'I think I shall have to buy another thirty-six pounds,' she said, 'otherwise there won't be anything for tomorrow.'

Pippi bought another thirty-six pounds, but

there was not much left for tomorrow in spite of it.

'Now we'll go to the next shop,' said Pippi and stalked into the toy shop. All the children followed. There were lots of nice things in the toy shop: trains and cars that could be wound up, pretty little dolls in beautiful dresses, dolls' china, and toy pistols, and tin soldiers, and soft toy dogs and elephants, and bookmarks, and jumping-jacks . . .

'Can I help you?' said the assistant.

'I'd like some of everything,' said Pippi, examining the shelves. 'We need, for instance, jumping-jacks and toy pistols,' she continued, 'but that can easily be put right, I expect.'

As she spoke Pippi pulled out a whole handful of gold coins, and then the children had to point out what they thought they needed most. Annika decided on a doll with fair, curly hair and a pink silk dress which could say 'mama' when you pressed its tummy. Tommy wanted a toy gun and a steam engine—and got them. All the other children pointed at what they wanted, and when Pippi had finished buying there was not much left in the shop, except for a few bookmarks and some building blocks. Pippi did not buy a single thing for herself, but Mr Nelson got a mirror.

Just before they left, Pippi bought each child a

toy ocarina, and when they were all out in the street again they played their ocarinas while Pippi beat time with the false arm. One little boy complained that his instrument would not work. Pippi took a look at it.

'No wonder, when there's chewing gum in it! Where did you pick up this treasure?' she asked, throwing away the large white ball. 'I don't remember buying any chewing gum.'

'I've had it since last Friday,' said the boy.

'Aren't you afraid your lips will grow together? That's what I thought usually happened to chewing gum chewers.'

She gave the boy back his ocarina, and he blew it merrily with the rest. There was such a noise in the High Street that at last a policeman came to see what was going on.

'What's all this?' he shouted.

'It's the Regimental March of the Grenadiers,' said Pippi, 'but I'm not sure all the children realize it. Some of them seem to think we're playing "Out roared the Dreadful Thunder".'

'Stop it!' yelled the policeman, covering his ears with his hands. Pippi patted him soothingly on the back with the false arm.

'You can thank your lucky stars we didn't buy trumpets,' she said.

One by one the ocarinas stopped playing.

Finally it was only Tommy's that gave a little squeak now and then. The policeman told them sternly that crowds were not allowed to collect in the High Street, and that the children must go home at once. The children did not mind. They were anxious to try out their toy trains and drive their motor-cars and make up the beds for their new dolls, so they all went home, happy and contented. They could not be bothered with supper that day.

It was time for Pippi and Tommy and Annika to go home, too. Pippi pulled the truck. She noticed all the shop signs as she passed them, and tried to spell as well as she could.

'*A pu-the-ca-ry*. Goodness! Isn't that where you buy meducin?' she asked.

'Yes, that's where you buy *medicine*,' said Annika.

'Ooh, then I must go in straight away and buy some,' said Pippi.

'But you're not ill,' said Tommy.

'I may not be ill now,' said Pippi, 'but I'm not taking any chances. Every year masses of people are taken ill and die, all because they didn't buy meducin in time: you bet I'm not going to be caught out that way.'

The apothecary was rolling pills, but he intended to roll only a few more because it was late, and near closing time. Then Pippi and Tommy and Annika walked up to the counter.

'Please can I have six pints of meducin?' said Pippi.

'What kind?' asked the apothecary impatiently.

'Well,' said Pippi, 'one that's good for illness.'

'What kind of illness?' asked the apothecary, still more impatiently.

'I think I'd like one that's good for whooping cough and blisters on the feet and tummy-ache and German measles and a pea that's got stuck in the nose, and all that kind of thing. It wouldn't be a bad idea if it could be used for polishing furniture as well. A real meducin, that's what I want.'

The apothecary said that no medicine was quite like that. There were different kinds of medicine for different illnesses, he explained, and when Pippi had mentioned about ten other complaints which she also wanted cured, he put a row of bottles on the counter. On some of them he wrote, 'Not to be taken,' which meant that the medicine was only meant to be applied to the skin. Pippi paid, took her bottles, thanked him and walked out. Tommy and Annika followed her. The apothecary looked at the clock and saw that it was time to close the shop. He locked the door carefully after the

272

children and thought how nice it would be to go home to a meal.

Pippi put her bottles down on the doorstep.

'Oh, dear me,' she said. 'I nearly forgot the most important thing.'

As the door was now shut, she put her finger on the bell and rang long and hard. Tommy and Annika heard the shrill sound inside the shop. Presently a small window in the door was opened; this was the window through which you could buy medicine for people who fell ill at night. The apothecary popped his head out. His face was rather red.

'What do you want now?' he asked Pippi in a gruff voice.

'Please, Mr Aputhecary,' said Pippi, 'I've just thought of something. You know all about illness: what's really best for a tummy-ache? To eat black pudding or to put the whole tummy to soak in cold water?'

The apothecary's face became redder still.

'Be off with you, this very instant,' he shouted, 'or else . . . !'

He shut the window with a bang.

'Goodness, he's bad-tempered,' said Pippi. 'You'd almost think I'd annoyed him.'

She rang the bell again, and it was not many seconds before the apothecary's head appeared once more in the window. His face was as red as a beetroot.

'Black pudding is perhaps a little indigestible?' suggested Pippi, looking up at him with friendly eyes.

The apothecary made no reply, but simply slammed the window shut.

'Very well, then,' said Pippi, shrugging her shoulders, 'I'll just have to try black pudding, that's all. He'll only have himself to blame if it does me harm.'

She calmly sat down on the steps outside the shop and arranged all her bottles in a row.

'My goodness, how unpractical grown-ups can be!' she said. 'There are—let's see—eight bottles, and one bottle would easily hold the lot. Lucky I've got some commonsense myself,' and she uncorked the bottles and emptied all the medicine into one of them. She shook it vigorously, and raising it to her mouth, she drank a large dose. Annika, knowing that some of the medicine was meant for putting on the skin, was rather worried.

'Oh, Pippi,' she said, 'how do you know that the medicine isn't poisonous?'

'I shall find out,' said Pippi gaily. 'I shall find out tomorrow at the latest. If I'm still alive then, it's not poisonous, and the smallest child can drink it.'

Tommy and Annika considered this. After a while Tommy said doubtfully, and rather dolefully:

'Yes, but supposing it is poisonous, after all, what then?'

'Then you'll have to use what's left over for polishing the dining-room furniture,' said Pippi, 'and poisonous or not, the meducin won't be wasted.'

She took the bottle and placed it on the cart. It already contained the false arm, and Tommy's steam engine and toy gun, and Annika's doll, and a bag with five small sweets which was all that was left of the two thirty-six pounds. Mr Nelson was sitting in it, too. He was tired, and wanted to go home.

'Besides, I can tell you, I think it's a jolly good meducin. I feel better already. I feel terrifically well, and fit for anything,' said Pippi, marching along jauntily. Off she went, with the cart, back to Villekulla Cottage. Tommy and Annika walked beside her feeling just a little queer in the tummy.

3
Pippi writes a Letter and goes to School

'Today,' said Tommy, 'Annika and I have written to our granny.'

'Have you?' said Pippi, while stirring the contents of a saucepan with an umbrella handle. 'I'm going to have a lovely dinner,' she said, sniffing the mixture. '"Boil for an hour, stirring vigorously, serve immediately without ginger."—What was that you said? You've written to your granny, have you?'

'Yes,' said Tommy from his place on Pippi's

wood-box, where he sat with his legs dangling. 'We're sure to have an answer soon.'

'I never have any letters,' said Pippi ruefully.

'But you don't write any,' said Annika. 'If you don't write, of course you don't get any letters. And that's because you don't want to go to school. You can't learn to write if you don't go to school.'

'I *can* write,' said Pippi. 'I know a whole lot of letters. Fridolf, who was mate in my father's ship, taught me heaps, and when you're short of letters, you can always make it up with numbers. Of course I can write! But I don't know what to write about. What sort of thing do they usually put in letters?'

'Well,' said Tommy, 'first I ask Granny how she is, and then I tell her that I'm well. Then I talk a little about the weather and things like that. Today I also said that I had killed a large rat in our cellar.'

Pippi stirred and thought.

'It's hard luck on me not having any post. Everyone else has letters. This can't go on. Even if I haven't a granny to write to me, I can jolly well write to myself. I'm going to do it straight away.'

She opened the oven door and looked in.

'There should be a pen in here if I'm not mistaken.'

There was a pen in there. Pippi got it out. Then she tore up a large white paper bag and sat down at the kitchen table. She frowned deeply and looked very thoughtful.

'Don't disturb me, I'm thinking,' she said.

Tommy and Annika decided to play with Mr Nelson. They took it in turns to put on and take off his small suit. Annika also tried to tuck him up in the green doll's bed which was his. She wanted to play nurse. Tommy was to be the doctor, and Mr Nelson the sick child, but he *would* wriggle out of the bed and jump up and hang from the lamp. Pippi glanced up from her writing.

'Silly Mr Nelson,' she said. 'Sick children mustn't hang by their tail from the lamp. At least not in this country. I've heard, though, that it does happen in South Africa. They hang up the children from the lamp as soon as they have the slightest temperature, and there they have to stay until they're well again. But we're not in South Africa now!'

Finally Tommy and Annika left Mr Nelson and began to groom the horse. The horse was very pleased when they came out in the porch to him. He sniffed their hands to see if they had brought any sugar. They hadn't got any, but Annika went inside immediately and fetched a couple of lumps.

Pippi kept writing and writing. At last the letter was ready. She had no envelope, but Tommy ran home for one. He gave her a stamp as well. Pippi wrote her name and address carefully on the outside: 'Miss Pippilotta Longstocking, Villekulla Cottage.'

'What does it say in the letter?' asked Annika.

'How should I know?' said Pippi. 'I haven't had it yet.'

Just then the postman passed Villekulla Cottage.

'I'm in luck,' said Pippi. 'Fancy finding a postman just when I was wanting one.'

She ran out into the road.

'Please take this letter to Pippi Longstocking at once,' she said. 'It's urgent!'

The postman looked first at the letter, and then at Pippi.

'Aren't you Pippi Longstocking?' he said.

' 'Course, who did you think I was? The Empress of Abyssinia?'

'Why don't you take the letter, then?' said the postman.

'Why don't I take the letter? Should I take it myself? That's some cheek! So people should deliver their own letters nowadays, should they? And what are postmen for, I wonder? They might as well all be done away with. I never heard anything so foolish! No, my boy, if that's how you do your job, you'll never be a postmaster, mark my words!'

The postman thought he had better do what she asked. He went up and put the letter in Villekulla Cottage's letterbox. No sooner had it dropped into the box than Pippi fetched it out in great excitement.

'Ooh,' she exclaimed to Tommy and Annika, 'I can't wait to see what's in it! It's the first letter I've ever had!'

All three children sat down on the porch steps while Pippi tore open the envelope. Tommy and Annika read over her shoulder. This is what it said:

DEER PIPPI U R NOT ILL I HOP IT WOOD B 2 SAD IF U WARE ILL I AM WELL NUFFING RONG WITH THE WETHER HEAR YESTERDAY TOMY KILLD A LARG RAT

LUV FROM PIPPI

'Oh,' said Pippi, delighted, 'my letter is just like the one you wrote to your granny yesterday, Tommy. That shows it's a proper letter. I shall keep it all my life.'

She put the letter back in the envelope and stowed it away in one of the small drawers of the big cupboard which she had in the parlour. There was hardly anything that Tommy and Annika enjoyed so much as looking at all the lovely things in Pippi's cupboard. Very often Pippi gave them a little present, but there was no end to the things in the drawers.

'But, Pippi,' said Tommy, when she had put the letter away, 'there were rather a lot of spelling mistakes in it.'

'Yes, you really *should* go to school and learn to write a bit better,' said Annika.

'Thank *you*,' said Pippi. 'I did it once, for a whole day, and I got so much learning into my head that it's still swimming about in it.'

'We're having an outing any day now,' said Annika, '—the whole class.'

'Gosh,' said Pippi, chewing one of her plaits. 'Gosh! And I can't go, I s'pose, 'cos I don't go to school. People seem to think they can treat you anyhow just because you don't go to school and learn pluttification.'

'Multiplication,' said Annika firmly.

'That's what I said—pluttification.'

'We're going to walk six miles, far into the forest, and there we're going to play games,' said Tommy.

'Gosh,' repeated Pippi once more.

The following day was so warm and sunny that the children at school in the little town found it difficult to sit still at their desks. The teacher opened all the windows and let the sunshine stream in. There was a birch tree just outside the school and at the top of it sat a small starling, chirruping so merrily that Tommy and Annika and the others in the form could not help listening to him, and did not care at all about nine times nine making eighty-one.

Tommy suddenly jumped high in surprise.

'Look, ma'am,' he shouted, pointing through the window, 'there's Pippi!'

The eyes of every child were turned in the same direction. Yes! There was Pippi, sitting on a branch of the birch tree. She was quite close to the window, because the branch nearly touched the window edge.

'Hello, ma'am,' she shouted. 'Hello, everybody!'

'Good morning, Pippi,' said the teacher. Pippi had once come to school for a whole day, so the teacher knew her quite well. Pippi and the teacher had agreed that perhaps Pippi would come back one day when she was a little older and more sensible.

'What do you want, Pippi dear?' said the teacher.

'Well, I thought I'd ask you to throw me a little pluttification through the window,' said Pippi, 'just enough so that I can come on the outing. If you've thought out any new letters, would you throw them as well at the same time?'

'Wouldn't you like to come in?' asked the teacher.

'I'd rather not,' said Pippi honestly, as she leant back comfortably on the branch. 'It only makes me dizzy. It's so thick with learning in there that you can cut it with a knife. But don't you think,' she went on hopefully, 'that a little learning flies out through the window and settles on me—just enough for me to come on the outing?'

'Maybe,' said the teacher, and continued the arithmetic lesson. All the children thought it was nice to have Pippi sitting in the tree outside. She had given all of them sweets and toys on the day when she visited the shops. Pippi had Mr Nelson with her, of course, and the children were very amused to see the way he threw himself from one branch to another. Sometimes he jumped down to the window, too, and once took a great leap right on to Tommy's head, and started to scratch his hair. Then the teacher told Pippi that she must call Mr Nelson, because Tommy had to divide three hundred and fifteen by seven, and it could not be done with a monkey in one's hair. It seemed impossible to keep on with the lesson. The spring sunshine, and the starling, and Pippi, and Mr Nelson—it was all too much for the children.

'I do believe you are quite out of your senses, children,' said the teacher.

'Yes,' said Pippi from the tree, 'honestly, this doesn't seem quite the right kind of day for pluttification.'

'We are doing division,' said the teacher.

'On this sort of day there shouldn't be any kind of "tion" at all,' said Pippi, 'at least, not anything except jollification.'

The teacher gave up the struggle.

'Perhaps you can supply the jollification, then,' she said.

'Oh, I'm not specially good at jollification,' said Pippi, hanging upside down from the branch by her knees, so that her red plaits almost trailed on the ground, 'but I know of a school where they have nothing else except jollification. "All day Jollification" it says on the time-table.'

'Really,' said the teacher. 'And where is that school?'

'In Australia,' said Pippi, 'in a village in Australia—in the south.'

She pulled herself upright on the branch, and her eyes began to shine.

'What do they do when they have jollification?' asked the teacher.

'Oh, all sorts of things,' said Pippi. 'They usually start by jumping through the window one after the other. Then they give a terrific roar and rush into the classroom again and hop around on the desks until they're tired.'

'And what does the schoolmistress say to that?' asked the teacher.

'Oh her,' said Pippi. 'She hops, too, with the best of them. Then the children fight for half an hour or so. The teacher cheers them on. If it's raining, all the children take their clothes off and run outside and dance and jump in the rain. The teacher plays a march on the organ to help them keep the time. Some of them stand under the gutter pipe to get a good shower.'

'I see,' said the teacher.

'Yes-s,' said Pippi, 'and it's a frightfully good school, one of the best in Australia—but it's very far south.'

'I can imagine that,' said the teacher. 'I don't think we are going to have quite such a jolly time in this school, though.'

'Pity,' said Pippi. 'If it had only been a matter of hopping on the desks, I might have ventured in for a while.'

'You will have to put off the hopping until we have our outing,' said the teacher.

'Then I *really* can come?' shouted Pippi joyously

so that she turned a back somersault and fell from the tree. 'I shall write and tell them that in Australia, and they can keep their old jollification as far as I'm concerned, because an outing is miles better.'

4

Pippi goes on a School Outing

There was a sound of the tramping of many feet on the road, and lots of chattering and laughter. Tommy with a rucksack on his back, and Annika in a brand new cotton dress, and the teacher, and all the other boys and girls in the class were there except one poor child who had developed a sore throat on the very day of the outing. In front of them all rode Pippi on her horse. Behind her sat Mr Nelson with his pocket mirror in his hand. He

287

caught the sunlight in it, and looked full of glee when he succeeded in dazzling Tommy with the reflection.

Annika had been quite sure it would rain on this day. She had been so sure of it that she nearly felt angry beforehand. But no, they were lucky; the sun kept shining from sheer force of habit, although it was the day of the outing, and Annika's heart leapt for joy as she walked along the road in her brand new cotton dress. All the children, for that matter, looked very happy and eager. Along the roadside there were baby willows, and once they passed a whole field full of cowslips. They all decided they would pick a bunch of willow and a big posy of cowslips on the way home.

'Isn't it a lovely, lovely day?' sighed Annika, looking up at Pippi who sat straight as a general on her horse.

'Yes, isn't it? I haven't had such fun since I fought a boxer in San Francisco,' said Pippi. 'Would you like a little ride?'

Annika said she would love it, and Pippi lifted her up and put her in front of herself on the horse, but when the other children saw this, they wanted rides, too, of course. So one after the other they had a ride, but Annika and Tommy had just a *little* longer than the rest. One girl had a sore foot, and Pippi let her sit behind her all the time, but Mr Nelson kept pulling her plait.

They were on their way to a forest which is called Monster Forest, because it is monstrously beautiful. When they were nearly there, Pippi jumped from the saddle, patted her horse, and said:

'Now you've carried us a long way, you must be tired. It isn't fair that one should do all the work.'

She lifted the horse in her strong arms and carried him all the way to a little glade in the forest where the teacher had called a halt. Pippi looked all round and shouted:

'Come on, you monsters, all of you! We'll see who's the strongest!'

The teacher explained that there were no monsters in the forest. Pippi was very disappointed.

'A Monster Forest without monsters! What will they think of next! Soon, I s'pose there'll be fires without fire, and Christmas parties without Christmas trees. It's jolly mean! The day they start having sweet shops without sweets I'll give them a piece of my mind. Well, there's nothing for it but to be a monster myself.'

She uttered such a terrifying roar that the teacher had to cover her ears, and several of the children were frightened out of their wits.

'Yes, let's pretend Pippi's a monster!' shouted Tommy in delight, clapping his hands. The children all thought this an excellent idea. The monster settled in a deep crevice in a rock which was to be its den. The children ran around outside, teasing it with shouts of:

'Silly, silly monster! Silly, silly monster!'

At this the monster rushed out uttering fierce howls, and chased the children who scattered in all directions to hide. Those who were caught were dragged into the hollow, and the monster said they were going to be cooked for dinner: but sometimes they managed to escape when the monster was out chasing other children. This meant climbing up the steep rock which formed the wall of the crevice, and that was quite difficult; there was only a small pine tree to hang on to, and it was a problem to know where to find a foothold. It was very exciting all the same, and the children thought it was the best game they had ever played. The teacher lay on the grass reading a book and glanced at the children every now and then.

'That's the wildest monster I ever saw,' she murmured to herself.

It was. The monster jumped, and howled, and threw three or four boys over its shoulder at a time, and dragged them back to the hollow.

Sometimes it climbed the highest tree at a terrific speed and leapt from branch to branch just like a monkey: sometimes it threw itself on to the horse and caught up with some of the children who were trying to escape between the trees. When the horse came galloping near them, the monster bent down and lifted them up in front and rode like lightning back to the hollow, shouting:

'I'm going to cook you for my dinner!'

The children had such a wonderful time that they did not want to stop, but suddenly there was complete silence. When Tommy and Annika came running to see what was happening, they found the monster kneeling on the ground, looking very queer. It was watching something clasped in its hand.

'He's dead! Look! He's quite dead!' said the monster.

It was a baby bird that was dead. It had fallen from its nest and been killed.

'Oh, what a shame!' said Annika. The monster nodded.

'Pippi! You're crying!' said Tommy suddenly.

'Crying? Me!' said Pippi. ' 'Course I'm not crying.'

'But your eyes are red,' persisted Tommy.

'Red?' exclaimed Pippi, and borrowed Mr Nelson's mirror to have a look. 'Is that what you call red eyes? Then you should have been with me and Daddy in Batavia! There was an old man there who had such red eyes that the police wouldn't let him show himself in the streets!'

'Why?' asked Tommy.

'Cos people thought he was a stop signal, silly! The traffic came to a standstill when he turned up. Red eyes? Me? Don't you believe I'm crying because of a stupid little bird like that!' said Pippi.

'Silly, silly monster! Silly, silly monster!'

The children came running from all over the place to see what the monster was up to. They found it putting the stupid little bird very gently on a bed of soft moss.

'If I could, I would make you alive again,' said Pippi with a deep sigh. There followed a colossal roar.

'Now I'm going to cook you for dinner,' she shouted, and with shrieks of joy the children disappeared among the bushes.

There was a girl in the class whose name was Ulla. She lived close to Monster Forest. Ulla's mother had promised that she could invite the teacher and everyone in her class (and Pippi, too, of course) home for refreshments in the garden. So, when the children had played the monster game for a long time, and had climbed the rock, and sailed bark boats on a big puddle, and seen who were brave enough to jump from a high stone, Ulla said she thought it was time they went to her house and had some orange squash. The teacher, who had read her book from cover to cover, thought so, too. She gathered the children together, and they left Monster Forest.

On the road they came upon a man with a cart loaded with sacks. The sacks were heavy, and there were many of them. The horse was old and tired. Suddenly one of the wheels ran into the ditch. The man, whose name happened to be Flowergrove, got terribly angry. He blamed the horse, and got out his whip. The next moment he was beating the horse violently. The horse tugged and pulled, trying with all its might to bring the load on to the road again, but he could not do it. Flowergrove got angrier and angrier and whipped harder and harder. Just then the teacher caught sight of him and was very distressed to see the poor horse being beaten.

'How *can* you treat an animal like that?' she said to Flowergrove. Flowergrove stopped for a second and spat before he answered:

'It's none of your business,' he said. 'If you don't shut up, I might give you a taste of the whip, too, the whole lot of you.'

He spat again and raised the whip. The poor

horse trembled all over. Then a streak of lightning seemed to tear through the flock of children. It was Pippi. She was white about the nose. And when Pippi was white about the nose, she was angry—Tommy and Annika knew that. She made a dash straight for Flowergrove, caught hold of him round the waist, and threw him high in the air. When he fell, she caught him, and threw him up again: four times, five times, six times he flew through the air. Flowergrove could not think what was happening to him.

'Help! Help!' he shouted in terror. In the end he landed with a bump in the road. He had dropped his whip. Pippi stood beside him with her hands on her hips.

'You're not going to beat that horse any more,' she said firmly. 'You're not going to, d'you hear? Once down in Cape Town I met another man who beat his horse. He had such a very smart and grand uniform, and I told him that if he whipped his horse any more, I would beat him so hard there wouldn't be a single thread left of his grand uniform. Fancy! A week afterwards he whipped his horse again! Pity about that grand uniform, wasn't it?'

Flowergrove remained sitting in the road, completely stunned.

'Where are you going with the load?' asked Pippi.

It was a frightened Flowergrove who pointed to a cottage a little way along the road.

'Over there,' he said.

Pippi unharnessed the horse, which was still trembling from exhaustion and fear.

'There you are, horsie,' she said. 'Now we'll see what we can do for you!'

She lifted him up in her strong arms and carried him home to his stable. The horse looked just as surprised as Flowergrove.

The children and the teacher were waiting in the road for Pippi. Flowergrove was standing by his load, scratching his head, wondering how he would get it home. Then Pippi came back. She picked up one of the big, heavy sacks and put it on Flowergrove's back.

'That's right,' she said, 'now we shall see if you're as clever at carrying as you are at whipping.'

Pippi took the whip.

'Really I ought to thrash you a bit with this as you seem so fond of thrashing, but the whip is just about finished,' she said, breaking off a piece, 'in fact, quite finished, worse luck,' she said, breaking the whip into small pieces.

Flowergrove staggered away with the sack

without saying another word: he just groaned a bit. Pippi took hold of the shafts of the cart and pulled it home for Flowergrove.

'That's all right. That won't cost you anything,' she said when she had put the cart outside Flowergrove's stable. 'It's a pleasure, and the flight won't cost you anything, either.'

Off she went. Flowergrove stood staring after her for a long time.

'Long live Pippi!' cried the children when Pippi returned. The teacher was very pleased with Pippi, too, and praised her.

'You did right,' she said. 'We should be kind to animals—and to humans too, of course.'

Pippi sat on her horse, looking pleased.

'Well, you can't say I wasn't kind to Flowergrove,' she said, 'all that air travel free!'

'That's why we are *here*,' continued the teacher, 'to show kindness to others.'

Pippi stood on her head on the horse's back, waggling her legs.

'Ha-ha,' she said, 'and why did the others come here then?'

In Ulla's garden there was a big table, laden with so many buns and cakes that the children's mouths watered. They quickly sat down round the table. Pippi was at one end. She immediately stuffed two buns into her mouth. It made her look like one of those cherubs with bulging cheeks.

'Pippi,' said the teacher reproachfully, 'you must wait till you are asked.'

'Don't pother about me,' Pippi managed to splutter through the buns. 'I'm not fusshy about mannersh.'

Then Ulla's mother came up to her, holding in one hand a jug of orange juice, and in the other a jug of chocolate.

'Will you have orange or chocolate?' she asked.

'Orange *and* shocolate,' said Pippi. 'Orange on one bun and shocolate on the other.'

Without further ado she seized the two jugs from Ulla's mother and took a long drink from each of them.

'She's been away at sea all her life,' whispered the teacher by way of explanation to Ulla's mother, who looked rather surprised.

'I quite understand,' nodded Ulla's mother, and decided not to take any notice of Pippi's bad manners.

'Ginger nuts?' she asked, offering a plate of them to Pippi.

'Oh? I hope they taste better than they look!' said Pippi, grabbing a handful. Then she caught sight of some delicious looking pink cakes further down the table. She gave Mr Nelson's tail a little tug, and said:

'Look here, Mr Nelson, get me one of those pink things over there. You might as well take two or three while you're about it.'

Mr Nelson scampered along the table, spilling the orange juice from the glasses.

When the party was over and Pippi went up to thank Ulla's mother, she said, 'I hope you've had enough to eat, dear.'

'No, I haven't, and I'm still thirsty,' said Pippi, scratching her ear.

'Yes, I'm afraid it wasn't much of a party,' said Ulla's mother.

'Could have been better,' replied Pippi amiably.

The teacher made up her mind to have a little talk with Pippi about how to behave.

'Look here, Pippi, my dear,' she said kindly. 'I'm sure you want to be a real lady when you are grown-up.'

'Oh, you mean one of those people with a veil over the nose and three chins underneath,' said Pippi.

'I mean a woman who knows how to behave, and who is always polite and considerate. A real lady—isn't that what you want to be?'

'I'll think it over,' said Pippi, 'because, you see,

I'd nearly made up my mind to be a pirate when I'm grown-up.'

She stood deep in thought for a while.

'Don't you think I could be a pirate and a Real Lady at the same time? Because then . . . '

The teacher did not think that this was possible.

'Dear, dear, which shall I choose?' said Pippi unhappily.

The teacher said that whatever career Pippi chose to follow, it would not hurt her to learn a few manners. Pippi must never behave at the table as she had done that afternoon.

'To think that it should be so difficult to know how to behave,' sighed Pippi. 'Couldn't you tell me the 'portantest rules?'

The teacher did her best, and Pippi listened with interest. You must not help yourself before being asked, you must not take more than one cake at a time, you must not eat with your knife, you must not scratch yourself while talking to other people, you must not do this, and you must not do that. Pippi nodded thoughtfully.

'I'll get up an hour earlier every morning to practise so that I shall get the hang of it in case I decide not to be a pirate,' she said.

Now the teacher told the children it was time to leave and march home. They all lined up. Only

Pippi remained on the lawn. She had her head cocked on one side as if she was listening for something.

'What's the matter, Pippi dear?' asked the teacher.

'Please, ma'am,' said Pippi, 'may a Real Lady's tummy gurgle?'

She was silent again listening.

'Cos if not,' she said at last, 'I might as well make up my mind straight away to be a pirate.'

5

Pippi goes to the Fair

I t was the day of the fair in the little town. Once a year they had a fair, and on each occasion the children in the little town were wild with joy that anything so exciting could happen. The town did not look its usual self at all on this day. There were crowds jostling everywhere, flags were hoisted, and the market-place was full of stalls where you could buy the most wonderful things. There was such a noise, and such a commotion that it was quite a thrill just to walk about in the streets. Best of all, down by the toll gate there was a big fairground with a merry-go-round, and rifle ranges, and a theatre, and all sorts of amusements. A menagerie, too: a menagerie with every kind of wild animal imaginable—tigers, and giant snakes, and monkeys, and sea lions. If you stood outside the menagerie, you could hear queerer growls and roars than you had ever heard in all your life. If you had any money, you could, of course, go in and see it all, too.

It was no wonder that Annika's hair ribbon seemed to quiver with excitement when she was dressed and ready in the morning of that day, or that Tommy nearly swallowed his breakfast whole in his haste. Tommy and Annika's mother asked her children if they would like to go to the fair with her. Tommy and Annika looked a little uncomfortable and said that if their mother did not mind, they would really rather go with Pippi.

'Because, you see,' explained Tommy to Annika as they shot through Villekulla Cottage's garden gate, 'it's sure to be much more fun with Pippi.'

Annika agreed.

Pippi was dressed, and waiting for them in the centre of the kitchen. She had at last found her big cartwheel hat—in the wood-shed.

'I quite forgot that I'd used it for carrying

wood the other day,' she said, pulling the hat down over her eyes. 'Don't I look grand?'

Tommy and Annika had to admit that she did. Pippi had blackened her eyebrows with coal and painted her mouth and nails with red paint. She had put on a very grand, long evening dress, which was cut so low at the back that her red bodice was showing. Her big black shoes could be seen below the hem, and they looked smarter than usual, because she had tied the green bows on to them which she only used on special occasions.

'I thought I ought to look a Real Lady when I'm going to the fair,' she said, tripping along as daintily as anyone can in such large shoes. She held up the hem of her skirt, and said at regular intervals in a voice which was quite different from her usual one:

'Delaightful! Delaightful!'

'What's delightful?' asked Tommy.

'Me,' said Pippi in a satisfied tone of voice.

Tommy and Annika thought *everything* delightful on the day of the fair. It was delightful to mix with the crowds in the streets, and to go from one stall to another in the market and look at all the things which were spread out. To celebrate, Pippi bought a red silk scarf for Annika, and Tommy received a peaked cap of a kind that he had always longed for but which his mother did not want him to have. At another stall Pippi bought two glass clocks. They were full of pink and white hundreds and thousands.

'You *are* kind, Pippi,' said Annika, hugging her clock.

'Oh, yes, delaightful,' said Pippi. 'Delaightful,' she said, holding up her skirt with an air of great elegance.

A long stream of people was pouring down towards the toll gate. Pippi, Tommy, and Annika followed.

'What a lovely noise!' said Tommy joyfully. The barrel organs were playing, and the merry-go-round was spinning round: people shouted and laughed. Arrow shooting and china breaking were in full swing. At the rifle ranges people jostled to show their skill at shooting.

'I'd like to have a closer look at that,' said Pippi, tugging Tommy and Annika with her to a rifle range. Just then there was no one at that particular rifle range, and the woman who was in charge of handing out rifles and taking the money was rather cross, and three children were not what she would choose for customers. She took no notice of them at all. Pippi looked at the targets with interest. They consisted of three paper figures painted blue, and each had a face as round as a ball. In the middle of the face was a very red nose. The nose was the bull's eye. If you could not manage to hit the nose, you should at least try to get somewhere near it. Shots that did not hit the face were not counted.

By and by the woman became annoyed at seeing the children standing there. She wanted customers who could shoot and pay.

'So you're still hanging around,' she said crossly.

'No,' said Pippi seriously, 'we're sitting in the market-place, cracking nuts.'

'What're you staring at?' said the woman still more crossly. 'Are you waiting for someone to come and shoot?'

'No,' said Pippi, 'we're waiting for you to start turning somersaults.'

However, at that moment a customer came along. He was an impressive-looking man with a gold chain across his waistcoat. He took hold of a rifle and weighed it in his hand.

'I might as well fire a few rounds,' he said, 'just to show how it should be done.'

He looked round to see if he had an audience, but there was no one near except Pippi and Tommy and Annika.

'Watch me, children,' he said, 'and I will give you a first lesson in the art of shooting. This is how it should be done!'

He lifted the rifle to his cheek and fired the first shot: it missed! The second shot also. The third and the fourth missed, too! The fifth hit one figure on the lower part of its chin.

'Rotten rifle,' said the impressive-looking man, and threw down the weapon. Pippi picked it up and loaded it.

'You are clever,' she said. 'Another time I shall do *exactly* as you've taught us, not like this!'

Bang, bang, bang, bang, bang! Five shots had hit a paper figure bang in the middle of its nose. Pippi handed a gold coin to the woman and walked away.

The merry-go-round was so splendid that Tommy and Annika caught their breath with delight when they saw it. There were black and white and brown wooden horses. They had real manes and looked almost alive. They had saddles and reins, too. You could choose whichever horse you wanted. Pippi spent a whole gold coin on tickets. She got so many that there was hardly enough room for them in her big purse.

'If I'd given them another gold coin, they'd probably have given me the whole roundabout thing,' she said to Tommy and Annika who were waiting for her.

Tommy chose a black horse and Annika a white one. Pippi sat Mr Nelson on one of the black horses that looked very wild. Mr Nelson immediately started to inspect its mane to see if it had fleas.

'Is Mr Nelson going on the merry-go-round too?' asked Annika in surprise.

''Course!' said Pippi. 'If I'd thought of it I would have brought my horse, too. He could have done with a bit of fun, and a horse riding on a horse—that would have been something very special in the horse line.'

As for herself, Pippi leapt into the saddle of a brown horse, and a moment later the merry-go-round started off to the music of a barrel organ playing the tune: 'Do you remember childhood's happy days with its fun and laughter?'

Tommy and Annika both thought it was wonderful to go on a merry-go-round. Pippi looked pleased too. She stood on her head on the horse, with her legs right up in the air. Her long evening dress fell down round her neck. All that the people standing round could see was a red bodice, a pair of green knickers, Pippi's long thin legs with one brown and one black stocking, and her big black shoes which waved playfully backwards and forwards.

'That's how it's done when a Real Lady goes on a merry-go-round,' said Pippi when the first turn was over.

The children stayed a whole hour on the merry-go-round, but in the end Pippi felt quite cross-eyed and said that she saw three merry-go-rounds instead of one.

'Then it's difficult to know which to choose,' she said, 'so I think we might as well go somewhere else.'

She had heaps of tickets left, and those she gave to some little children who were standing near, and had not had a ride, because they had no money for tickets.

Outside a tent nearby a man stood shouting:

'Another performance starting in five minutes! You must not miss this unique drama! *The Murder of the Countess Aurora*, or *Who is Creeping in the Bushes?*'

'If anyone's creeping in the bushes, we must find out who it is straight away,' said Pippi to Tommy and Annika. 'Let's go in!'

Pippi went up to the box-office.

'Can I go in half price if I promise to look with one eye only?' she enquired, with a sudden attack of economy.

The ticket lady would not hear of it.

'I don't see any bushes, and no one creeping in them, either,' said Pippi crossly when she and Tommy and Annika had placed themselves in the front row close to the curtain.

'It hasn't started yet,' said Tommy.

At that moment the curtain went up, and they could see the Countess Aurora pacing the floor of the stage, wringing her hands and looking very worried. Pippi followed it all with keen interest.

'I think she's unhappy about something,' she said to Tommy and Annika, 'or else she's got a safety-pin sticking into her.'

The Countess Aurora *was* unhappy. She raised her eyes to the ceiling and said in a plaintive voice:

'Is there anyone so unhappy as I? My children have been taken from me, my husband has disappeared, and I myself am surrounded by scoundrels and bandits who want to kill me.'

'This is terrible to hear,' said Pippi, and her eyes went rather red.

'I wish I were dead already,' cried the Countess Aurora.

Then Pippi burst into a flood of tears.

'Please don't say that!' she sobbed. 'Things will get better, you'll see. I'm sure the children will turn up, and perhaps you can have another husband. There are so ma-any me-en in the wo-orld,' she hiccuped between sobs.

Then the theatre manager came up to Pippi— he was the man who had been standing outside the tent, shouting—and said that if she did not stop all that noise, she would have to leave the theatre immediately.

'I'll try,' said Pippi, rubbing her eyes.

It was a terribly exciting play. Tommy kept turning his cap round and round and inside out from sheer nervousness, and Annika's hands were clasped tight. Pippi's eyes were wet and did not leave the Countess Aurora for a minute. Things were going from bad to worse for the poor Countess. There she walked in the palace garden, suspecting nothing. Suddenly there was a shriek. It came from Pippi. She had caught sight of a man behind a tree, and he was looking far from friendly. The Countess Aurora seemed to have noticed the rustling, too, because she said in a frightened whisper:

'Who is creeping in the bushes?'

'I can tell you,' said Pippi eagerly, 'it's a sly, horrid man with a black moustache. Hide in the wood-shed and lock the door, for goodness' sake!'

Now the theatre manager came up to Pippi and said that she must go at once.

'And leave the Countess Aurora alone with that ruffian? You don't know me!' said Pippi.

On the stage the play continued. Suddenly the horrid man rushed out of the bushes and threw himself at the Countess Aurora.

'Your last hour has come,' he hissed between his teeth.

'We'll see about that,' said Pippi taking a leap on to the stage. She seized the bandit round the waist and threw him into the audience. She was still weeping.

'How could you?' she sobbed. 'What've you got against the Countess, I'd like to know? Think of it! She's lost her children and her husband. She's quite al-o-o-one!'

She went up to the Countess who had collapsed on a garden seat.

'You can come and live with me at Villekulla Cottage if you like,' she said soothingly.

Sobbing loudly, Pippi stumbled out of the theatre, closely followed by Tommy and Annika—and by the theatre manager. He shook his fists at her. The people in the theatre, however, clapped their hands and thought it was a splendid performance.

When they were outside Pippi blew her nose loudly and said:

'My goodness, that was a sad affair! Let's do something to cheer ourselves up!'

'The menagerie!' said Tommy. 'We haven't been to the menagerie.'

So off they went. But first they visited a sandwich stall where Pippi bought six sandwiches for each of them, and three big bottles of fizzy lemonade.

'Cos crying always makes me hungry,' said Pippi.

In the menagerie there were lots of interesting things to see: elephants, and two tigers in a cage, and several sea lions who could play ball, a whole lot of monkeys, and a hyena, and two giant snakes. Pippi immediately took Mr Nelson to the monkey cage to say 'How-do-you-do' to his relations. There sat a sad-looking old chimpanzee.

'Now, come on, Mr Nelson,' said Pippi, 'say "How-do-you-do" nicely! I should think that's your grandfather's cousin's aunt's little third cousin!'

Mr Nelson raised his straw hat as politely as he could, but the chimpanzee could not be bothered to return his greeting.

The two giant snakes were in a big box. Once an hour they were taken out of the box by the beautiful snake charmer called Mademoiselle Paula, who showed them on a platform. The children were in luck. A performance was just about to begin. Annika was very much afraid of snakes, so she took firm hold of Pippi's arm. Mademoiselle Paula lifted up one of the snakes, a big horrible ugly thing, and laid it round her neck like a fur.

'It's a boa constrictor,' whispered Pippi to

Tommy and Annika. 'I wonder what the other one is.'

She went to the box and lifted out the other snake. It was bigger, and more horrible still. Pippi laid it round her neck just as Mademoiselle Paula had done with the other. Everyone in the menagerie gave a shout of terror. Mademoiselle Paula threw her snake into the box and rushed forward to save Pippi from certain death. The noise made Pippi's snake frightened and angry. He could not understand at all why he should be hanging round the neck of a little red-haired girl instead of round Mademoiselle Paula's which he was used to. He decided to give the red-haired girl something to remember, and he coiled his body round her in a grip which would have squeezed an ox to death.

'Don't you try that old trick on me!' said Pippi. 'I've met bigger snakes than you, you know—in Indo-China.'

She loosened the snake and put him back into his box. Tommy and Annika had turned pale.

'That was a boa constrictor, too,' said Pippi, fastening one of her suspenders which had come undone. 'Just what I thought!'

Mademoiselle Paula kept on scolding Pippi in some foreign language. Everyone in the menagerie heaved a deep sigh of relief, but they sighed too soon. This was obviously a day when anything might happen. Afterwards, no one knew how it occurred. The tigers had been fed with large chunks of red meat, and later the keeper swore that he had shut the door properly, but soon someone screamed in terror.

'There's a tiger loose!'

The yellow striped brute lay curled up outside the menagerie, ready to spring. People fled in all directions, but one little girl was squeezed into a corner close to the tiger.

'Don't move!' people shouted to her. They hoped the tiger would leave her alone if she stayed still.

'What are we to do?' they said.

'Run for the police!' suggested one.

'Call the fire brigade!'

'Fetch Pippi Longstocking!' said Pippi, and stepped forward. She crouched down a few yards from the tiger, calling out to him:

'Puss, puss, puss!'

The tiger gave a dreadful growl and showed his fearful teeth. Pippi raised a warning finger.

'If you bite me, I'll bite you, and no mistake,' she said.

The tiger leapt straight at her.

'What's the matter with you? Can't you take a joke?' said Pippi, flinging him away from her.

With a growling roar, which made everyone shiver all over, the tiger threw himself again at Pippi. It was evident that he meant to break her neck this time.

'Have it your own way,' said Pippi, 'but don't forget it was you that started it!'

With one hand she pressed the tiger's jaws together, and then she carried him tenderly in her arms back to the cage while she hummed a little tune:

'I love little pussy, her coat is so warm.'

For the second time everyone heaved a sigh of relief. The little girl who had squashed herself into the corner ran to her mother crying that she never wanted to go to a menagerie again.

The tiger had torn the hem of Pippi's dress. Pippi looked at the torn bits and said:

'Has anyone got a pair of scissors?'

Mademoiselle Paula had a pair. She was not cross with Pippi any more.

'Here you are, you brave leetle girl,' she said, handing Pippi the scissors. Pippi promptly cut the dress off short, well above the knees.

'Good,' she said, 'now I look even better with my dress cut low at the top and high at the bottom. No one could possibly look twice as elegant!'

She walked in such an elegant way that her knees knocked together at each step.

'Delaightful,' she said, as she walked along.

You would expect that things would have become quieter by this time, but fair days are never really quiet, and this day was no exception.

In the town there was a ruffian who was very strong. All the children were afraid of him, and not only the children, for that matter. Everyone was frightened of him. Even the police liked to keep out of the way when Laban, the ruffian, was on the warpath. He was not angry always, but only when he had been drinking beer. He had been doing so on that market day. He rolled along the High Street, shouting and roaring, and hitting out with his dreadful arms.

'Get out of my way!' he shouted. 'Here comes Laban!'

People pressed anxiously against the walls of the houses, and many of the children wept with fright. The police were nowhere to be seen. By degrees Laban made his way to the toll gate. He was a horrible sight with long black hair hanging over his forehead, a big red nose, and a yellow tooth sticking out of his mouth. The people who were gathered down by the toll gate thought he looked more horrible than the tiger.

A little old man stood at a stall, selling sausages. Laban stalked up to him, banged his fist down on the counter, and shouted:

'Give me a sausage! And be quick about it!'

'That'll be three pence,' the man said politely.

'So you expect to be paid for it, too?' said Laban. 'You should be ashamed of yourself when you've got the chance to sell to a fine gentleman like me, you old blockhead. Hand over another sausage.'

The old man said he would rather have the money first for the sausage that Laban had already had. Laban seized the old man and shook him by the ear.

'Give me another sausage,' he ordered. 'Quick!'

The old man did not dare to disobey, but the people round could not help muttering disapprovingly. One of them was even brave enough to say:

'It's a shame treating a poor old man like that!'

Laban turned round. He looked them over with bloodshot eyes.

'Did someone open his mouth?'

The people became frightened and started to go away.

'Stay where you are!' bawled Laban. 'If anyone moves I'll beat him to a jelly. Stay where you are, I said! Because now Laban is going to show you a thing or two.'

He seized a handful of sausages and started to play ball with them. He threw the sausages in the air and caught some of them with his hands, but dropped many of them on the ground. The poor old sausage man nearly wept. At that moment a small figure came forward out of the crowd.

Pippi stopped immediately in front of Laban.

'And whose little boy might this be?' she said quietly. 'And what has his mother to say to him about flinging his breakfast around?'

Laban uttered a terrible roar.

'Didn't I tell you to stay where you are, all of you?' he shouted.

'D'you always turn on the radio full blast?' asked Pippi.

Laban raised a threatening fist, shouting, 'Brat!!! Do I have to mash you into pulp to make you quiet?'

Pippi stood with her hands on her hips, watching him with interest.

'Now, what exactly was it you did with those sausages?' she said. 'Was this it?'

Throwing Laban high up in the air, she played ball with him for a minute or two. People cheered loudly, and the old sausage man clapped his small, wrinkled hands and smiled.

When Pippi had finished, it was a very frightened Laban who sat on the ground, looking about him, dazed.

'I think it's about time he went home,' said Pippi.

Laban had no objection to this.

'But first there's a number of sausages to pay for,' said Pippi.

Laban got up and paid for eighteen sausages. Then he left without saying another word. He never behaved in quite such a bullying fashion again.

'Three cheers for Pippi!' shouted the crowd.

'Hooray for Pippi!' said Tommy and Annika.

'We don't need a policeman in this town,' said one, 'so long as we have Pippi Longstocking.'

'No, we don't!' said another. 'She takes care of tigers and ruffians.'

''Course there must be a policeman,' said Pippi. 'Someone has to see that all the bicycles are wrongly parked properly.'

'Oh, Pippi, you're wonderful,' said Annika as the children marched home from the fair.

'Oh, yes! Delaightful,' said Pippi. She held up her skirt which already ended halfway up her legs. 'Absolutely delaightful.'

6
Pippi is Shipwrecked

Every day when school was finished Tommy and Annika rushed over to Villekulla Cottage. They did not even want to do their prep. at home, but took their books over to Pippi's.

'Good,' said Pippi. 'You sit here and work, and perhaps a little learning will stick to me, too. Not that I feel I need it, exactly, but I think perhaps I can't become a Real Lady if I don't learn how many hottentots there are in Australia.'

Tommy and Annika were sitting by the kitchen

table with their geography books open. Pippi was sitting cross-legged in the middle of the table.

'But supposing,' said Pippi, putting her finger on her nose in a thoughtful manner, 'supposing, just when I've learnt how many hottentots there are, one of them goes and gets pneumonia and dies! Then it's all been for nothing, and here I am, no more of a Real Lady than before.'

She thought hard.

'Someone ought to tell the hottentots to behave, so that your books don't go wrong,' she said.

When Tommy and Annika had finished their homework the fun began. If the weather was fine, they went in the garden, rode on the horse for a little or climbed up on the roof of the shed where they sat down to drink coffee, or else they climbed the old oak which was quite hollow, so that they could get right inside the trunk. Pippi said it was a very remarkable tree, because ginger beer grew in it. It must have been true, because each time the children climbed down into their hiding-place in the oak, there were three bottles of ginger beer waiting for them. Tommy and Annika could not understand where the empties went, but Pippi said that they faded away as soon as the ginger beer was drunk. A remarkable tree, Tommy and Annika thought.

'Sometimes bars of chocolate grow in it, but

only on Thursdays,' said Pippi, so Tommy and Annika were most particular about going there every Thursday to collect bars of chocolate. Pippi said that if only the tree was watered properly now and then, she thought they could get it to grow bread rolls as well, and perhaps even a sirloin of beef.

If it was rainy weather they had to stay indoors, and that was fun, too. They could look at all the fine things in Pippi's drawers, or they could sit in front of the stove and watch Pippi making waffles and roasting apples; or they might pop down into the big box where the firewood was kept and sit there, listening to Pippi's stories of exciting adventures from the time when she sailed the ocean.

'The storm was terrible,' Pippi would say. 'Even the fishes were seasick and wanted to go ashore. I saw, with my own eyes, a shark which was green in the face, and an octopus holding its forehead with all its many arms. Shocking storm, that.'

'Oh, weren't you frightened, Pippi?' asked Annika.

'Yes, supposing you'd been shipwrecked!' said Tommy.

'Well,' said Pippi, 'I've been shipwrecked— more or less—so many times it doesn't scare me.

It takes a lot more to do that. I wasn't frightened when the raisins blew out of the Spotted Dick while we were having dinner, nor when the false teeth blew out of the cook's mouth, either. But when I saw the ship's cat losing his fur and sailing off in the air towards the Far East with nothing on, I began to feel a bit queer.'

'I've got a book all about a shipwreck,' said Tommy. 'It's called *Robinson Crusoe*.'

'Oh, yes, it's awfully good,' said Annika. 'Robinson Crusoe came to a desert island!'

'Have you really been shipwrecked, Pippi?' asked Tommy, making himself comfortable in the wood-box. 'And on a desert island?'

'I should jolly well think so,' said Pippi emphatically. 'You would have to look hard before you could find anything as shipwrecked as me. Robinson, he's miles behind. I should think there are only about eight or ten islands in the Atlantic and the Pacific where I *haven't* landed after a shipwreck. They're on a special black list in the tourist handbooks.'

'It must be fun to be on a desert island!' said Tommy. 'I'd love it!'

'That's easily arranged,' said Pippi. 'There's no shortage of islands.'

'No,' said Tommy, 'I know of one not far from here.'

323

'Is it in a lake?' asked Pippi.

'' Course,' said Tommy.

'Splendid!' said Pippi. 'Cos if it had been on dry land it wouldn't have been any good.'

Tommy was wild with excitement.

'Let's go!' he shouted. 'Straight away!'

In two days' time Tommy and Annika's summer holidays would begin. Then their mother and father were going away. They would never have a better chance to play Crusoe.

'To play shipwreck,' said Pippi, 'we must first have a boat.'

'And we haven't got one,' said Annika.

'I've seen an old broken rowing-boat at the bottom of the stream,' said Pippi.

'But it *has* been shipwrecked already,' said Annika.

'All the better,' said Pippi. 'Then it knows how to do it.'

For Pippi it was a simple matter to raise the sunken boat. She then spent all day on the bank of the stream making the boat water-tight, and the whole of a rainy morning she worked in the wood-shed making a pair of oars.

And then Tommy and Annika's summer holidays began, and their parents went away.

'We shall be back in two days' time,' said their mother. 'You must be very good and obedient, and remember to do exactly as Ella tells you.'

Ella was the maid, and she was supposed to look after Tommy and Annika while their mother and father were away. But when the children had been left alone with Ella, Tommy said:

'Ella, you needn't look after *us*, we shall be at Pippi's all the time.'

'Besides, why shouldn't we look after ourselves?' said Annika. 'Pippi *never* has anyone to look after *her*, so why shouldn't we be left in peace—for a couple of days, anyway?'

Ella had no real objection to a two days' holiday, and Tommy and Annika begged and prayed so hard that at last Ella agreed to go home and stay with her mother. But the children must promise faithfully to eat and sleep properly and not be out in the evening without a woolly on. Tommy said he would gladly wear a dozen jerseys if only Ella went.

So it was all settled. Ella went off, and two hours later Pippi, Tommy and Annika, the horse, and Mr Nelson began their journey to the uninhabited island.

It was a mild evening in early summer; the air was warm though the sky was cloudy. They had quite a long way to go before they reached the lake with the uninhabited island. Pippi carried the boat upside down on her head. She had packed an enormous sack and a tent on the horse's back.

'What's in the sack?' asked Tommy.

'Food and weapons and blankets and an empty bottle,' said Pippi. 'You see, I thought we'd have a fairly comfortable shipwreck as it's your first. Usually when I'm shipwrecked I always shoot an antelope or a llama and eat the meat raw, but there mightn't be any antelopes or llamas on this island, and it would be tiresome if we died of hunger because of such small details.'

'What are you going to do with the empty bottle?' asked Annika.

'What am I going to do with the empty bottle? What a silly question! A boat, of course, is the most important thing when you're going to be shipwrecked; but next comes an empty bottle. My father taught me that when I was in my cradle. "Pippi," he said, "it doesn't matter if you forget to wash your feet when you're going to be presented at Court, but if you forget the empty bottle when you're going to be shipwrecked you're done for."'

'Yes, but what's it for?' persisted Annika.

'Haven't you ever heard of bottle post?' said Pippi. 'You write a letter asking for help, then you put it into the bottle, push the cork in, and throw the bottle into the water, and it floats

326

straight to someone who will come and save you. How else did you think you could survive a shipwreck? Leave everything to chance? Certainly not!'

'Oh, is that what you do?' said Annika.

Soon they arrived at a little lake, and there in the middle was the uninhabited island. The sun was just coming out from behind the clouds, casting a friendly glow over the pale green of the early summer landscape.

'Well,' said Pippi, 'if that isn't one of the nicest uninhabited islands I've ever seen!'

Quickly she heaved the boat into the lake, relieved the horse of his load and stowed it all in the bottom of the boat. Annika and Tommy and Mr Nelson jumped in. Pippi patted the horse.

'Dear old horsie, much as I'd like to, I can't invite you to come in the boat. I hope you can swim. It's as simple as anything. Watch me!'

She plunged into the water with her clothes on and did a few strokes.

'It's terrific fun, you know, and if you want more fun still, you can play whales. Like this!'

Pippi filled her mouth with water, lay floating on her back, and spouted like a fountain. The horse did not look as if he thought it was particularly amusing, but when Pippi went aboard, took the oars, and rowed off, the horse threw himself into the water and swam after her. But he did not pretend he was a whale. When they had nearly reached the island, Pippi shouted:

'All hands to the pumps!'

And a second later:

'In vain! Abandon ship! Everyone who can, save himself!'

She stood on the stern and threw herself head first into the water. Soon she was up again, caught hold of the painter and swam towards land.

'The provisions must be saved anyway, so the crew might as well stay on board,' she said. She made fast the boat to a stone and helped Tommy and Annika ashore. Mr Nelson managed to get ashore by himself.

'A miracle has happened,' shouted Pippi. 'We are saved. At least for the time being. Provided there aren't any cannibals and lions here.'

The horse had by now also reached the island. He stepped out of the water and shook himself.

'Oh, look, here's our first mate, too,' said Pippi, pleased. 'Let's hold a council of war!'

From the sack she brought out her pistol which she had once found in a sailor's chest in the attic of Villekulla Cottage. With the pistol cocked she crept cautiously forward looking in every direction.

'What's the matter?' said Annika anxiously.

'I thought I heard the growl of a cannibal,' said Pippi. 'You can't be too careful. It wouldn't be much use saving yourself from drowning only to be served with two vegetables as dinner for a cannibal!'

But there were no cannibals in sight.

'They've retreated and are lying in ambush,' said Pippi. 'Or else they're probably studying the cookery book to see how to cook us. And I must say that if they serve us with carrots and white sauce I shall never forgive them. I loathe carrots.'

'Pippi, don't talk like that,' said Annika shuddering.

'Oh! So you don't like carrots either? Well, anyway we'll start putting the tent up.'

This Pippi did, and soon it was pitched in a sheltered spot, and Tommy and Annika crawled in and out and were thrilled. A little distance from the tent Pippi laid a few stones in a ring and on these she put sticks and twigs which she gathered.

'Oh, how lovely to have a fire!' said Annika.

'Yes, rather!' said Pippi. She took two pieces of wood and started to rub them together. Tommy was very interested.

'Oh, Pippi,' he said in delight, 'you're making a fire like the cannibals do!'

'No, I'm warming my fingers,' said Pippi, 'and this is just as good as beating one's arms. Let me see now, where did I put that box of matches?'

Soon the fire was burning brightly, and Tommy said he thought it was very cosy.

' 'Tis, and keeps the wild animals away, too,' said Pippi.

Annika caught her breath.

'What wild animals?' she asked in a trembling voice.

'The mosquitoes,' said Pippi, thoughtfully scratching a big mosquito bite on her leg.

Annika heaved a sigh of relief.

'And the lions, too, of course,' continued Pippi. 'But it's not supposed to be any good against pythons or bisons.'

She patted her pistol.

'But don't worry, Annika,' she said. 'With this I'll manage all right, even if a field mouse should come.'

Then Pippi brought out coffee and sandwiches, and the children sat round the fire, eating and drinking and having a lovely time. Mr Nelson sat on Pippi's shoulder. He was eating, too. Every now and then the horse put his nose forward for a piece of bread and some sugar, and he also had lots of beautiful green grass to graze on.

There were clouds in the sky, and it was

becoming dark among the bushes. Annika moved as close to Pippi as she could get. The flames from the fire threw strange shadows. The darkness beyond the little circle of light from the fire seemed somehow alive.

Supposing there was a cannibal behind that juniper bush, or a lion hiding behind the big stone!

Pippi put her coffee cup down.

'Fifteen men on the Dead Man's Chest—
Yo-ho-ho, and a bottle of rum!'

she sang in a hoarse voice.

Annika shivered still more.

'That tune is in another of my books,' said Tommy eagerly. 'One about pirates.'

'Is it really?' said Pippi. 'Then it must be Fridolf that wrote the book, because he taught me the tune. Many a time I've sat on the afterdeck of my father's ship on starlit nights with the Southern Cross straight above my head and Fridolf beside me, and heard him sing like this:

'Fifteen men on the Dead Man's Chest—
Yo-ho-ho, and a bottle of rum!'

Pippi sang once more in a hoarser voice still.

'Pippi, it makes me feel very queer when you sing like that,' said Tommy. 'It's frightening and lovely all at the same time.'

331

'It's only frightening to me,' said Annika, 'but perhaps a little lovely, too.'

'I shall go to sea when I'm grown up,' said Tommy firmly. 'I shall be a pirate, just like you, Pippi.'

'Good!' said Pippi. 'The Terrors of the Caribbean Sea, that'll be you and me, Tommy. We shall make off with gold and jewels and precious stones and have a hiding-place for our treasures deep in a cave on a desert island in the Pacific, and three skeletons to guard the cave. We'll have a flag with a skull and two crossbones on it, and we'll sing "Fifteen men" so it can be heard from one end of the Atlantic to the other and all the seafarers will grow pale and think of throwing themselves into the sea to escape our bloody, bloody vengeance!'

'What about me?' said Annika plaintively. 'I'm afraid to be a pirate. What shall *I* do?'

'You can come all the same,' said Pippi, 'to dust the pianola!'

The fire was dying down.

'Time for bed,' said Pippi. She had laid branches of spruce on the floor of the tent and several thick blankets over the branches.

'Would you like to sleep like sardines with me in the tent?' said Pippi to the horse. 'Or would you rather stay out here under a tree with a horse blanket over you?—What was that you said?—You always feel sick sleeping in a tent. Just as you like,' and Pippi gave him a friendly pat.

Soon all three children and Mr Nelson were rolled in their blankets in the tent. Outside, the waves lapped against the shore.

'Hear the roar of the ocean,' said Pippi dreamily.

It was pitch dark, and Annika clutched Pippi's hand because everything seemed less dangerous then. Suddenly it started to rain. The drops splashed on the canvas, but inside the tent it was warm and dry. The sound of the rain outside made it seem all the cosier. Pippi went out to put another blanket on the horse. He was standing under a thick spruce, so he was all right.

'Isn't it grand?' sighed Tommy when Pippi returned.

'Rather,' said Pippi. 'And look what I found under a stone! Three bars of chocolate!'

Three minutes later Annika was fast asleep with her mouth full of chocolate and her hand in Pippi's.

'We've forgotten to brush our teeth,' said Tommy and fell fast asleep.

When Tommy and Annika woke up, Pippi had disappeared. Eagerly they crawled out of the tent. The sun was shining. A fresh fire was burning in front of the tent and Pippi was sitting by it frying bacon and making coffee.

'Happy Easter!' she said when she caught sight of Tommy and Annika.

'Easter?' said Tommy. 'It's not Easter!'

'Isn't it?' said Pippi. 'Well, save it up for next year then!'

The children sniffed the delicious smell from the bacon and the coffee. They squatted by the fire, and Pippi passed them bacon and eggs and potatoes. Afterwards they had coffee with ginger nuts. Never before had a breakfast tasted so good.

'I think we're better off than Robinson Crusoe,' said Tommy.

'Well, if we have a little fresh fish for dinner as well, you bet Robinson would be green with envy,' said Pippi.

'Ugh, I don't like fish,' said Tommy.

'I don't either,' said Annika.

Pippi, however, cut a long thin branch, tied a piece of string at one end, bent a pin into a hook, put a bread pellet on to the hook and sat herself on a big stone on the shore.

'Now we shall see what happens,' she said.

'What're you fishing for?' asked Tommy.

'Octopus,' said Pippi. 'It's a delicacy beyond compare.'

She sat there for a whole hour, but no octopus nibbled. A perch came up and nosed at the bread crumb, but Pippi quickly pulled up the hook.

'No, thank you, my boy,' she said. 'I said octopus, and I mean octopus, so it's no use you coming sponging.'

After a while Pippi threw the fishing rod into the lake.

'You were lucky that time,' she said. 'It looks like pancakes instead. The octopus is obstinate today.'

Tommy and Annika were well content. The water glittered invitingly in the sunshine.

'What about a swim?' said Tommy.

Pippi and Annika were all for it. The water was rather cold. Tommy and Annika dipped their big toes in, but quickly withdrew them.

'I know a better way,' said Pippi. There was a rock close to the water's edge, and on the rock grew a tree. The branches stretched out over the water. Pippi climbed the tree and tied a rope round a branch.

'Look!' She took hold of the rope, threw herself into the air and slid down into the water. 'This way you get wet straight away,' she shouted when she reached the surface.

Tommy and Annika were at first rather doubtful, but it looked such fun that they decided to have a go, and once they had tried it they did not want to stop. It was even more fun than it looked. Mr Nelson wanted to join in, too. He slid down the rope, but a second before he would have splashed in the water he turned round and started to climb up at a terrific speed. He did that each time although the children called to him that he was a coward. Pippi then hit upon the idea that they could sit on a plank of wood and slide on it down the rock into the water—and that was great fun, too, because there was such a tremendous splash when it reached the water.

'That chap Robinson, I wonder if he slid on a plank of wood,' mused Pippi when she sat at the top of the rock ready to start off.

'No-o—at least, it doesn't say so in the book,' said Tommy.

'That's what I thought. His shipwreck wasn't much to write home about, *I* don't think. What did he do with himself all day long? Sew cross-stitch? Yippy! Here goes!'

Pippi slid downwards, her red plaits flying.

After the bathe the children decided to explore the uninhabited island properly. They all three mounted the horse, and he trotted along good-naturedly. Up hill and down dale they went, through thickets and among dense spruce, over marsh land and across beautiful little glades where masses of wild flowers were growing. Pippi sat with her pistol at the ready, and now and then she fired a shot. This made the horse cut great capers with fright.

'There a lion bit the dust,' she said, pleased. Or:

'*That* cannibal has planted his last potato!'

'Let's keep this for our own island always,' said Tommy when they had returned to camp and Pippi had started making pancakes.

Pippi and Annika agreed.

Pancakes taste very good when you eat them smoking hot. There were no plates and no forks and knives handy, and Annika asked:

'Can we eat with our fingers?'

'I don't mind,' said Pippi, 'but myself, I'd rather stick to the old method of eating with my mouth.'

'You know what I mean,' said Annika. She picked up a pancake with her little hand and put it with great relish into her mouth.

Once more it was evening. The fire had been put out. Pressed against each other, their faces smeared with pancake, the children lay in their blankets. A big star shone through a slit in the tent canvas. The lapping of the water soothed them to sleep.

'We've got to go home today,' said Tommy gloomily next morning.

'It's an awful shame,' said Annika. 'I'd like to stay here all summer, but Mummy and Daddy are coming back today.'

After breakfast Tommy took a stroll down by the lake. Suddenly he gave a terrific yell. The boat! It was gone! Annika was very upset. How were they to get away now? It is true, she very much wanted to stay on the island for the whole summer but it was a different thing to know that you *could* not go home. And what would their poor mother say when she realized that Tommy and Annika had disappeared? Tears came into Annika's eyes as she thought of it.

'What's the matter with you, Annika?' said Pippi. 'What's your idea of a shipwreck, I'd like to know? What d'you think Robinson would have said if a ship had come to fetch him when he'd been on his desert island for two days? "Here you are, Mr Crusoe! Will you please go on board and be saved and bathed and shaved and have your toenails cut!" No, *thank* you! I'm pretty well sure Mr Crusoe would have run away and hidden behind a bush, because once you've managed to get to a desert island, you certainly don't want to stay less than seven years.'

338

Seven years! Annika shuddered, and Tommy looked very doubtful.

'Well, I don't mean that we're going to stay here for simply ages,' said Pippi reassuringly. 'When it's time for Tommy to do his National Service, I s'pose we've got to let them know where we are. But perhaps he can get a deferment for a year or two.'

Annika felt more and more desperate. Pippi looked at her thoughtfully.

'Well, if you're going to take it like that,' she said, 'I s'pose there's nothing for it but to send off the bottle.'

She went and dug out the empty bottle from the sack. She also managed to find a paper and pencil. She put them all on a stone in front of Tommy.

'You write,' she said. 'You're much more used to writing than me.'

'But what shall I write?' asked Tommy.

'Let's see,' said Pippi, thinking hard. 'Write: "Save us before we perish! For two days we have pined away without snuff on this island."'

'Pippi, we can't write that,' said Tommy reproachfully. 'It isn't true.'

'What isn't?' said Pippi.

'We can't write "without snuff",' said Tommy.

'Why not?' said Pippi. 'Have you got any snuff?'

'No,' said Tommy.

'Has Annika got any snuff?'

''Course not, but—'

'Have I got any snuff?' asked Pippi.

'P'raps not,' said Tommy, 'but we don't take snuff.'

'And that's exactly what I want you to write: "For two days without snuff . . . "'

'But if we write that I'm sure people will think we take snuff,' persisted Tommy.

'Look, Tommy,' said Pippi. 'Tell me this, who's without snuff *oftenest*? The ones that take it or the ones that don't take it?'

'The ones that *don't* take it, of course,' said Tommy.

'Well, what's all the fuss about then?' said Pippi. 'You're to write what I tell you!'

So Tommy wrote: 'Save us before we perish! For two days we have pined away without snuff on this island.'

Pippi took the paper, pushed it into the bottle, put the cork in, and threw the bottle into the water.

'Our rescuers should soon be here,' she said.

The bottle bobbed about, and soon it came to rest among the roots of an alder by the shore.

'We have to throw it further out,' said Tommy.

'That'd be the silliest thing to do,' said Pippi.

'If it floated far away, our rescuers wouldn't know where to look for us, but if it's here we can shout to them when they've found it, and we'll be saved immediately.'

Pippi sat down on the shore.

'We'd better keep our eye on the bottle all the time,' she said. Tommy and Annika sat down beside her. After ten minutes Pippi said impatiently:

'People seem to think we've got *nothing* else to do except sit and wait to be rescued. Where are they, I'd like to know?'

'Who?' asked Annika.

'The people who're going to rescue us,' said Pippi. 'The carelessness and negligence of it is quite shocking when you think that lives are at stake.'

Annika began to think that they were really going to pine away on the island, but suddenly Pippi put her finger up and shouted:

'Goodness me! What a scatterbrain I am! How *could* I forget?'

'What?' asked Tommy.

'The boat,' said Pippi. 'I carried it up on land last night when you'd gone to sleep. Now I remember.'

'But why?' said Annika reproachfully.

'I was afraid it might get wet,' said Pippi.

In a twinkling she had fetched the boat which

had been well hidden under a spruce. She heaved it into the lake and said grimly:

'There! Let 'em come! Cos when they come to rescue us, it'll be for nothing, cos we're going to rescue ourselves. That'll serve them right. It'll teach them to be quicker another time.'

'I hope we'll be home before Mummy and Daddy,' said Annika when they had got into the boat and Pippi was rowing with strong strokes towards land. 'Mummy will be terribly worried otherwise.'

'I don't think so,' said Pippi.

Mr and Mrs Settergreen did reach home half an hour before the children. There was no trace of Tommy and Annika. But in the letter-box they found a piece of paper, and on it was written:

DO NOT FINK YOR CHILREN DED OR DISAPPEERD FOR EVER COS THA ARNT ONLE A LITTL SHIPRECKD AND COMING HOM SOON I PROMMIS

LUV FROM PIPPI

7

Pippi has a Grand Visitor

One summer evening Pippi and Tommy and Annika sat on Pippi's front door-step eating wild strawberries which they had picked that afternoon. It was such a lovely evening with bird song and the scent of flowers and—yes, the strawberries. It was all very peaceful. The children ate and hardly talked at all. Tommy and Annika sat thinking how lovely it was that it was summer time and what a blessing school would not be starting for a long time yet. What Pippi was thinking no one knows.

'Pippi, you've been here at Villekulla Cottage for a whole year now,' said Annika suddenly, and squeezed Pippi's arm.

'Yes, time flies, and I'm getting old,' said Pippi. 'I shall be ten in the autumn and then I s'pose I shall be past my prime.'

'Will you live here always, d'you think?' asked Tommy. 'I mean, until you're big and old enough to be a pirate.'

'No one knows,' said Pippi, 'because I don't suppose my father will stay on that Cannibal Island for ever, and as soon as he's got a new boat ready I expect he'll come and fetch me.'

Tommy and Annika sighed. Suddenly Pippi sat bolt upright on the steps.

'Look! Why, there he is!' she said pointing down towards the gate. She was down the garden path in three leaps. After some hesitation Tommy and Annika followed and saw her throw her arms round the neck of a very fat man with a red, clipped moustache and wearing blue sailor's trousers.

'Darling Daddy!' shouted Pippi, waggling her legs so vigorously as she hung round his neck that her big shoes fell off. 'Daddy! How you have grown!'

'Pippilotta Provisiona Gaberdina Dandeliona Ephraims-daughter Longstocking, my darling child! I was just about to say that *you* have grown.'

'Ha-ha, I knew that!' laughed Pippi. 'That's why I said it first!'

'My child, are you as strong as you used to be?'

'Stronger,' said Pippi. 'Let's have a tug-of-war!'

'Right-o,' said her father.

There was only one person in the world as strong as Pippi, and that was her father. There they were, tugging with all their might, but neither succeeded in beating the other. At last, however, Captain Longstocking's arm began to tremble and Pippi said:

'When I'm ten, I'll get the better of you, Daddy.'

Her father thought so, too.

'But, goodness me,' said Pippi, 'I'm forgetting the introductions. This is Tommy and this is Annika. And this is my father, the sea captain and His Majesty Ephraim Longstocking—because you are a Cannibal King, aren't you, Daddy?'

'Exactly,' said Captain Longstocking. 'I'm the king of the Canny Cannibals of Canny-Canny Island. I floated ashore there after I'd been blown into the sea, you remember.'

'That's just what I thought,' said Pippi. 'I knew all along that you weren't drowned.'

'Drowned! 'Course not! It's as impossible for me to sink as for a camel to thread a needle. My fat keeps me afloat.'

Tommy and Annika looked at Captain Longstocking wonderingly.

'Why haven't you got any Cannibal King clothes on?' asked Tommy.

'They're here in my bag,' said Captain Longstocking.

'Put them on! Put them on!' shouted Pippi. 'I want to see my father in royal attire.'

They all went into the kitchen. Captain Longstocking disappeared into Pippi's bedroom, and the children sat down on the wood-box and waited.

'This is just like the theatre,' said Annika expectantly.

Then—bang—the door opened, and there stood the Cannibal King. He was wearing a straw skirt and on his head was a crown of gold. Round his neck there were strings and strings of beads. In one hand he was carrying two arrows and in the other a shield. And that was all. No, not quite; below the straw skirt his fat, hairy legs were decorated with gold rings round the ankles.

'Ussamkussor mussor filibussor,' said Captain Longstocking, puckering his eyebrows in a threatening manner.

'Ooh, he's talking cannibal language,' said Tommy delightedly. 'What does it mean, sir?'

'It means, "Tremble, my enemies!"'

'Daddy,' said Pippi, 'weren't the cannibals surprised when you floated ashore on their island?'

'Yes, they certainly were,' said Captain Longstocking, 'they were terrifically surprised. At first they thought they'd eat me up, but when I uprooted a palm tree with my bare hands they thought better of it, and made me king. So then I ruled in the mornings and worked at building my boat in the afternoons. It took me a long time to get it finished as I had to do it all myself. It was only a little sailing boat, of course. When I was ready I told the cannibals that I should have to leave them for a little time, but that I would soon return and then I would bring a Princess whose name was Pippilotta. Then they beat their shields and shouted, "Ussumlussor! Ussumplussor!"'

'What does that mean?' said Annika.

'It means, "Bravo! Bravo!" Then I ruled really strongly for a fortnight so that it would last for the whole time that I was going to be away, and then I hoisted the sail and made a bee-line for the open sea, and the cannibals shouted, "Ussumkura kussomkara!" That means, "Come back soon, fat white chief!" I set my course for Sourabaya, and what do you think was the first thing I saw when

I jumped ashore there? My staunch old schooner the *Hoppetossa* with my faithful old Fridolf standing by the rail waving for all he was worth. "Fridolf," I said, "I am back to resume command." "Aye, aye, Cap'n," he said. And I went on board. Every man of the old crew is still on it, and now the *Hoppetossa* is lying at anchor in the harbour here, so you can go and see all your old friends, Pippi.'

This made Pippi so happy that she stood on her head on the kitchen table and waggled her legs. But Tommy and Annika could not help feeling a little sad. They felt as if someone was taking Pippi away from them.

'This calls for a celebration!' shouted Pippi when she was on her feet again. 'A celebration that'll make the whole of Villekulla Cottage creak.'

So she laid a substantial supper on the kitchen table and they all sat down and ate. Pippi swallowed three hard-boiled eggs, shell and all. Every now and then she bit her father's ear just because she was so pleased to see him. Mr Nelson, who had been asleep, suddenly came leaping over, and he rubbed his eyes in surprise when he caught sight of Captain Longstocking.

'Oh, so you've still got Mr Nelson,' said Captain Longstocking.

'Yes, rather, and I've other domestic animals, you know,' said Pippi, fetching the horse, and he, too, got a hard-boiled egg to chew.

Captain Longstocking was very pleased that his daughter had arranged things so cosily for herself at Villekulla Cottage, and he was glad that she had her suitcase of gold coins, so that she had not suffered want while he was away.

When everyone had had enough to eat, Captain Longstocking took a tom-tom out of his suitcase, one of those that the cannibals used to beat time on when they had their dancing and religious feasts. Captain Longstocking sat down on the floor and beat the drum. It sounded muffled and eerie, different from anything that Tommy and Annika had ever heard.

'It's cannibalish,' said Tommy by way of explanation to Annika.

Pippi took her big shoes off and danced in her stockinged feet a dance which was eerie, too. Finally King Ephraim danced a savage war dance which he had learnt at Canny-Canny Island. He swung a spear and gesticulated wildly with the shield and stamped so hard with his bare feet that Pippi shouted:

'Watch out, or the kitchen floor will crack!'

'Won't matter,' said Captain Longstocking,

whirling on, 'cos now you're going to be a Cannibal Princess, daughter mine!'

Pippi darted forward and danced with her father. They posed to each other and heigh-hoed and shouted, sometimes taking such big leaps that Tommy and Annika felt dizzy from watching them. It seemed that Mr Nelson did, too, because he covered his eyes all the time.

Gradually the dancing changed into a wrestling match between Pippi and her father. Captain Longstocking threw his daughter so that she landed on the hat shelf. But she did not stay there long. With a yell she took a huge leap right across the kitchen straight for her father. A second later she had thrown him like a rocket head first into the wood-box. His fat legs were pointing straight up in the air. He could not get out by himself, partly because he was too fat and partly because he laughed so much. It sounded like the roar of thunder down in the wood-box. Pippi took hold of his feet to pull him up, but that made him laugh so much that he nearly choked. The fact was that he was extremely ticklish.

'D-d-d-don't t-t-t-ti-i-ck-ck-l-le me,' he groaned. 'You can throw me into the lake or heave me out of the window, anything, but d-d-d-don't t-t-t-ti-i-ck-ck-l-le me under my feet!'

He laughed so much that Tommy and Annika were afraid the wood-box might crack. At last he managed to wriggle out of the box. As soon as he was on his feet again, he made for Pippi and threw her right across the kitchen. She landed with her face on the stove which was full of soot.

'Ha-ha, here we have the Cannibal Princess—hey presto,' shouted Pippi with glee, turning a face as black as soot to Tommy and Annika. With a howl she threw herself on her father, giving him such a beating that his straw skirt crackled and clouds of straw whirled about the kitchen. The gold crown fell off and rolled under the table. In the end Pippi succeeded in throwing her father on to the floor and she sat down on him, saying:

'Do you give in?'

'I do,' said Captain Longstocking, and they both laughed so much that they cried and Pippi bit her father's nose lightly.

'I haven't enjoyed myself so much since you and I cleaned up that sailors' pub in Singapore!' he said.

He crawled under the table and picked up his crown.

'The cannibals should see this,' he said, 'the State Regalia lying under the kitchen table at Villekulla Cottage!'

He put on his crown and combed out the straw skirt which was looking rather thin.

'It seems to me that you'll have to send it for invisible mending,' said Pippi.

'It was worth it, though,' said Captain Longstocking.

He sat down on the floor and wiped the sweat from his brow.

'Well, Pippi, my child,' he said, 'd'you tell fibs at all nowadays?'

'Yes, I do, when I've got time, but that's not very often, I'm afraid,' said Pippi. 'And what about you? You weren't so bad at it either.'

'Oh, I usually tell the cannibals a few tall stories on Saturday nights if they've behaved well during the week. We generally have a little yarn and sing-song evening to the accompaniment of drums and torchlight dancing. The taller my stories the harder they beat the drums.'

'I see,' said Pippi, 'but no one beats the drum for me. Here I am all alone telling myself fibs that I'm simply full of and that it's a joy to hear, but no one even plays on a comb because of that. The other night when I'd gone to bed I thought up a long story about a calf who could make lace and climb trees—just imagine! I believed every word of it. But beat a drum! No, indeed! No one does that!'

'Well, then! *I'm* going to do it,' said Captain Longstocking. And he rolled the drum for a long time for his daughter, and Pippi sat on his lap with her sooty face against his cheek, so that he got as black as she was.

A thought had occurred to Annika. She did not know if it was proper for her to mention it, but she could not help doing so.

'It's wrong to tell lies,' she said. 'Mummy says so.'

'Don't be silly, Annika,' said Tommy. 'Pippi doesn't tell real lies, it's pretend lies. She makes up stories, you see.'

Pippi looked at Tommy thoughtfully.

'Sometimes you talk so wisely it makes me think you might be a great man one day,' she said.

Evening had come. It was time for Tommy and Annika to go home. It had been an eventful day and it was interesting to have seen a real live Cannibal King, and of course it was lovely for Pippi to have her father at home, but still . . . still . . .

When Tommy and Annika had crept into bed they did not talk as they usually did. There was complete silence in the nursery. Then a sigh was heard. It came from Tommy. After a time there was another sigh. This time it came from Annika.

'Why do you keep on sighing?' said Tommy irritably.

There was no reply. For Annika was underneath the bedclothes, weeping.

8
Pippi gives a Farewell Party

When Tommy and Annika walked through the kitchen door of Villekulla Cottage next morning, the whole house was echoing with the most terrific snores. Captain Longstocking had not yet woken up. Pippi, however, was standing in the kitchen doing her early morning exercises when Tommy and Annika came and interrupted her.

'It's settled,' said Pippi. 'Now my future is assured. I'm going to be a Cannibal Princess. For six months in the year I'm going to be a Cannibal

Princess and for the other six I'm going to sail on all the oceans in the world in the *Hoppetossa*. Daddy thinks that if he rules firmly over the cannibals for six months in the year, they'll manage without a king for the other six months. You do see, don't you, that an old sea dog must feel a deck under his feet now and then? Besides, he must think of my education. If I'm to be a really good pirate one day, it won't do for me only to live at Court. It makes you soft, Daddy says.'

'Aren't you going to be at Villekulla Cottage at all?' asked Tommy in a small voice.

'Yes, when we retire,' said Pippi, 'in about fifty or sixty years' time. Then you and I can play and have a nice time together, can't we?'

Neither Tommy nor Annika could find much comfort in what she said.

'Imagine! A Cannibal Princess!' said Pippi dreamily. 'Not many children become that. I shall look grand! I shall have rings in all my ears and a slightly bigger ring in my nose.'

'What else are you going to wear?' asked Annika.

'Nothing else,' said Pippi. 'Not another scrap! But I shall have a cannibal of my own to polish me all over with shoe polish every morning. All I'll have to do will be to put myself in the passage at night together with my shoes.'

Tommy and Annika tried to picture what Pippi would look like.

'D'you think the black will look well with your red hair?' asked Annika doubtfully.

'We'll see,' said Pippi. 'If not, it's easy to dye hair green.' She sighed in rapture. 'Princess Pippilotta! What pomp! What grandeur! And how I shall dance! Princess Pippilotta dancing in the light of the camp fire to the rolling of drums. My goodness, how my nose ring will rattle then!'

'When—when—are you going?' asked Tommy. His voice sounded a little husky.

'The *Hoppetossa* is weighing anchor tomorrow,' said Pippi. All three children were silent for a long time. It seemed there was nothing more to be said. But at last Pippi turned a cartwheel and said:

'Tonight a farewell party will be held at Villekulla Cottage. A farewell party—I will say no more! Everyone who wants to come and say goodbye to me is welcome.'

The news spread like wild-fire among all the children of the little town.

'Pippi Longstocking is leaving town, and she is giving a farewell party tonight at Villekulla Cottage. Anybody who wants to can come!'

There were many who wanted to come; thirty-

357

four children to be exact. Tommy and Annika had persuaded their mother to allow them to stay up as long as they liked that evening. Their mother realized that she could not do otherwise.

Tommy and Annika would never forget the evening when Pippi had her farewell party. It was one of those delightfully warm and beautiful summer evenings when you keep thinking: 'This is what it's really like when it's summer!'

All the roses in Pippi's garden glowed with colour and gave out their scent in the dusk. The old trees seemed to whisper secretly among themselves. It would all have been wonderful, if only—if only . . . Tommy and Annika did not want to think of the rest.

All the children from the town had brought their ocarinas. They blew them gaily as they came tramping up the garden path of Villekulla Cottage, led by Tommy and Annika. The moment they reached the steps to the porch the front door was thrown open and Pippi stood in the doorway. Her eyes shone in her freckled face.

'Welcome to my humble dwelling!' she said with a sweet smile. Annika took a long look at her so that she would always be able to remember what Pippi looked like. Never, never would she forget her, standing there with the red plaits and the freckles and the happy smile and the big black shoes.

Nearby there was the muffled beat of a drum. Captain Longstocking was sitting in the kitchen with the cannibal drum between his knees. He had dressed in his Cannibal King clothes today as well. Pippi had specially asked him to do so, because she knew that all the children would very much want to see a real live Cannibal King.

The whole kitchen became filled with children who crowded round King Ephraim to look at him. Annika thought it was lucky no more had come, because then there might not have been room for them. As she was thinking this the music from a concertina was heard in the garden. The entire crew of the *Hoppetossa* was coming, with Fridolf in the lead. It was Fridolf who was playing the concertina. Pippi had gone down to the harbour that same day to greet her friends and invite them to the farewell party. Now she rushed up to Fridolf and hugged him till his face began to go blue. Then she let him go, shouting:

'Music! Music!'

Then Fridolf played his concertina, King Ephraim beat his drum, and all the children blew their ocarinas.

The lid of the wood-box was shut and on it stood long rows of bottles of ginger beer. There were fifteen iced cakes on the big kitchen table, and a giant saucepan full of sausages on the stove.

King Ephraim began by grabbing eight sausages. Everyone followed his example, and soon the only sounds to be heard in the kitchen were those of sausages being munched. Then everyone was allowed to help himself to as much cake and ginger beer as he wanted. It was rather a squash in the kitchen, and the guests overflowed on to the porch and into the garden, and you could see the gleam of white icing here and there in the dusk.

When no one could possibly eat another thing Tommy suggested shaking down the sausages and the iced cakes with a game like 'Follow my leader', perhaps. Pippi did not know how to play it, so Tommy explained to her that someone had to be leader and all the others were to copy everything that the leader did.

'Right-o,' said Pippi. 'Doesn't sound a bad idea. I think I'd better be the leader.'

She began by climbing the shed roof. To get there she had first to climb the garden fence, and then she was able to edge herself up on her tummy on to the roof. Pippi and Tommy and Annika had done it so many times before that to them it was easy, but the other children thought it rather difficult. The sailors from the *Hoppetossa* were, of course, used to climbing the rigging so it was nothing to them, either, but Captain Longstocking got into difficulties because he was so fat, and also he got tangled up with his straw skirt. He breathed heavily as he heaved himself on to the roof.

'This straw skirt will never be the same again,' he said gloomily.

From the shed roof Pippi jumped down to the ground. Some of the younger children were, of course, afraid to do this, but Fridolf was a good sort. He lifted down all those who dared not jump. After that Pippi turned six somersaults on the lawn. They all copied her, but Captain Longstocking said:

'Someone will have to give me a push from behind, otherwise I shall never do it.'

Pippi did. She gave him such a big push that once he had started he could not stop, but rolled like a ball across the lawn and turned fourteen somersaults instead of six.

Then Pippi ran into Villekulla Cottage, racing up the porch steps, and climbed out through a window. By standing with her legs wide apart she could just reach a ladder outside. Quickly she skipped up the ladder, leapt on to the roof of Villekulla Cottage, rushed along the top of the roof, jumped up on the chimney and stood on one leg crowing like a cock. Then she threw herself head first into a tree by the side of the house, slid down to the ground, rushed into the wood-shed, caught hold of an axe and chopped down a plank in the wall, crept through the narrow chink, jumped up on the garden fence, walked along the top of the fence for fifty yards, climbed an oak and sat down to rest in the very top of it.

Quite a crowd of people had collected in the road outside Villekulla Cottage, and later they went home and told everybody that they had seen a Cannibal King standing on one leg on Villekulla Cottage's chimney shouting 'cock-a-doodle-do' so that you could hear it for miles. But no one believed them.

When Captain Longstocking tried to squeeze through the narrow hole in the wall of the wood-shed the inevitable happened—he got stuck and could move neither forwards nor backwards. That was why the game stopped short, and all the children gathered round to watch Fridolf sawing Captain Longstocking out of the wall.

'It was a rollicking good game,' said Captain Longstocking, very pleased when he was free again. 'What shall we think up next?'

'Years ago,' said Fridolf, 'the Cap'n and Pippi

used to have a match to see who was the strongest. It was good fun to watch.'

'Not a bad idea,' said Captain Longstocking, 'but the worst of it is that my daughter is getting to be stronger than me.'

Tommy was standing close to Pippi.

'Pippi,' he whispered, 'I was so 'fraid that you were going to creep into our hiding-place in the oak when we played "Follow my leader". I don't want anyone else to know about it. Not even if we never go there again.'

'No, it's our secret,' said Pippi.

Her father took hold of an iron poker. He bent it in the middle as if it had been made of wax. Pippi took another poker and did the same.

'That's nothing,' she said, 'I used to amuse myself with simple tricks like that when I was in my cradle. Just to pass the time.'

At this Captain Longstocking unhinged the kitchen door. Fridolf and five other sailors stood on the door and Captain Longstocking lifted them all high in the air and carried them round the lawn ten times.

It was now quite dark, so Pippi fixed burning torches here and there and they shone beautifully, casting a fairy light over the garden.

'Are you ready now?' she said to her father after the tenth round. He was. So Pippi put the horse on the kitchen door and on the horse's back she put Fridolf and three of the other sailors, and each of the four had two children in their arms. Fridolf held Tommy and Annika. Then Pippi lifted the kitchen door and carried them round the lawn twenty-five times. It looked marvellous in the light from the torches.

''Pon my word, child, you *are* stronger than me,' said Captain Longstocking.

After that everyone sat down on the lawn and Fridolf played the concertina, and all the other sailors sang the most beautiful sea shanties. The children danced to the music. Pippi took a torch in each hand and danced more wildly than anyone.

The party ended with a firework display. Pippi set off rockets and Catherine wheels, so that the whole sky hissed with them. Annika sat in the porch watching. It was all so very beautiful. So truly lovely. She could not now see the roses, but she could smell them in the darkness. How wonderful it would all have been if only—if only . . . An icy hand seemed to clutch at Annika's heart. Tomorrow—what would things be like then? And all the rest of the summer holidays? And forever? There would be no Pippi at Villekulla Cottage any more. There would be no Mr Nelson, and no horse standing in the porch. No more rides, no outings with Pippi, no pleasant evening hours in the kitchen of Villekulla Cottage, no tree where ginger beer grew. Well, the tree would be there, of course, but Annika had a strong feeling that there would not be any ginger beer growing in it when Pippi was gone. What would she and Tommy do tomorrow? Play croquet, probably. Annika sighed.

The party was over. All the children said thank you and goodbye. Captain Longstocking went back with his sailors to the *Hoppetossa*. He thought Pippi might as well come, too. But Pippi said she wanted to stay one more night at Villekulla Cottage.

'Tomorrow morning at ten o'clock we weigh anchor, don't forget,' shouted Captain Longstocking as he went.

Now only Pippi and Tommy and Annika were left. They sat silent on the porch steps in the darkness.

'Do come here and play just the same,' said Pippi at last. 'The key will be hanging on a nail beside the door. You can have everything in the drawers. And if I put a ladder inside the oak, you can climb down there by yourselves, although there might not be quite so much ginger beer growing. It's the wrong time of year.'

'No, Pippi,' said Tommy solemnly, 'we shall never come here again.'

'No! Never, never,' said Annika, thinking that after this she would shut her eyes every time she had to pass Villekulla Cottage. Villekulla Cottage without Pippi . . .

9
Pippi goes Aboard

Pippi carefully locked the door of Villekulla Cottage. She hung the key on a nail just beside it. She lifted the horse from the porch—lifted him from the porch for the very last time. Mr Nelson was already sitting on her shoulder looking important. He seemed to realize that something unusual was about to happen.

'Well, I suppose that's all,' said Pippi.

Tommy and Annika nodded. Yes, they supposed it was.

'We're quite early,' said Pippi. 'Let's walk and then it'll take longer.'

Tommy and Annika nodded again, but said nothing. They began their walk to the town. To the harbour. To the *Hoppetossa*. They left the horse to follow as he pleased.

Pippi glanced back over her shoulder at Villekulla Cottage.

'Not a bad cottage that,' she said. 'Free from fleas and pleasant in every way. I may not be able to say that much for the cannibal mud hut where I'm going to live from now on.'

Tommy and Annika said nothing.

'If there should be a terrible lot of fleas in my cannibal mud hut,' continued Pippi, 'I shall tame them and keep them in a cigar box and play with them in the evenings. I shall tie little bows round their legs and the two most faithful and most affectionate fleas I shall call "Tommy" and "Annika" and they're going to sleep in my bed at night.'

Not even this roused Tommy and Annika from their silence.

'What on earth's the matter with you two?' said Pippi irritably. 'I can tell you it's jolly dangerous to be silent for long. Your tongue shrivels up if you don't use it. I once knew a fireplace builder in Calcutta who kept on being silent. Perhaps you can imagine what happened. Once he wanted to say to me, "Goodbye, dear Pippi, happy voyage and thanks for everything!" And can you guess what became of it? First he screwed his face up dreadfully, because the hinges of his mouth had gone completely rusty, so I had to oil them with sewing-machine oil, then out came, "Coo pi ank ing!" I then took a look in his mouth, and would you believe it? There lay his tongue like a withered little leaf! And as long as he lived that fireplace builder could never say anything except "Goo pi ank ing!" It would be dreadful if the same thing happened to you. Let's see if you can say it better than the fireplace builder: "Happy voyage, dear Pippi, and thanks for everything!" Try!'

'Happy voyage, dear Pippi, and thanks for everything,' said Tommy and Annika obediently.

'Thank goodness for that,' said Pippi. 'You certainly gave me a fright! If you'd said, "Coo pi ank ing" I don't know what I should have done.'

There was the harbour. There lay the *Hoppetossa*. Captain Longstocking stood on deck, shouting his orders. The sailors rushed to and fro to make everything ready for departure. On the quay all the people in the little town had gathered to wave goodbye to Pippi, and there she was together with Tommy and Annika and the horse and Mr Nelson.

'Here's Pippi Longstocking! Make way for Pippi Longstocking!' the folk cried, and stood aside to let Pippi pass. Pippi waved and greeted people to right and left. Then she took the horse and carried him up the gangway. The poor animal glowered suspiciously round him, for horses do not like boat trips much.

'So there you are, dear child,' said Captain Longstocking, breaking off in the middle of an order to give Pippi a hug. They squeezed each other till their ribs creaked.

Annika had been going around with a lump in her throat all morning, and when she saw Pippi lifting the horse on board the lump loosened. Standing pressed against a packing-case on the quay she began to cry, at first quietly, but gradually more and more loudly.

'Shut up,' said Tommy angrily. 'You're disgracing us in front of everybody!'

This only resulted in Annika bursting into an absolute flood of tears. She wept so much that she quivered. Tommy gave a stone such a kick that it rolled down over the edge of the quay and fell into the water. Actually he would have liked to have thrown it at the *Hoppetossa*. Miserable boat to take Pippi from them! In fact, if no one had been looking, Tommy would have liked to cry a little too. But that would not do. He kicked another stone savagely.

Now Pippi came running down the gangway from the ship. She made straight for Tommy and Annika. She clasped their hands in hers.

'Ten minutes left,' she said.

Then Annika threw herself down across a packing-case and wept as if her heart would break. There were no more stones for Tommy to kick. He clenched his teeth and looked very, very angry.

All the children in the town crowded round Pippi. They brought out their ocarinas and played a farewell tune for her. It sounded dreadfully sad, because it was a very, very plaintive tune. Annika was now weeping so much that she could hardly stand upright. At that moment Tommy remembered that he had written a little farewell rhyme in Pippi's honour. He hauled out a paper and began to read. Only it was awful that his voice should tremble so!

> 'Farewell, Pippi dear, you leave us now,
> But remember how
> Good friends you've here always
> For all your days.'

'Gosh, it rhymed!' said Pippi, pleased. 'I shall

learn it by heart and say it to the cannibals when we're sitting round the camp fire at night.'

The children were pressing in from every direction to say goodbye. Pippi raised her hand to call for silence.

'Children,' she said, 'after this I shall only have little cannibal children to play with. What we're going to amuse ourselves with I don't know. Perhaps we'll play catch with rhinoceroses, and do snake charming, and ride on elephants and put up a swing in the coconut palm round the corner. I expect we'll manage to pass the time somehow.'

Pippi paused. Both Tommy and Annika felt they hated those cannibal children that Pippi was going to play with from now on.

'But,' continued Pippi, 'there may come a day during the rainy season—a boring day, because even if it's fun to skip about without clothes on when it's raining, you can't do more than get really wet; and when we've done that properly perhaps we'll crawl into my mud hut, provided it hasn't all turned into clay, of course, because in that case we can make mud pies, but if it hasn't turned into clay we'll sit down inside, the cannibal children and I, and then perhaps the cannibal children will say, "Pippi, tell us a story"! Then I shall tell about a tiny little town which is far far away in another part of the world, and about the little white children who live there. "You can't imagine what dear children they are," I shall tell the cannibal children. "They're white like little angels all over except their feet, they play ocarinas, and—best of all—they know pluttification." Only the little black cannibal children might get upset that *they* don't know pluttification, and then I shan't know what to do with them. Well, if the worst comes to the worst, I'll have to pull down the mud hut and make clay of it and then we can make mud pies and dig ourselves down into the clay right up to our necks. By that time I should be much surprised if I hadn't managed to make them think of something else besides pluttification. Thank you, all of you! And goodbye very much!'

The children blew on their ocarinas an even sadder tune than before.

'Pippi, it's time to go on board,' called Captain Longstocking.

'Aye, aye, Cap'n,' said Pippi.

She turned to Tommy and Annika, gazing at them.

Her eyes look queer, thought Tommy. His mother had looked just like that once when Tommy was very, very ill. Annika was lying in a little heap on the packing-case. Pippi lifted her up in her arms.

'Goodbye, Annika, goodbye,' she whispered. 'Don't cry!'

Annika threw her arms round Pippi's neck and made a mournful sound.

'Goodbye, Pippi,' she managed to sob.

Then Pippi took Tommy's hand and squeezed it hard. She ran up the gangway. That when a big tear rolled down Tommy's nose. He clenched his teeth, but it was no use. Another tear came. He took hold of Annika's hand, and together they stood there watching Pippi. They could see her up on deck, but things are always rather blurred when you see them through a mist of tears.

'Three cheers for Pippi Longstocking,' shouted the people on the quay.

'Pull up the gangway, Fridolf,' shouted Captain Longstocking.

Fridolf did so. The *Hoppetossa* was ready for her voyage to foreign parts. But then—

'Daddy,' shouted Pippi. 'I can't! I can't bear it!'

'What is it you can't bear?' asked Captain Longstocking.

'I can't bear that anyone on God's green earth should weep and be sad because of me, least of all

Tommy and Annika. Put the gangway down again! I'm staying at Villekulla Cottage.'

Captain Longstocking said nothing for some minutes.

'You do as you think best,' he said at last. 'You always did!'

Pippi nodded in agreement.

'Yes, I always did,' she said quietly.

Pippi and her father hugged each other again so that their ribs creaked, and they agreed that Captain Longstocking would come and see Pippi at Villekulla Cottage very often.

'When it comes to the point, Daddy,' said Pippi, 'it's really best for a child to have a proper home and not wander about on the sea so much and live in cannibal huts, don't you think?'

'You're right as always, my daughter,' said Captain Longstocking. ''Course your life is more regular at Villekulla Cottage, and I'm sure that's best for little children.'

'Exactly,' said Pippi, 'it's definitely best for little children to have a regular life, especially if they can regulate it themselves.'

And so Pippi said goodbye to the sailors on the *Hoppetossa* and hugged her father a last time. Then she lifted the horse in her strong arms and carried him down the gangway. The anchor of the

Hoppetossa was hauled up. At the last moment an idea occurred to Captain Longstocking.

'Pippi,' he shouted, 'you must have some more gold coins! Catch!'

And he threw across another case of gold coins, but unfortunately the *Hoppetossa* was too far away and the case missed the quay. There was a splash and the case sank. There was a murmur of disappointment among the crowd of people. Then there was another splash. That was Pippi diving. In a moment she rose clutching the case between her teeth. She climbed up on the quay, at the same time pulling away some seaweed which was clinging behind her ear.

'Ha, I'm rich as a troll again,' she said.

Tommy and Annika had not yet grasped what was happening. They were staring open-mouthed at Pippi and the horse and Mr Nelson and the case and the *Hoppetossa* which was steering with full sail out of the harbour.

'Aren't you—aren't you going in the ship?' said Tommy doubtfully at last.

'Guess three times,' said Pippi, wringing the water out of her plaits.

Then she lifted Tommy and Annika and the suitcase and Mr Nelson up on the horse and swung herself up behind them.

'Back to Villekulla Cottage,' she shouted loudly.

Then at last it was all clear to Tommy and Annika. Tommy was so thrilled that he instantly started on his favourite song:

'Here come the Swedes with a hullabaloo!'

Annika had cried so much that she could not stop immediately. She was still sobbing, but they were happy little sobs which would soon cease. Pippi's arms were firmly round her. It felt wonderfully safe. Oh, how wonderful everything was!

'What shall we do, today, Pippi?' asked Annika when she had stopped sobbing.

'Well—play croquet, perhaps,' said Pippi.

'Let's,' said Annika. She knew that even croquet would be quite different with Pippi.

'Or else,' said Pippi thinking.

All the children in the little town crowded round the horse to hear what Pippi was saying.

'Or else,' she said. 'Or else we might nip down to the stream and practise walking on the water.'

'You can't walk on the water,' said Tommy.

'Oh yes, it's not at all impossible,' said Pippi. 'In Cuba I once met a carpenter who . . . '

The horse started galloping and the little children who were crowding round could not hear the rest. But for a long, long time they stood looking after Pippi and her horse galloping in the direction of Villekulla Cottage. Soon all they could see was a small dot far away. Finally it disappeared altogether.